Roses are Dead

Elise Noble

Published by Undercover Publishing Limited

Copyright © 2017 Elise Noble

V1

ISBN: 978-1-910954-73-7

Edited by Nikki Mentges, NAM Editorial

www.undercover-publishing.com

www.elise-noble.com

You can complain because roses have thorns,
Or you can rejoice because thorns have roses.

CHAPTER 1

AN INSISTENT BEEPING interrupted what had been a peaceful sleep. No dreams, no nightmares, just a delicious void of nothingness. How long had I been out? I tried to lift an eyelid, but neither played ball. Okay, I'd take things slowly. And as I waited for my body to catch up with my mind, I thought back to yesterday's good news.

At midday, my little shop had received its first ever order from Hollywood. In all honesty, Velvet Jones wasn't my favourite actress, but she'd bought six corsets. Six! And not the cheap ones either. "Queen of the Night" retailed at eight hundred pounds, and she wanted it in two different colours. The other four weren't far off it. Suki, my best friend and assistant, had squealed loudly enough for the whole of Soho to hear then rushed out to buy cupcakes in eight different flavours.

And yes, we ate them all.

Still in the mood to celebrate when I finished work, I'd put on a party frock and caught the Tube to my sister's apartment to surprise her with a bottle of wine and a takeaway. Oh, who was I kidding? Rose would have knocked back the wine, laughed at the idea of food, and then dragged me out to a bar. Wouldn't she? I scrunched my eyes, doing my best to remember. Try as I might, I couldn't recall getting to her place. Everything after the pervert who squeezed my bottom on his way out of the carriage at Stockwell was a blur.

Still, I must have got there, and we must have partied the night away. Why else would I feel this bad? My head throbbed as sensation came back, and aches pulsed through my muscles with every breath. Had Rose let me drink Southern Comfort again? She knew what that did to me.

My lungs felt squashed, sore, and as I struggled to take in air, something tickled the end of my nose. I wanted to wipe it away, but my hand refused to move, and when I tried to force it, a fresh wave of pain swept through me. That did it. With God as my witness, I was never touching alcohol again. I hadn't felt so rough since that morning in college when I woke up on the couch with a blow-up unicorn, a lightsabre, and half a kebab.

I gave a delicate sniff. Well, at least I couldn't smell vomit. Had I managed to keep one shred of dignity before passing out in my sister's guest room? Because that was where I was, wasn't it? I sniffed again. My sister's flat always smelled like the Italian deli down below—the price she had to pay for cheap rent in a half-decent area. This room didn't. Instead, the aromas of hand sanitiser and bleach lingered in my nostrils.

Come to think of it, this bed was much softer than her futon too. And what was that damn beeping?

I tried again with my eyes and succeeded in lifting one lid halfway. An expanse of white filled my vision, broken only by the harsh glare of a strip light. Unless Rose had decided to redecorate in the last two days, this wasn't her apartment. Sweat popped through the pores on my back as I struggled to sit up, and my heart sped out of control. Where was I? The beeping hurried in sympathy, muffled by the blood whooshing in my ears. I managed to roll onto my left side, but not all the way. Something tugged at my right hand, and when I attempted to shake it off, a new noise started—a loud screech that made my teeth hurt.

Someone flung a door open, and it crashed into the wall behind, making me jump. Running footsteps got closer...closer...

"Miss? Are you awake?"

A female voice, but not my sister. Who the hell was she? I tried to ask, but my words didn't work. My tongue felt too big for my mouth, a pair of old socks someone had stuffed in there as a cruel prank.

"Doctor's on his way," a second voice called.

Doctor? I didn't need a doctor. I needed another twelve hours of sleep and maybe an aspirin.

"Lie still, Miss. Everything'll be all right."

Okay, I could manage that one. I leaned back, welcoming the softness of the pillow, and succumbed to the darkness once more.

The beeping woke me again. Would I have more luck with my eyes this time? After a brief moment of resistance as my eyelashes gummed together, they popped open. The strip lights shone down at me, bright and unrelenting.

"She wakes." A man's voice this time.

I didn't know whether to run or beg for water. My mouth tasted as though someone had dumped the contents of a compost bin in it.

In the end, I opted for middle ground. "Who are you?" It came out as a croak, foreign to my ears.

"Detective Sergeant Nash."

The police? Oh, heck, had I been arrested? I rolled my head to face him, wincing as a searing pain shot across the back of my skull. Not only that, the beeping sped up, and my eyes widened as I saw my heartbeat on screen next to the man sitting at my bedside.

With some effort, I glanced down at my hands. No handcuffs. That was a good sign, right? I squinted to focus as another figure arrived, this one dressed in pale blue and smiling.

"How are you feeling?" the nurse asked.

"Ugh." I tried again. "Not so good."

"That's only to be expected. It's almost time for your next lot of painkillers."

"What happened?" I managed to spit out the question burning through my brain.

The woman looked away and met the policeman's eyes. He gave his head a small shake, and a spider of fear crawled up my spine. What wasn't she telling me?

She turned back, smiling again, but this time it was all fake. "We'll talk about that later."

Her voice was too bright, her tone too cheery.

"Why not now?"

She ignored the question. "The doctor'll be through in a minute—he's just finishing up with another patient." Her grin got wider, the lie bigger. "You'll be feeling better in no time."

With practised efficiency, she reached up and changed my drip for a full bag then smoothed out my blankets. "Would you like a drink?"

I supposed gin would be out of the question. "Yes, please."

She reached over to the nightstand and picked up a plastic cup with a straw sticking out of the top, then threaded it between my lips. I sucked. The water tasted metallic, lukewarm, but I swallowed it down. My insides felt shrivelled, as though I'd been left in the sun to dry like a raisin.

She didn't bother to close the door on her way out, and it turned out she'd been telling the truth about the doctor. He swept in before I'd had a chance to question the policeman again, his hangdog expression a contrast to the nurse's false sunshine. In a way, I preferred that —at least he wasn't trying to pretend the situation was anything other than miserable.

"I need to check a few things." He poked and prodded, scribbling on his chart as he went. When he got to my head, I let out a yowl and jerked away as he pressed on the back of it. Even Detective Nash grimaced.

"Nasty lump, that," the doctor said, stepping back.

"How did I get it?"

It was his turn to look at the policeman. Another shake of his head.

I gritted my teeth, both from pain and frustration. "Will one of you tell me what's going on?"

The doctor made a show of looking at his watch. "Sorry, late for my next patient."

His footsteps had gone out of earshot before the door swung closed behind him.

That left me, Detective Nash, and a roomful of still, dead air, so thick and cloying every breath weighed heavy on my chest.

"What do you remember?" he finally asked. "Your name?"

"Lily Ann Matthews."

He pulled a notebook out of his pocket and wrote that down. "What else?"

"Being on the Tube. I was on my way to visit my sister."

"You remember getting off the Tube? Leaving the station?"

I shook my head and instantly regretted it as sparks burst behind my eyes.

"No. Wait, was I mugged? Is that it?"

I shuffled up the bed and looked for my bag—a small black clutch I didn't like much but cared more for now that I no longer had it.

He shook his head again, which seemed to be his full repertoire of movement.

"No. Maybe. We're not sure."

I waited for him to make up his mind and continue. He shifted in his seat, sinking lower on the ugly floral fabric.

"A passer-by found you unconscious in a concrete planter just after ten last night. From the marks on your arms, it looks like you were in a fight."

I lifted my arms into my field of vision, noticing the bandages wound around them for the first time as well as the tubes snaking from the back of my right hand.

"I don't fight. I never fight."

Rose always said I was a lover not a fighter, although I disagreed with her on the lover part. The first man I dated left me for a girl who, I quote, would "put out," and the second didn't even have the decency to let me know before he took my ex-flatmate on a romantic minibreak to Venice. Still, that didn't change the fact that I was more likely to hug someone when I got drunk than punch them.

Nash shrugged. "The evidence says otherwise."

"What else does the evidence say?" I asked, trying to keep the snark out of my voice.

"That you got in an altercation and hit your head, probably on the edge of the planter." He shrugged again, and although I'd denied being prone to violence, I wanted to smack him. "Wouldn't be the first time a girl's got in a bust-up after one too many."

I reached up and gingerly felt my way along the satsuma-sized bump on the back of my head. He was right about that part. "Did anybody see what happened?"

"Nobody's come forward so far."

"And where's my handbag?"

"Did you have it with you?"

"Of course I did. What kind of girl goes out without her mobile? Oh, hell, my sister's gonna freak when she can't get hold of me." Rose may have only been a year older, but since our mum went into a care home, she'd assumed the role of parent. "I need to call her."

For the first time, something approaching sympathy appeared on Nash's face. "Give me her number, and I'll let her know where you are."

I recited it, and he jotted the digits down. "Is there any chance you could not tell her where I am? Perhaps pretend you're a friend and I'm crashing at your place?"

He stifled a laugh. "No can do. It wouldn't make a good impression if the police started lying, would it?"

I was about to say it didn't usually make a difference, but I bit my tongue. I needed his help—

there was no point in annoying him.

"Besides," he continued. "You'll need somebody to bring you clothes. Your dress got trashed and the nurses cut you out of the remains of it."

I groaned as I looked down at the paper gown. Nash was right—I could hardly catch a cab looking like that, even if I had the cash to do so.

"Fine, you win."

I tried to fold my arms and roll over, but the wires and tubes got in the way. I had to settle for giving him a dirty look.

"I'll call her, but when I come back, we need to talk about the rest of this."

Oh, I couldn't wait. And I couldn't remember either. While Nash stepped out of the room, I made an effort to push aside the quicksand in my brain and grab some thoughts, but they wouldn't come. A planter? How on earth had I got into one of those?

Nash had been gone less than a minute before he returned. "She's not answering."

"She always answers."

We had a standing joke that Rose would self-destruct if she got more than three feet from her phone.

"Well, she didn't today."

The ripple of fear I'd felt earlier returned. What if we'd gone out after all? She could have got hurt at the same time as me. I pushed myself up and swung my legs over the side of the bed, ignoring the pain that shot through my lower spine.

"Hey, lie back down. You're not supposed to get up until they've run more tests."

"I need to check on my sister." I tugged a plastic clip off my finger, and the machine next to me went haywire.

"Congratulations. Now they think you're dead."

Seconds later, the door crashed open and a team of wide-eyed nurses ran in. The first one quickly assessed the situation.

"You need to get back into bed," she said, hands on hips.

"Not until I've spoken to my sister."

"You can speak to her later," Nash said.

"No, I can speak to her now." Asserting myself felt uncomfortable, but no matter what they thought I'd done, they had no right to keep me away from Rose.

I struggled to my feet and took a shaky step, tugging the drip trolley along behind me. Cool air on my bottom told me the gown was gaping, and I reached behind to hold it closed. No sense in embarrassing myself more than I already had.

Nash huffed in exasperation. "Look, if I send an officer round to fetch her, will you lie down?"

I paused and considered his offer. Even as I stood still, my legs trembled. I'd never make it to Clapham on my own. His small victory smile as I sank back on the bed made me hate him even more.

"Fine, you win again," I said, barely able to get the words out between gritted teeth.

"Give me the address."

"Thirty-seven Brook House, Melrose Street, Clapham. It's a block of flats."

He'd started writing, but his pen paused halfway through. "Above Gino's Deli?"

"You know the area?"

He shook his head. "Never went there before this morning." He hesitated. "It's where we picked you up.

In the planter outside the deli."

I dragged an image out of my mind. I saw that concrete trough every time I walked to Rose's. Two days ago, petunias had overflowed down the sides, a riot of colour against the spiky phormiums in the centre. And now they had a Lily-shaped dent in the middle. Another image popped up, this time of me looking down at the display from above, glass of wine in hand as I stood on the...

"Holy crap! I fell off my sister's balcony."

"Huh?"

"Her balcony's right above that planter."

His brow crinkled. "That might explain the bump on your head, but what about the scratches on your arms?"

"I don't know. Maybe something happened before..." I trailed off, and his loss of colour suggested he shared the same thoughts.

"Lie down." His voice took on an urgency lacking before, and his sallow complexion turned a shade paler. "I'll send a unit around."

He strode out of the room, and I had no choice but to follow his instructions. My muscles refused to hold me up any longer. As I strained to hear his mutterings in the corridor, ice ran through my veins. What had happened in my sister's apartment?

CHAPTER 2

AN HOUR PASSED, then two. The nurse came back with lunch, but I was in no mood to eat the lukewarm mashed potato and greyish chicken. Where was Rose? How on earth hadn't she noticed when I fell off the balcony? Her flat only had four rooms—surely she must have wondered where I went?

I needed to know.

Right up until three o'clock when I found out. Nash came back, trailed by a black guy wearing jeans and a leather jacket. Even without a uniform, he had "cop" written all over him. Neither of them spoke. They didn't need to. Rose's fate was written on their faces, in the lines on their foreheads, the set of their mouths, the haunted depths of their eyes.

"She's dead, isn't she?"

Relief flickered across Nash's face before his sombre expression returned. I'd saved him from having to break the news. He only had to nod. "I'm sorry, ma'am."

I'd asked the question, but nothing could have prepared me for the answer. A chill ran through me again. At this rate, I'd need antifreeze in my drip, not saline. I pressed my head into the pillow to try and stop the whooshing sound in my ears.

"Are you okay, ma'am? Should we call the nurse?"

Was I okay? *Was I okay?* How could he even ask that question?

"What happened?" I choked out.

"I'm not sure—"

"Please, just tell me what happened."

Nothing he said could be as bad as the thoughts swirling around in my head. Did Rose die by accident? Or was it...was it...?

Nash's colleague stepped forward. "Detective Sergeant Bridges."

He held out a hand, then looked at mine with their collection of wires and tubes and thought better of it. Instead, he perched on the seat and leaned forward so his eyes were level with mine.

"We found Rose in bed. I'm afraid there was nothing we could do."

"But how? Did she hit her head? Was it alcohol poisoning?"

He glanced at the bandages on my arms, and then I realised. We hadn't been alone in her flat last night, had we?

"Somebody killed her?" I whispered.

I didn't want to know the details, but at the same time, I needed to. What had happened to my sister?

Bridges nodded.

"How?"

He looked at Nash, who gave a tiny shrug. "We'll have to wait for the medical examiner to confirm that."

"But you must have a clue! Did you see her?"

"Yes."

I'd steeled myself for his answer, but even so, that one word broke through to my core and shattered me. The heart-rate monitor went crazy again as I sobbed, and the nurse reappeared with a handful of pills.

"Take these. They'll make you feel better."

Was she crazy? I shoved her hand away.

"They won't bring my sister back, will they?" I yelled.

And that was the only thing that would help.

Nash hovered by the door, looking as though he'd rather be anywhere but stuck in a room with a hysterical female. Bridges's eyes didn't waver, though. He conveyed a practised air of sympathy and calm in the manner of a man who'd done it many times before. How awful must it be to live through this every day? To have a job that revolved around death?

A vision floated into my head of Rose the last time I saw her. The previous Sunday, we'd curled up on her sofa for a marathon session of *The West Wing*, accompanied by her homemade chocolate brownies and copious amounts of ice cream. Now, I'd never eat them again, and that stupid thought made the tears flow harder. I'd tried making brownies myself, but all I got was a ruined pan and charcoal.

"Is there someone we can call?" Bridges asked. "Your parents?"

"My father's dead and my mother lives in a nursing home. She's got dementia."

And perhaps that was the only saving grace in all of this. I'd have to tell Mum that Rose had left us, of course, but she'd forget by the next day.

"Someone else? A friend maybe?"

"Suki. She's my friend, and I work with her."

"Can you give me her number?"

I recited it while Nash wrote it down, and then he dashed from the room, no doubt pleased to escape.

An uncomfortable minute passed before Bridges spoke again. "We'll need to ask you a few questions about what went on yesterday."

"I don't know what went on. I can't remember anything." I ended on a near shriek, almost as high pitched as the damn machine next to me.

"Talking about things can sometimes help. You know, stir up thoughts you didn't realise you had."

At that moment I wasn't sure what would be worse —remembering or not remembering. While any recollection could give the police a lead to the man who killed Rose, I didn't want my last memories of her to be those moments.

Bridges leaned forward a little more. "It doesn't need to be right away. Take a few hours to get your head straight."

Hours? I'd need years, no, decades. My whole life could pass, and I'd still miss Rose with every atom in my body. But what of the person who killed her? Did he, or she, feel remorse? Or emptiness? Or a sick thrill?

Maybe I'd never find out those details, but I did know whoever did it was walking around free at the moment, and that had to change.

"Okay. Fine. Ask what you need to ask."

"Thank you. I know this can't be easy. Let's take a break for an hour or two, and we'll talk this afternoon after Detective Nash comes back. Do you want me to bring you anything? Something to drink?"

I shook my head. The one thing I wanted was Rose, but nobody could help there.

An hour later, Detective Nash brought the next best thing—Suki. She rushed in like a tiny Tasmanian devil, a whirl of blonde hair and energy half-hidden by a belted trench coat. Judging by the black streaks of mascara across her cheeks, she'd already been told the news.

I prepared to have the breath squashed out of me as usual, but she stopped short inches from the bed. "Are you okay? I mean, stupid question, do you hurt? Like, do you need a hug?"

I nodded, and she flung her arms around me. The monitors didn't appreciate that either.

"Shut up," she hissed at them. "I can't believe it. Rose died?"

I nodded.

"That's crazy. Who would want to hurt her? Everybody loved Rose."

It was true. My sister may have been awkward at times, but even if she told you something you didn't want to hear, she said the words with a smile on her face.

"I don't know. I've thought of nothing else for the past hour."

Suki turned to Nash and Bridges and put her hands on her hips. "Why are you two standing around? Why aren't you out detecting?"

Irritation flashed in Nash's eyes, but Bridges stifled a grin. The younger of the pair by at least two decades, he was also more personable.

"We'll go and spend your tax money just as soon as we've asked Lily here a few questions."

"What questions?"

"Well, from the bruises on her arms, it looks like

she's been in a struggle. We're hoping she can remember something about it."

Suki pointed at the empty seat. "So, get on with it."

This time, Bridges didn't bother trying to hide his smile. "We can't do that with you here. It's a police investigation. The only people allowed to be present are Miss Matthews and a lawyer if she wants one."

"A lawyer? Why would I need a lawyer?"

Bridges turned his smile on me. If he wasn't careful, he could use it as a weapon. "We need to offer you that option, but this is just a little chat so we can hear your side of the story."

That didn't sound too bad. After all, I wanted them to catch whoever did this.

"She's having a lawyer," Suki said.

"Miss Matthews?"

Suki planted herself in front of him. "Don't you 'Miss Matthews' her. Lily's just gone through hell, and I know all about your 'little chats.' My brother's friend Carlson got invited in for coffee and biscuits at the cop shop once, and the next day he ended up in court."

"I can't afford a lawyer."

Bridges sighed. "We can find one for you."

"Off you go, then." Suki pointed at the door, and the two men shuffled before she plopped down on the bed.

Her face softened and she hugged me again, only this time I couldn't control my emotions. Tears poured out of me, dripping onto Suki's blonde bob. When my mum got diagnosed with dementia, I'd thought that was as bad as life got, but it turned out that was just the warm-up. Losing Rose tore me in two.

"Things can only get better," Suki whispered, reading my thoughts. "You'll see."

But she was wrong.

If I'd known what was to come, instead of wishing for Rose to return, I'd have prayed to join her on the other side.

CHAPTER 3

NASH AND BRIDGES returned as the nurse brought my dinner. I wasn't sure which was less appetising—gelatinous soup or a police interview. Another man hovered in the doorway, taking quick glances down the corridor even as Bridges beckoned him into the room.

"This is Marty Brogan, your lawyer."

Marty wiped his palms on his trousers and stepped forward. "Pleased to meet you." He stuck out a pudgy hand for me to shake, and it turned out he hadn't managed to get rid of the sweat. Yuck. Then as he squashed into the chair next to me, I caught sight of the damp patches under his armpits. Not a great start—my lawyer was more nervous than me.

"How are you feeling?" Bridges set up a digital recorder on the tray-table next to the soup while Nash dragged a couple of extra chairs over.

I stared at him. My sister just got murdered. How did he think I felt?

Undaunted, he tried again. "Nurses treating you okay?"

"Fine."

Fine. One tiny word, yet it was programmed to set off alarm bells in all but the dumbest of men. Bridges sucked in a hasty breath and stepped backwards, fumbling in his pocket as he took a seat.

"Are you ready to start?" He'd got his notepad out, and now he reached over and clicked the start button on the recorder. The green light blinking didn't give me much choice.

"I'll try to help. But everything after my Tube ride's a blank."

"Let's start a little earlier in the day. You said you spoke to your sister in the morning?"

"Yes."

"Did you call her? Or did she call you?"

"She phoned me."

"Is that normal?"

"That I talk to my sister? Of course."

A rare day passed without me speaking to Rose, but now I'd never hear her voice again. *Never*. Grief crawled up my throat, but I forced it back down. Crying in front of three men would be mortifying, and it wouldn't help to catch her killer either.

"Wasn't Rose at work yesterday?" Bridges asked.

"She often called me on her coffee breaks. What's this got to do with her death?"

I glanced sideways at Marty and found him eyeing up my soup.

"It's standard procedure to establish a timeline."

"Fine. She called. We spoke about the corset I'm...I was making her and arranged to see the new James Bond film at the weekend. Then a customer came in, so I had to go."

Nash took over. "You work in that bondage shop?"

He nearly ended up wearing the damn soup.

"Black Lily is *not* a bondage shop. We sell leather goods, bespoke corsets, and luxury underwear. And I don't just work there, I own it."

"What did your sister think of that? From the look of her flat, she wasn't into all that kinky stuff."

"Can you make him leave?" I asked Marty. "I'm not speaking to him anymore."

"Uh...well, n-n-no. Not really."

What exactly was the point of having a lawyer? So far, all he'd done was get a yellow legal pad out and doodle his name in one corner. Suki would have been more use.

Bridges cut back in. "Nash didn't mean to insult you. It's just that when we visited your sister's home, she seemed more into flowers than leather."

"So what if she was?"

She'd always loved pastels and florals. Usually, my corsets were made from leather or taffeta in strong shades of green, red, and purple. For Rose's birthday, I'd been sewing one in peach velvet with lace ruffles. She'd been bugging me to make it for months, and with three weeks to go, I only needed to sew on the miniature silk roses. Now, she'd never see it.

"Let's move on, shall we? What did you do after the phone call?"

"Served the customer, then a big order came in over the internet. Suki and I danced around a bit then had lunch."

Danced around? That was an understatement. Suki had whooped like an idiot, and I spilled coffee all over a pile of invoices.

"Just one customer came into the shop?"

"We cater to the higher end of the market, so we only get a few customers each day. Twenty, thirty if we're lucky. Each piece is made by hand, and we mainly work to order."

"Okay, you had lunch. Where did you go?"

"There's a sandwich shop next door. I go there most days."

"So the staff would recognise you?"

"Definitely. But why does that matter? Shouldn't you be asking about my sister?"

Bridges smiled again, and damn if it didn't chip a little bit of ice from my heart.

"We'll get to that in just a minute. As you were with her in the flat, we need to talk through everything in case there's a clue that could help us. We want to get to the bottom of this as much as you do."

"But it wasn't me who got…" I paused on the word, hating it. "Killed. Shouldn't you be finding out what Rose did yesterday?"

"Believe me, we will. Our colleagues are looking into that right now. But we need to ask you because you were in the flat too."

I nodded and tried to swallow, but a lump got caught in my throat. Talking about this was harder than I'd ever imagined. Bridges passed me a glass of water, and I took a sip, wishing with all my heart for the questions to end.

"What did you ask again?" I couldn't think straight.

"The staff in the sandwich shop…"

"Yes, they'd recognise me. Marek served me, and I bought an egg mayonnaise baguette and crisps."

"Did you eat in or out?"

"I ate in our shop. Then I worked on clothes for the rest of the afternoon while Suki dealt with enquiries."

"You work on clothes in the shop as well?"

"Yes. We've got a work area set up at the back. It's been good for business—our clients like to see with their own eyes that everything's handmade. So many other companies outsource, and although we can't compete on volume, we get a lot of repeat customers."

My voice sounded robotic to my own ears. Calm and collected while my guts writhed inside my belly like angry snakes.

"What time did you leave?" Bridges asked as his pen scratched across the pad.

"Just after six. I wanted to finish some stitching before I went."

"Where did you get on the Tube?"

"Piccadilly Circus."

"And then you travelled to Clapham?"

I shook my head, then regretted it as pain shot through my neck. "No. I went from Paddington to see her. I live there."

He wrote that down. "You went home first? Why?"

"I wanted to change into something more comfortable. You try wearing a corset all day and see if you'd fancy keeping it on in the evening as well."

The corner of his lip quirked up, and a vision of Mr. Tough Cop in a leather outfit popped into my mind. I bit my lip to stop the giggle that wanted to escape. Totally not appropriate in that situation. And Bridges was watching me. Did he know what I was thinking? I flipping well hoped not.

"Did you notice anyone following you?" he asked, ever the professional. "Paying you any extra attention?"

I couldn't help rolling my eyes at him. "This is London. There are people everywhere."

"Is that a no?"

"Yes, it's a no. When I get on the Tube, I keep my eyes down." If you made eye contact with another passenger on the London Underground, you were immediately labelled a freak. "One guy pinched my bottom, but he got off at Stockwell. Besides, that's nothing unusual."

Bridges gazed up and down my body, and I shrank back under the thin blanket. I already got stared at enough at work without him joining in.

"So, when did you last see your sister? That you remember?"

"Almost a week ago. Sunday."

"Did she mention her plans for yesterday evening? Was she expecting anybody besides you to visit?"

"She wasn't even expecting me. I thought I'd surprise her. When I spoke to her in the morning, she had a meeting at work due to finish at five, and then she was going to binge on Netflix."

"Was she seeing anyone? A boyfriend?" He met my eyes. "Girlfriend?"

"Neither." My sister would have mentioned a little thing like that. "She was living with a guy—Damien—but they broke up a few months ago, and he moved out. Since then she's been singing the praises of the single life."

I choked as I caught myself using the present tense. How many more times would I make that mistake before reality sank in?

"So, she hasn't been out with a man since? Is that right?"

"Not exactly. She joined an online dating site, just looking for something casual. I don't think she was ready for commitment again."

"Which site?"

"I don't know. Can you find out from her

computer?"

"I'll have a word with the tech team. I'm sure they're already looking at it."

This discussion left me feeling sick. Time and time again, I'd warned Rose against hook-ups with strangers, but she'd disregarded my fears.

"It's just a bit of fun," she'd said. "You should try it. Get out a bit more and meet new people. It's not healthy to work as many hours as you do."

"But you don't know any of these guys."

"How well do you ever know anyone? I thought Damien was the one for me until I caught him with his tongue down that trollop's throat."

"Be careful, okay."

"Look, if it makes you feel better, I'll message you the details each time I go on a date. How about that?"

And she had. Once or twice a week for the last couple of months, I'd received a message in the afternoon with a man's name, his picture, and a brief biography. Some of them were even cute, but she'd never mentioned the same man twice. I told all of this to Bridges.

"Do you still have the messages?"

"They were in my phone, which was in my bag. I don't know what happened to it."

"We'll check Rose's flat. Did you get a message yesterday?"

"No, nothing."

"And did you ever take her advice?"

"What, and try online dating?"

He nodded.

"No."

"And you're single?"

"Yes." Unless you counted my deep and meaningful relationship with Ben and Jerry.

"Have you had any break-ups yourself recently?"

"I haven't been out on a date in a while."

He kept his eyes fixed on his notepad. "How long's a while?"

Oh great. Now I had to admit to the rather nice-looking cop just how long my dry spell had lasted. "Over a year."

"A year? Are you serious?"

"Yes. Can we move on to something else?"

He jotted a few notes down. My non-existent love life recorded in black and white for posterity. Wonderful.

"You mentioned she was at work until early evening. What did she do?"

I noted he'd remembered to use the past tense. Probably in his job, he got used to it.

"She was a PA at a software company in Victoria. Mediforce. She'd worked there since she left school."

"Software. What kind of software?"

Rose had tried to explain it to me on several occasions over the years but lost me every time.

"Uh, something for compliance on medical trials. I never really understood."

And I could barely turn my own computer on. Apart from Facebook and email, technology and I weren't really on speaking terms. I left all that stuff to Suki.

"Okay, we can find out more if we need to. Did your sister have a tiff with anyone lately? Doesn't matter how minor. Sometimes even tiny things can set off someone who's not quite wired up right."

A tiff? What kind of freak murdered someone over a

bloody tiff?

"Nothing that she told me. Only Damien, but that was ages ago. He cheated on her."

Bridges raised an eyebrow and scribbled something. "I'll put him at the top of our list."

"Oh, and one of the neighbours kept playing his music too loud. She mentioned having a word, but I don't know if she got around to it."

"Do you remember their name?"

I forgot and shook my head again, then sucked in a sharp breath.

"Do you need some painkillers? I can call the nurse."

I gritted my teeth. The last lot of pills they brought had left me spaced out and nauseous, and I hated that feeling.

"No. No more pills. I'm not sure I ever knew the person's name. But Rose said she hammered on the ceiling to try and get the music to stop, so I think whoever was playing it lived above her."

"We'll be speaking to everyone in the building, so I'll make sure we identify him. Or her. And I have to ask, what about you? Have you had issues with anyone lately?"

A bubble of laughter escaped at his question. To suggest I'd had a bust-up would be suggesting I had a life outside work, and right now, I didn't. I spent five days a week at my shop, and even when I wasn't behind the counter, I'd turned my lounge into a workshop. Each evening, I sewed until my fingers ached.

"No, nobody."

"And how was your relationship with Rose?" He chuckled. "I'm always getting into squabbles with my sister. Drives me nuts sometimes."

"We didn't fight. Never. We only had each other."
Us against the world, that was what Rose always said.
"Surely you can't think I had something to do with
this?"

"We have to explore every avenue. And at the
moment, you're the only other person we can find who
was in the flat that evening."

I held up my bandaged arms. "I didn't do this to
myself, you know."

"No, but your sister looked like she'd been in a fight
as well."

Was he suggesting what I thought he was? "How
can you even contemplate me hurting my sister?"

"Statistically speaking, most victims are killed by
someone close to them."

"Screw you, and screw your damn statistics." First, I
pointed at Marty. "You might as well go home. If you
can't help to keep the questions sensible, there's no
point in you being here." Then I turned my glare on the
two alleged detectives. "And if you insist on wasting
your time here, you can do it in silence. I'm done."

I turned over, ignoring the machine's howl of
protest, and put the pillow over my head.

My brain hurt, my heart ached, and I needed to
sleep.

CHAPTER 4

CONCUSSION, THE DOCTOR said. That was why they wouldn't let me go home, and why I was stuck in my cell-like room reading a six-month-old copy of *Knitting World* magazine. I didn't even know how to knit. Suki had tried to get me something more entertaining before she left, but the kiosk in the hospital foyer closed before she got there. With visiting hours over, all she could give me was a promise to come back the next morning with supplies.

"What about Black Lily?" I'd asked. Saturday was usually our busiest day at the shop.

"I called Brenda. She's going to watch Cindy's son while Cindy opens up."

Brenda, Cindy, and Susan were my three part-timers. When sales began to build up, Suki and I had struggled to make all the clothes ourselves, so I advertised for help. Brenda had retired from her job making theatre costumes three years ago and got bored with doing nothing every day, and Cindy and Susan wanted to work part-time from home so they could be there for their children.

Before I ended up an invalid, I'd been on the lookout for a sixth person to join our team. My girls worked all the hours they could, but stock levels had dropped to the bare minimum over the past few weeks.

"They're gems. I don't know what I'd do without them."

"Brenda said she'd help out with babysitting next week. She offered to come into the shop too, if we get desperate, but I'm not sure what our clients would think of a seventy-year-old in leather."

The thought made me smile for the first time all day. Suki and I acted as walking advertisements while we worked, and the idea of Brenda in a basque was... interesting.

"She could always wear the velvet corset jacket with that long organza skirt."

Both were prototypes and hideously fiddly to make.

"Hopefully they'll let you out before it comes to that."

I didn't want to be stuck in hospital, but returning to work filled me with trepidation as well. How could I face people when I didn't even want to face my own mind?

I didn't have an answer, but I didn't have a choice either. I needed to work if I wanted to eat.

Head throbbing, I flung the knitting magazine down and tried to sleep, hoping it would heal me. But my subconscious had other plans. Over and over again, I ran through the events of yesterday, but every time I got to the Tube journey, the movie stopped. Poof. Like somebody pulled out the plug.

After I'd lain awake for five hours, I gave in. The nurse came back with her pills, and I swallowed every last one without even asking what they were.

Temporary oblivion was a better option than thinking.

The day of my release came all too soon and not soon enough. I say release because the hospital felt like a prison, but at the same time, I hated the thought of going home alone. I'd had a flatmate up until two months ago, an accountant on secondment at one of the big firms, but he'd moved back to India. With stock and half-finished corsets spread all over my spare bedroom, I hadn't got around to replacing him.

Suki saved the day again by offering her couch. I knew from experience it wasn't the most comfortable place to sleep, but at least I'd have company, and that was what I needed at the moment.

Before I left, Bridges stopped by one last time. He'd been to visit every afternoon—four times in total, twice alone and twice with Nash trailing along behind him. Out of the two detectives, I much preferred Bridges. He seemed human compared to Nash's cyborg. Bridges had assured me of his partner's investigative skills, and perhaps they were excellent, but his interpersonal ones sure needed work.

Each time Bridges arrived, I'd asked the same question and got the same answer:

"Anything?"

"Nothing concrete's turned up."

I began to think Suki was right, and they spent all day playing solitaire and eating donuts. "But you found my phone?"

Nash, in one of his cheerier moments, had told me my bag turned up under Rose's sideboard, as if it had slid under there in the struggle with her murderer.

They'd stopped thinking I had anything to do with her death, which I'd thought was a blessing until I found out why.

Bridges had put on his sympathetic face as he broke the news yesterday. That the sick bastard who killed my sister got off on it. They'd found semen on the outfit she'd worn to work that day, a navy shift dress she'd left draped over the end of her bed.

Of course, they couldn't prove it belonged to the killer, but I knew what they thought because I thought it too. Rose would never have worn a stained dress to work, and she wasn't the type to pop into the stationery cupboard for a quickie at lunchtime. However the traces got on there, it happened after she left the office. The part of me that hadn't been frozen into paralysis prayed Rose hadn't been alive as her killer got his kicks.

Bridges didn't put it into words, but his expression said the same.

And today, his mask was one of determination as he took a seat and handed over a pastry from the bakery down the road. The first day he came, the nurse had served up stew so foul I wasn't sure whether it had been cooked or simply vomited up, and since then Bridges had taken to bringing me little treats. Underneath his slightly officious exterior, a kind heart lurked.

"Yes, we've found your phone, but it takes time to track people down, especially when they haven't used their real names. We've eliminated two of the men Rose met through the dating site so far, and the team's working to find the other seven." He crouched at the side of my bed. "I want to catch this man as much as you do."

"I just wish I could remember."

The doctors said memory loss was common with head injuries, and it might only be temporary. I could remember everything, nothing, or anything in between. Which meant that right now, I potentially had the key to a murderer locked up in my head, and I couldn't do a damn thing about it.

"You and me both, Miss Matthews. You and me both."

Suki hailed a cab outside King's College Hospital and helped me inside. The twenty-five-minute car journey seemed to take twice as long as we crawled past Hyde Park. Tourists wandered in the road, oblivious to traffic as they looked for anything vaguely British to photograph. As we neared Paddington, the grey clouds above let go of their load and fat plops of rain fell, getting heavier as we dashed from the vehicle to my flat. I needed to pick up enough clothes to last...well, I wasn't sure, plus some of my half-finished pieces. If nothing else, sewing would keep my hands busy.

For the next three days, I hid myself away in Suki's one-bedroom flat with no desire to speak to anybody. The only call I answered was from Bridges, but he didn't have the news I hoped for.

"We found the neighbour who kept playing the loud music."

"And?"

"The reason it took so long is because he just got back from a trip to Ibiza with his girlfriend."

"Let me guess, they were away on the night Rose got...got..." I couldn't say the word.

"Sorry. He had a prior for assault too. We'd felt hopeful on that one."

"Is there anyone else?"

"We've spoken to all of Rose's colleagues, and half of the men on the list from your phone. Nobody could think of a reason to hurt her, and all but one of the phone guys had an alibi."

"What about that one?"

"The semen stain we found didn't contain any DNA, but—"

"Wait! How is that possible? Was your test faulty?"

"It's rare, but it can happen if the man's had a vasectomy. As I was saying, the suspect's sample didn't contain DNA. While it's possible the semen stain could have been unrelated to the murder, we don't consider that a likely scenario. It was right on the front of the dress, and none of her colleagues recall seeing it. A neighbour remembers her arriving home a few minutes before *EastEnders* started, which means Rose didn't have time to go anywhere after she left work."

"So you've got nothing?"

"We've eliminated people. Your sister's ex doesn't look good for it either. He swears he spent that night in front of the TV, although he can't prove it, and we've had him under surveillance. He spends most of his time watching anime."

Which had been one of Rose's complaints about him. And when he'd done the dirty on her, he'd done it with a girl who liked to dress up as a Pokémon in her spare time. Racking my brain, I remembered one more thing. "He hasn't had a vasectomy either, or at least he hadn't when he was with Rose. I went to the clinic with her to get the morning-after pill when a condom broke.

She was in a right state, and Damien didn't have time to take her."

"He said that too. Asshole," Bridges added under his breath.

"So what now?"

"We'll carry on hunting for the rest of the men from the internet, and we're waiting on forensic evidence from the lab."

"Still? It's been over a week." What were my taxes paying for?

"Cutbacks. We were lucky to get the sample from the dress processed as fast as we did. Had to call in a favour for that one."

"Will you let me know what happens?"

His voice softened. "Believe me, you'll be the first person I call."

When he hung up, I crawled back under the duvet, drained. Work could wait. Everything could wait. Life could wait.

The blows kept coming. Suki arrived home early the next day carrying a bottle of wine and a pint of ice cream.

"What's wrong?"

She led me over to the sofa and sat me down, then poured us a glass each.

"The police called today."

"Why didn't they call me?"

"They did. You didn't answer."

I glanced at my phone on the coffee table, now up to forty-seven missed calls. I'd ignored them all while I concentrated on watching television game shows, but I hadn't noticed Bridges's number among them. Mind you, I didn't seem to notice an awful lot at the moment.

"Did they find anything?"

She shook her head, then put her wine down and gripped my hand. "Sweetie, they're releasing Rose's body."

Ahh, now I understood the need for wine. I grabbed my glass and swallowed the lot, then went to pour myself another. Before the glass was full, I gave up and swigged from the bottle instead.

The worst moment in all this, the absolute worst, had been when Bridges led me into the morgue to identify Rose's body. Even in death, she'd looked beautiful, and if I imagined hard enough, she could have been asleep. Only the sheet, pulled right up to her chin, gave the game away. It hid the ligature mark I now knew was there. The post-mortem results had come through the day before, and Bridges shared that little gem with me. And then after I'd pressed my hand up against the glass viewing window and sobbed into his handkerchief, I'd had to walk away from my sister for the last time. My soul parted, with the stronger half left behind in that stark white room with Rose.

And now I needed to bury her.

Suki shuffled close and squeezed my shoulders. "Do you want me to organise the funeral? The wake?"

Yes. "No, I should do it."

"Well, I'll help. Just let me know what you need."

"Could you bring another bottle of wine?"

Chapter 5

SIX PALL-BEARERS trudged slowly down the aisle of the chapel, carrying my sister on their shoulders as if she weighed nothing. Maybe she did? The important part of her, the soul that laughed and smiled and cried and loved, that was long gone. Where to? I liked to imagine she'd moved on to a new place, one without pain or heartache. Anything but nothing.

"Is someone getting married?"

I squeezed my mum's hand tighter. "No, Mum. It's a funeral. Rose's funeral."

"I remember Rose. We used to play bridge together when your father was alive. Now, there was something about her…"

She lapsed into silence, and the carer sitting to her right wrapped the fallen end of her scarf back around her neck. Mum had always felt the cold, and I'd inherited that trait. Rose got my father's love of winter, which led to endless battles over the thermostat as we grew up.

The vicar stood as the casket was lowered onto its stand, the spray of white roses stark against the dark wood. The irony of their presence wasn't lost on me—it always amused both of us that I was allergic to lilies, while roses made Rose sneeze. Their sweet scent drifted over as the vicar started speaking, reminding me more than his words ever could of what I'd lost.

My icy fingers gripped the necklace I always wore—a silver lily Mum gave me for my fourteenth birthday, three years before she got sick. Rose got a matching one for her namesake. Only now it was missing. I'd asked Bridges if I could have it back, and he'd gone around to her flat personally to search for it, but to no avail. He suspected the killer might have taken it as a sick souvenir, and that thought made bile rise in my throat.

"Cats," my mum whispered. "That's it. Rose had cats everywhere. Or was it dogs? My memory's not what it was."

"Shhh." I pointed to the front.

Mum's eyes lit up. "Is the bride coming soon?"

"Are you ready?" Suki asked.

I nodded, and she gave me a hug before we filed out of the chapel. As we shuffled past the rows of pews, I spotted Nash and Bridges in the corner, watching. Bridges had warned me they'd be there, something about killers revisiting the scene of the crime. Apparently, they liked funerals too. So, I knew why the police had to come, but even though Bridges caught my eye and smiled, I felt sick because their presence was a grim reminder of the hell Rose went through at the end.

"You did good," Suki said.

"Did I?" If my tears during the eulogy were anything to go by, she was using a different scale to judge. I'd rate myself as bad with a hint of awful.

"Yes. Getting up there in front of everyone must

have been doubly difficult for you."

I didn't tell her about the shot of whisky I'd knocked back in the toilet before they brought the coffin in. For my whole life, I'd longed to overcome my terror of public speaking, and driven by tragedy, I'd managed to get up in front of a hundred people and talk for three entire minutes. If Rose could have seen me, she'd have been laughing. Time and time again, she'd told me I just needed the right motivation and I could do anything. Suki and Rose used to kid about my plans for domination—first lingerie, then the world.

I tried to smile, but my mouth fought against it. "Next thing you know, I'll be running for office."

Suki laughed and steered me in the direction of the waiting car. Despite my vow to organise the funeral, she'd sorted out most of it as well as running the shop and sewing until two in the morning while I stared into space. Now that today was over, I needed to start pulling my weight again.

But not yet, it seemed.

"Let's get some food first, eh?" Suki suggested.

Mum and her carer came with us, and I felt sad that Mum's first trip out for ages was to attend her daughter's funeral. State-run nursing homes didn't budget for excursions, and I'd been so busy with the shop lately I hadn't had time to visit much. At least, that was what I told myself. If I cared to face the truth, I'd admit how much I hated seeing the shell of the woman who brought me up, who barely remembered her own name, let alone mine.

Still, today she was smiling, and she looked more like Rose than ever.

"Who are you, dear?" she asked Suki as we settled

her in the seat between us.

"Suki," she replied for the fourth time that day. "Lily's friend."

"Suki. Isn't that Japanese? You don't look Japanese."

"Yes, it is, and no, I'm not. My mum read *Memoirs of a Geisha* and developed an obsession with Japan. It means 'love.'"

It also meant *bitches* in Russian, but Suki only admitted that when she got drunk.

"That's nice. If I ever have children, I think I'll name them after flowers. So pretty..."

I clutched my head in my hands and took a deep breath. Mum didn't mean to upset me, but when she said things like that, I felt as if she'd stabbed me in the heart. Both damn ventricles. I tried to block out the rest of the words as she chattered away for the journey to The Watchman's Arms, the pub where Suki had organised the wake.

"We'll just stay for a few minutes, and then I'll take her back," the carer whispered as we walked in, and I nodded, grateful she understood.

The atmosphere seemed entirely too cheery for the occasion, but with free food and drink, what could I expect? Instead of hiding in the toilets as I longed to do, I plastered on an expression that passed for bland as I helped Mum to fill a plate with sandwiches. A few people came up to offer condolences, but most left us alone. For that I was grateful.

"Are you ready to go now, Linda?" the carer asked once Mum finished her cake.

She nodded. "I do feel a little tired. But where's Rose? I haven't seen her yet."

I took her arm and led her towards the door. "Rose died, Mum."

"Oh, such a shame. Who's going to look after all the cats?"

I was on the verge of throwing up as I went back inside, but a glass of wine helped. I nibbled on a slice of cake as well, because even if there was edible food left in my flat, I wouldn't feel like eating it when I got back home. And I *was* going back home. Tonight. No more putting it off.

A girl wandered over, skinny with thick-rimmed glasses. I vaguely recognised her from somewhere. Rose's salsa class? Her book group?

She smiled hesitantly. "I'm not sure if you remember me?"

I shook my head.

"Sonya. I used to work with Rose. And this is Ned." She indicated the man standing at her elbow, who looked distinctly uncomfortable in his tie. "He's one of the programmers."

What was I supposed to say? "Oh. I'm sure you must be missing her as well."

Ned... That name sounded vaguely familiar. I was sure Rose went out for dinner with him once, and probably more. Or was it Ted?

A tear dripped down Sonya's cheek. "Every day. We always used to eat lunch together, and on Mondays, we'd started Spanish lessons in the evenings."

"I remember Rose mentioning that."

"Have the police caught anyone yet? I watch the news every day, just in case they say anything."

I'd restricted myself to box sets and crappy game shows. No news. I didn't want to see my sister reduced to a thirty-second sound bite on the BBC. "Not yet. They say they're looking, but..."

She gripped my hands. "They should do more. I mean, if this person killed once, they could do it again."

Another voice joined in. "I'm sure they're doing their best, Sonya."

I recognised the glum face of Rose's boss, Andrew. Although he was ten years older than her, she'd had a secret crush on him when she first joined the company. I didn't understand it myself—he was hardly the epitome of handsome, and she usually went for looks. Still, nothing ever came of it. She lost interest and he got married a couple of years back. I'd even made her an outfit to wear to the wedding. She'd looked so damn pretty. I gave another sniffle, wishing I'd brought more tissues.

Sonya turned to face him. "Their best isn't enough, is it?"

He gave her a sad smile, then addressed me. "We were all devastated to hear the news. Rose was a key member of the team and a friend. She'd been with us for so long. Eight years, wasn't it?"

"Longer than me and I've been there five," Sonya said.

Another man joined the group, hovering on the edges as if he wasn't sure whether to stay or leave. Sonya waved at him. "This is Steve, from HR."

Now, that guy, he was Rose's type. He was anyone's type. Older again, by six or seven years at a guess, but he had the most gorgeous blue eyes—midway between a summer sky and the cornflowers beneath it—and my heart gave an inadvertent flutter as he addressed me.

"Is there any way we can help you?" he asked, the

epitome of politeness. "I imagine things can't be easy after such a tragedy."

I shook my head, not trusting myself to speak without breaking down.

"If you do think of something, you can always call. Have you got the office number?"

"I don't think so."

He pulled out a business card and handed it over. "There. Just give me a shout if you need anything. Anything at all."

"Thanks."

"That offer goes for any of us," Ned put in. "We all loved Rose."

Sonya echoed him, bringing a tear to my eye. Why did people have to be so damn nice? It hurt.

Their approach opened the floodgates, because soon people were queuing up to offer sympathy I didn't want. More people Rose worked with, and dozens of people from her social circle. Who would have turned up to say goodbye to me? Suki, the other girls from work, Rose, and Mum. That was all. Face it, I had no life compared to my sister. As I accepted condolences from what had to be the hundredth person, I longed for my bed and a bottle of something strong. Sweet oblivion.

Finally, we managed to escape. Well, Suki forced a way through the crowd and shoved me towards the exit, living up to her pseudo-Russian roots. She'd just gone to flag down a cab when someone tapped my shoulder.

"Can I have a quick word?" Steve asked. His smile

had a sadness around the edges.

What now? "Sure."

"This may not be the best time, but I thought you should know. All of Medicorp's employees are enrolled in the company life insurance scheme, and it pays out twice their salary in the event of death. Rose nominated you as her beneficiary. It'll be about sixty thousand pounds."

Bloody hell! I'd never dreamed of having that much money. I sank down onto a bollard bordering the road and sucked in air. Part of me hated the thought of Rose being reduced to numbers on a cheque. But...that was a lot of zeroes.

Steve squeezed my shoulder. "Like I said, now might not be the best time. Rose put your address on the form, so I'll send you a letter confirming everything."

"It's okay. I mean, thank you. I don't really know what to say."

"It's been a hard day for you—I can see that. Why don't you go home and get some sleep? Nothing'll change between now and the morning."

I nodded dumbly.

"Do you need a lift home? My car's around the corner. I'd just need to track down my girlfriend inside." He glanced sheepishly back towards the pub. "She does like to talk."

I looked up to find Suki had already stopped a cab. "No, it's fine. But thanks again."

He smiled again, more warmly this time. "Take care of yourself, Lily."

"Who was he? What did he want?" Suki asked as the car pulled away.

"One of Rose's colleagues. Apparently, she had some life insurance through work." Sixty thousand flipping pounds! Although until I saw the cash for myself, I didn't quite believe it.

"That's good, right? I mean, it's terrible that she died, but at least...you know."

"It seems like blood money."

And I'd feel dreadful if I simply used it to pay off my credit cards. What sort of tribute was that? No, the sum would need to go towards something special.

"Don't be ridiculous. Millions of people have insurance policies. It's perfectly normal."

"It still makes me uncomfortable."

"Then why don't you donate some to charity?"

I could always trust Suki to come up with a good plan. "I like that idea. Rose gave money towards gorilla conservation every year. Perhaps I could too?"

"Or cats. Don't forget the cats. Or was it dogs?"

Even in the face of darkness, I burst into laughter. "I'll never forget the cats."

CHAPTER 6

AND SO LIFE went on. The day of the funeral, I closed the door on what came before and faced my future. A future all the more lacklustre because I'd live it without Rose.

My flat smelled musty when I opened the door, and the weeping fig in the corner of the lounge had shed half its leaves in protest at being abandoned for so long. On the other hand, the mould on the loaf of bread in the fridge was positively thriving. I took an almost-full bottle of white wine out and shut the door. Cleaning could wait until tomorrow. Or maybe the weekend. Sunday sounded like a good plan.

Other than that, the place remained as I left it. Everything neat and in its place, with my DVDs arranged in alphabetical order and the bottles on my dressing table lined up biggest first. The only hint at disarray was the jumble of leather on the table in the spare room—I'd been halfway through sewing a corset the night before I visited Rose, and when my eyes started closing of their own accord at 3:00 a.m., I abandoned it and went to bed. Fortunately, it was a stock item rather than a custom order, so at least I wouldn't have an irate client on the phone demanding to know when it would be ready.

My phone trilled as I poured myself a glass of wine.

"Suki? Why are you calling?"

"I just wanted to check you're okay."

"You only saw me half an hour ago."

"I know, but..."

"I'm fine, really," I lied. "I'm going to bed in a minute, so I'll see you in the morning."

"You want me to pick you up?"

"I can get the Tube." Because I couldn't ask Suki to travel all the way to Paddington from her flat in Whitechapel, then go back to Soho again.

"I'll open up, so don't worry about coming in early."

It was sweet of her to say, but I'd be there at nine, come rain, come shine.

Or come headache. I glared at the empty wine bottle as I pulled my corset tight the next morning and gritted my teeth at the worst part of my job. I loved corsets, don't get me wrong, but having to squash myself into one every day was purgatory.

Today, I didn't even feel pretty. When I stood on the scales, I found I'd lost over a stone in weight, and my pale complexion had gone all blotchy. My smokey eyes looked bruised, and the slash of red lipstick I wore looked less sexy and more like I'd done myself an injury. I closed my eyes at my reflection in the mirror, hating the girl staring back at me. My mood matched my hair colour: black.

Before I could change my mind about working and crawl back to bed, I slipped into a maroon velvet trench coat—another of my experiments—and pulled on my trainers. At least I could put off changing into my heels until I got to the shop.

Black Lily Designs. The business I'd started by accident then grown to be proud of. I'd adored my little shop in its tiny Soho backstreet from the moment I opened it, but right now I struggled to care about its future. Still, I needed money, so I had to work. Mind over matter. I had to put mind over matter.

"I was going to offer you a coffee, but I'm thinking an aspirin may be more appropriate," Suki said when the tinkling of the old brass bell over the door announced my arrival.

"I need both."

"How much wine did you drink last night?"

"One."

"One glass?"

"One bottle."

"Oh. That's probably for the best."

"What? Why?"

"Bridges phoned."

Why did those two words make my stomach do a backflip? "Since when did he start calling you and not me?"

"Since you stopped picking up. Have you even looked at your phone since we last talked?"

I fished around in my handbag, which was where I'd flung the thing yesterday after I spoke to Suki. Seventeen missed calls, five of them from Bridges. "Oops."

"Anyway, he got worried. I told him you'd drunk yourself silly and gone to bed."

Great, so now he thought I was an alcoholic. Although if the last fortnight was any indication, he wasn't far from the truth. "Thanks so much. Did he say anything else?" Suki had that look, the one where she twitched her lip before she told you something you didn't want to hear.

"They've finished processing Rose's apartment, so they're releasing it."

I sat down with a bump on one of the padded velvet stools that dotted the shop floor. "I don't know what I'm supposed to do with it."

Suki crouched beside me and rested a hand on my knee, her fingers warm to the touch. "I know you don't want to think about the place, but the landlord won't wait forever. He'll want it back unless you keep paying the rent."

Just when I thought I'd reached the point where I didn't need to cry anymore, another tear fell. "I can't afford to pay two lots of rent."

"How about I call him and explain the situation, and then we can go around there on Sunday and make a start with the clearing? We could box everything up and take it to one of those storage places, and you could sort through it properly when you feel better."

"I guess we'll have to." Then, realising how ungrateful I sounded, I added, "I mean, thanks for offering to help."

"It's okay. Now, I suggest you spend the day in the work area while I deal with the customers. People want to see a smile when they buy their kinky undies."

Head down, I traipsed to the back of the shop. Everything looked exactly like it did last time I was there, but it felt different. *I* felt different. Hollowed out inside, cracked, and the cracks were widening into chasms with every passing day. With nothing more to occupy me, I sat on my stool and began to sew.

I'd made three corsets, two skirts, and a jacket by the time Sunday came. All in black. All with the same grim aura of madness about them. Suki thought they were wonderful, but she'd always tended towards the darker side of the gothic trend.

"We need a hat to go with the jacket. Something with a veil."

"Neither of us knows how to make hats."

"Maybe we could do a collab. Remember that fashion student who stopped in the other day, looking for work experience? The one from Central Saint Martins? I'm sure she said something about hats. Hmm... Leave it with me."

Knowing Suki, I had no doubt we'd be selling hats next week. The project she set up with a shoe designer a few months back had earned us rave reviews and plenty of column inches, so it didn't sound like a bad idea. I wished I could share her enthusiasm, but right now, all I wanted to do was sleep.

On Sunday morning, she paced my lounge, flicking through her phone while I dithered around getting ready to go out. I needed to tidy my hair, put lipstick on, and find the right coat to go with my jeans. Okay, so I didn't really need to do all that, but anything that put off the agony of visiting Rose's flat became essential in my eyes.

Eventually, as I changed my shoes for the third

time, Suki grabbed my hand and tugged me towards the door. "Come on. It'll be dark by the time we get there at this rate."

Oh, good. Then we could come straight home again.

The Tube ride to Clapham, one I'd done so many times before but always in happier times, seemed to go more quickly than usual, and we emerged at Clapham North Underground station before I'd had a chance to steel myself properly. Every day, the station staff wrote an inspiring quote on the noticeboard in the ticket hall, and today's made me more depressed than ever.

In the end, we only regret the chances we didn't take.

There would be no more chances for Rose. And I regretted all the things we'd planned to do together but never got around to. That trip to Paris to visit the Montmartre and the Moulin Rouge we'd been putting off. The extra Christmas in June she kept talking about, just so she could celebrate her favourite time of year twice. I didn't want to do those things by myself.

Suki pulled me out of the exit, past the coffee stand, and along the high street. Rose lived on a side road halfway between Sainsbury's and the florist, in a block of flats that had seen better days. Gino from the deli below waved as we walked past. Usually, I got a wide grin as well, but today he barely mustered up a smile.

Suki and I climbed up the steps inside to Rose's door on the first floor. Why couldn't I remember the last time I'd made this journey? Weeks had passed, but the events of that night still showed no sign of coming back to me. Secretly, I hoped this trip might shake something loose. Painful though it may be, the agony of my sister's killer being on the loose, going about his daily life while she'd lost hers, was slowly making me lose my mind. I wanted the bastard to pay for what he did.

Suki took the key from me and swung the front door open. It took a second for my eyes to adjust to what I saw in front of me.

"What the..."

Suki's gasp told me she'd had the same thought. "I know the police said they needed to do a thorough search, but this is ridiculous."

All around, Rose's possessions lay strewn on the floor. Broken, torn, barely anything was intact. I stooped to pick up the cuddly dog she'd brought back from our visit to Blackpool last year. An ugly thing, but she'd been so proud when she won it from one of those grab machines in an amusement arcade. Now its head lolled at an unnatural angle, stuffing spilling from a hole in its neck.

While I sank to the floor, Suki's disbelief gave way to anger. "They can't leave it like this." She pulled her phone out and jabbed at the screen. "Bridges? You're an asshole."

I didn't hear his response, only the tirade Suki unleashed at him.

"Because the place is a tip. You've left so much shit everywhere we can't even see the floor. And half of it's broken... No, it's not just a few bits out of place. It looks like a hurricane's been through... Yes, the door was locked when we got here."

As I watched, the colour drained from her face, and her voice dropped. "Okay, we'll wait in the hall."

Once she hung up, she pulled me to my feet. "Bridges said last time he came here it was tidy. The only damage was in the bedroom, but they took some of the furniture from there and cleaned up as best they could."

"You mean someone else did this?"

"Bridges is on his way over. Let's just wait for him to get here, okay?"

He arrived a few minutes later, dressed in Lycra. Suki's gaze dropped to his package at the same time as mine, an automatic response. Not bad. I may have been grieving, but I wasn't dead myself, okay? He coughed, and both our gazes snapped upwards.

"Sorry about the outfit, ladies. I was out riding my bike."

Suki recovered first. "Well, we didn't think you wore that while you watched TV."

He chuckled, then quickly grew serious. "Let's have a look at this flat, then."

His muttered "fuck" as he pushed the door open gave us our answer, and within the hour Rose's former home became a crime scene for the second time in as many months.

I leaned against the stained wall in the hallway, clutching a cup of tea Bridges had magicked up from somewhere, as uniformed officers and a forensics team arrived. Then the inevitable questions came.

"When did you last come to the flat?"

Suki glared at Bridges and answered for me. "The night she fell off the balcony. Your people were here last. Are you sure you locked up properly?"

"I wasn't here myself, but they're usually damn careful about things like that. I know we've still got the spare key from the kitchen drawer in the evidence locker. Who else had a key?"

"Just me and Rose. And Damien had one. I don't know if he gave it back when he moved out."

"I already asked him that. He said he did, but nothing would have stopped him getting a spare cut first." He leaned against the wall beside me and sighed. "I'm more worried about Rose's key. We never found it."

My eyes widened. "She always carried it in her bag."

"We don't know where that is either."

Suki smacked him in the arm, and I groaned as he winced. Couldn't she be arrested for assault on a policeman?

"You prick! A murderer's been wandering around with the keys to Rose's flat and you didn't think to tell us? What if we'd been in there when he came back?"

"Whoa. We don't know it was him. There's been a spate of burglaries in this area, and the results look exactly like that." He jerked his thumb at the mess.

I barely heard him. "And my flat," I whispered.

"What?" Two faces turned towards me.

"Rose kept a key to my place on her key ring."

Bridges's voice took on an urgent tone not there before. "Would she have had anything in her bag with your address on? Or lying around here?"

I sifted through my brain, what little of it still functioned. "I don't think so. She only carried the bare minimum."

He nodded, the worry lines on his forehead softening a little. "That's something, at least. Even so, we need to get your locks changed."

"Do you know a locksmith?" Suki asked.

"I'll give a guy a call. He owes me a favour."

Bridges got a colleague to take his bike back to the

station while we rode to Paddington in a squad car. The locksmith arrived before we did.

"Thanks for coming, mate." Bridges shook hands with the guy.

"Not surprised you need a new lock for this place. The old one's shit. A child could get through it."

Oh boy, this day got better and better. "Could you fit something more secure? And perhaps an extra bolt for the inside?" Plus I could drag the dining table in front of the door when I was home. And an armchair or two.

He rapped on the door with his knuckles. "Whole door's crap, really, but I'll do my best."

Bridges insisted on going in first, just in case, and Suki put the kettle on as he did a thorough check of each room.

"I don't like the look of that fire escape. I'll get Spike to put something else on that as well," he said once he was done.

"Will I still be able to use it?" With my cooking, burning the place down was a very real possibility.

"Yes, we'll just make it a little more difficult to get through the window from the outside."

Suki handed me a cup of tea, and I almost choked when I sipped it. "How much sugar did you put in this?"

She shrugged. "Four spoons. Maybe five. I don't want you going into shock."

I supposed that was a small consolation—one terrible event after another had hardened my nerves a little. I didn't feel faint at all this time.

"I'll be okay. Not sure when I'll be up to facing that mess again, though."

Bridges took a swig of his own drink. "I've got next Sunday off. I'll round up a couple of mates and give you a hand."

"You don't have to do that."

"I know, but I want to. Too much bad shit happens to good people, and if I can help clear a bit of it up, then I will."

I laid a hand on his, my pale skin a contrast against his much darker tone. "Thank you... I can't keep calling you Bridges?"

"Jason. My name's Jason."

He gave me a warmer smile than I'd ever seen before, and I couldn't help but return it, even as a tear ran down my cheek. "Thank you, Jason." I clasped Suki's hand with my other one. "I don't know what I'd have done without both of you."

CHAPTER 7

TRUE TO HIS word, Bridges—Jason, although I still struggled to think of him by his first name—turned up at ten the following Sunday with Spike, Nash, two more guys, and a stack of flattened cardboard boxes. Suki had arranged a storage locker for the stuff while I slowly alternated between stitching a corset and stabbing my finger with the needle.

"Where do you want us to start?" Bridges asked once we'd taped the first few boxes together.

I glanced towards the darkened doorway in the corner. "Do you think you could pack up the bedroom? I can't... I just can't..."

"No problem. We'll have it squared away in no time."

Three of them headed in there while the other two made a start on the kitchen. Suki and I stayed in the lounge, which with the standard lamp in the corner broken and the grey clouds hovering outside had taken on a post-apocalyptic air.

"I suggest we make three piles," she said. "Anything that's broken goes in one, another for the charity shop, and the bits you want to keep go straight into boxes."

I nodded, not trusting myself to speak as I lifted up the remains of the lamp and placed it next to the door. Four hours later, the "broken" pile was by far the largest. Rose's life, what little was left of it, was stacked into a dozen boxes in Spike's van.

"What can I do to thank you?" I asked Bridges. "We'd never have got through this lot on our own."

"Only one thing." He met my eyes, solemn. "Don't let the bastard win, Lily. Just don't let him win."

Easier said than done, but I vowed to try.

I took Bridges's words to heart over the next week, at least in public. At work, I forced a smile, served customers, and sketched a whole pad of new designs for our next spring collection. The Black Rose collection. Morbid, maybe, and Suki cast more than one worried glance in my direction, but I had to do it as my own tribute to my sister.

I gave myself that, but the following week I needed to sew again. I'd looked at the accounts on Friday and seen what a loss we'd made over the last two months. A couple more like that, and we'd struggle to cover the rent.

I'd just told Suki exactly that at closing time on Saturday, right before her phone rang.

"Is everything okay?" she asked.

Who was calling?

She flicked her gaze towards me. "Yeah, she's here. Why?... Oh, shit."

"What?" I mouthed.

She hung up. "Are you sitting down?"

A chill ran through me. "Enough with the sitting down. Just tell me, would you?"

"Jason's on his way over. One of your neighbours

reported hearing a loud bang in your flat."

No...please, no. I sank down onto the nearest seat and stuck my head between my legs as dizziness overcame me.

"Are you going to be sick? Should I get a bucket?"

I shook my head. "Give me a minute."

The wave of nausea passed, but as I sat up, I started shivering and not from the cold. I kept the shop at a balmy twenty-five degrees all year around. An unnecessary expense, some might say, but as my work uniform consisted of a corset and a short skirt, I'd argue the toss.

"That's it?" I whispered, trying to stop my teeth from chattering. "That's all he said?"

"I think that's all he knows. He said he'd be here in ten minutes."

I paced between the mannequins, wobbling on my heels. Was someone in my home? The flat was an old Victorian, and the previous occupant had installed extra soundproofing so he could practise playing his saxophone, or so the landlord had told me. Whatever my neighbour heard must have been damn loud.

A car pulled up outside, and Suki shoved my arms into a coat. Not my usual velvet trench, but an old ski jacket of hers. She must have thought I needed the warmth.

Bridges didn't bother stopping the engine, and as soon as Suki slammed the door behind us, he took off.

"Shouldn't you put the siren on?" she asked.

"Not really supposed to do that on trips like this."

"Isn't it an emergency?"

"The panda car'll beat us there."

A string of unintelligible numbers crackled out of

the radio, and Jason swore.

Suki leaned between the gap in the seats. "What did that mean?"

I watched in the rear-view mirror as his brow creased into a frown. "It's the code for a burglary. There's a bit of a mess."

Well, wasn't that an understatement? Whoever got in had bypassed Spike's new lock by simply taking a crowbar to the door. It swung on its hinges, dropping splinters all over the carpet.

As Jason held up a hand to keep us outside, the next door along the hallway opened and an old lady shuffled towards us, leaning on her walking frame.

"Are you the police?" She peered over her half-moon glasses at me.

I jerked a thumb towards Jason. "He is."

She focused on him and drew herself up to her full height, which meant she came to his navel. "Did you catch that man?"

"Which man?"

"The one who caused all that mess." She peered through the doorway, taking in the shambles in my lounge.

"How do you know it was a man?"

"I saw him leave. Through the peephole in my door."

I glanced at my own door. No peephole. She had better security than me.

Jason took a notepad out of his pocket and fumbled for a pen. "Can you describe him?"

"Well, I didn't see his face. He had one of those hoods like teenagers wear. That's all changed since my day. What's wrong with a nice cap to keep your head warm?"

My heart sank as a possible lead floated away.

"If you didn't see his face, how do you know he was male?"

"He walked like a man." She nodded confidently. "Yes. Big strides. And no chest." She motioned with her hands. "Flat."

Bridges asked more questions, but the lady couldn't remember anything more useful. I was near enough to hear his thin sigh as he changed tack.

"Was it you who called us?"

Her grey curls bobbed up and down. "There was a heck of a bang. I thought maybe the young lady who lived there had hurt herself." She peered more closely at me. "Is that you?"

Jason answered for me. "It is. What kind of bang? Like an explosion?"

"My hearing's not what it was, but it sounded more like something falling over. I went to check, but I saw the state of the door, all broken and swinging open. So I hurried back home and shouted I'd be calling the police, then locked myself inside."

"That was the right thing to do."

"Was it a burglar?"

"We think so."

An invisible thread drew me forward, and I left Jason to finish up his interview while I looked at the damage. Four uniformed policemen stood in my lounge, surveying the mess. I realised what the noise must have been—the old dresser I'd found in an antique shop in East London lay on its front, a lifetime's worth of knick-knacks strewn across the floor.

A sense of déjà vu settled over me. The place looked like Rose's except in darker colours. I bent to pick up the china donkey she'd brought me back from a trip to Spain, now minus a leg. A few years back, we'd started a competition to see who could find the tackiest holiday souvenirs, although the donkey got eclipsed by a wind-up plastic pharaoh from her week in Sharm el Sheikh last year. The remains of that lay next to a miniature straw hat from her Portuguese break with Damien.

Why? Why had someone done this?

Was it connected to Rose's death, or had someone nominated me as London's unluckiest resident this year? If so, I'd gladly return the award.

One of the policemen picked a sofa cushion off the floor, returned it to its place, and motioned for me to sit down. "This room took the worst of it. Reckon whoever it was got halfway through the second bedroom before your neighbour disturbed him."

"The kitchen and bathroom are okay?"

"Pristine."

A sigh escaped. I should be thankful for the small things, right?

Bridges came in a minute later and crouched beside me. "It's best if we wait in the hallway. I've called the forensics team."

I followed him out. "It's him, isn't it? The same guy?"

"We don't know that."

But I did. I felt it in my stomach. That queasy fluttering that told me the worst was yet to come. "What, you think this is all a big coincidence?"

He stayed silent and I got my answer.

"Why me? Why Rose?"

"I don't know. We need to go through everything again. From the way both your flats have been turned over, I'd say he was looking for something."

"But what? I don't own anything valuable."

"Now, that's the question we'd all like to answer. Given that he took off before he finished the search, either he found it or your neighbour scared him off."

"So you think he might come back?" The shakes returned, and Bridges settled an arm around my shoulders.

"I wish I could say no, but..."

I slithered down the wall and landed with a bump.

"I'll leave someone here to watch the place until Spike sorts your door out tomorrow." He turned to Suki. "Can she stay with you tonight?"

"Of course."

As they led me down to the car, my mind was a jumble of thoughts. Rose, the mess, the shadowy man who seemed to have it in for me. When we arrived at Suki's, I'd got myself in such a state I couldn't see straight. Bridges half-carried me into the flat, and Suki tucked me into her bed.

"Do you want me to call a doctor?" she asked.

"No."

What would a doctor do apart from giving me pills? I didn't want to go down that route again.

In the end, I fell into a troubled sleep as she sat next to me, stroking my hand. Before everything went black, I said a silent prayer that things would look better in the morning.

Sheer exhaustion let me sleep until eleven, and when I woke, I found Suki sitting on the edge of the bed. Sunlight streamed in through her east-facing window and made my fledgling headache ten times worse.

"How do you feel?" she asked.

I rolled to see her better, and my temples throbbed. "Not good."

"You want something to drink?"

A stiff whisky. "Coffee would be good."

The noise of cups clinking made my eyes widen. "Who's out there?"

"Jason."

"He didn't leave?"

"He slept in the chair, and I took the sofa. He's worried about you. We both are."

Wow. Talk about going above and beyond his job. When I first met Bridges in the hospital, I'd cast him as a cop out to tick the boxes and move on, but he'd proven otherwise with all his phone calls and the help he'd given to clear Rose's flat. Perhaps I should be considering him a friend rather than simply a policeman?

I thought back to his wise words from last week. "I'm not going to let that bastard win. I can't."

"You can stay here as long as you want," Suki offered. "We can pick up more of your stuff."

I shook my head. "That's not fair on you."

"But—"

"And besides, if I'm not in my apartment, it'll be easier for the man to break in again."

"You're crazy."

Maybe, but if I gave up and lived the rest of my life in fear, I might as well not live at all.

By evening, my flat sported a new door, more solid
than the last one. Spike had talked about strike plates,
mortise locks, and side-hinge units, all of which flew
right over my head, but I understood the function of
the peephole and door chain.

Bridges gave the place one last look-over before he
left. We'd cleared it up as best we could, although the
dining room table now had a permanent wobble and
my table lamp was lighting Rose's way in heaven.
Despite the chaos, nothing seemed to be missing.

"You'll give some consideration to moving?"
Bridges asked. He'd mentioned it several times through
the course of the afternoon.

"I still can't see the point. Whoever broke in would
only have to follow me home from work, and he'd have
my new address."

"A more modern flat would be easier to secure. This
building's full of shadows, and the street's quiet."

"Okay, I'll think about it," I said, more to keep him
happy than anything else. What were the chances of
lightning striking a fourth time?

"And you need to keep your phone fully charged
and close to you at all times."

That I could do. I fished it out of my pocket and
waved it. "Look, one hundred percent."

"Good." He took my hands in his and gave them a
squeeze. "I'll call tomorrow. Remember to answer this
time, yeah?"

"Are you sure you can't put someone on
surveillance outside?" Suki asked.

"Wish I could, but our budgets don't run to that, I'm afraid. One of my mates'll drive by a couple of times each night until we get this sorted, though."

At least he was optimistic. With few clues and no sign of my memory returning, surely the phrase was "if" rather than "when" the case got solved.

"Thanks for arranging that," I said.

"Stay strong."

After one final plea for me to stay with her, Suki left as well, and I crawled into bed. Sleep didn't come easy. In fact, it didn't come at all. When I got into work the next morning, Suki gave me one glance and pointed to the tiny break-room at the back. "Go and lie down. You look terrible."

Well, that was what happened when you jumped at every creak of the building settling, every footstep in the hallway, every car door slamming outside. I grabbed an extra couple of hours' sleep at work and bought a bottle of wine on my way home. A glass of white before bed would help to settle my nerves, right?

Wrong.

By the third night, I almost wanted the bastard to turn up, because I was angry enough to kill him with the kitchen knife I'd taken to keeping on my nightstand.

"You can't carry on like this." Suki put her hands on her hips, and I looked up from where I'd passed out at the sewing table in the shop.

"Well, what do you suggest?" I snapped, irritable. My temper had suffered along with my sanity.

"Have you thought about Jason's suggestion?"

"Yes, all right? I even called my landlord, and he said I can only leave early if I pay the rest of the year's rent up front."

"Did you explain the circumstances?"

"What do you think? He said he was a businessman and reminded me I'll need to leave the place perfect when I go if I want my security deposit back."

She slammed her coffee cup down, and cappuccino sloshed over the edge. I reached for a tissue as she ranted.

"That asshole! I've got a good mind to speak to him myself. How can he think it's okay for you to be terrified in your own home?"

"Because he's just that. An asshole."

She snapped her fingers. "How about you get a new roommate? Then you wouldn't be alone."

I'd thought about that too. "I can't. It wouldn't be fair to drop someone else into the middle of all this."

She tapped a finger on her lips and got a worrying glint in her eye. "In that case, you need a bodyguard. There's no other option left. Like Kevin Costner and Whitney Houston."

Suki must have seen that movie at least a dozen times, and she'd dragged me along to the stage show twice. "I doubt a bodyguard will work for twenty euros and a creased-up cinema ticket, and that's all I've got in my wallet."

"Didn't you say you were getting some life insurance money?"

"It's not here yet." But it had been confirmed. Steve wrote to me personally to say the paperwork was in hand, although it would take a few weeks to process. I'd filed the letter behind the china bulldog Rose brought me from Blackpool, and after the burglary, it had ended up on the floor along with everything else from the dresser.

"I can lend you money in the meantime. My credit card's almost up to date."

"You can't do that."

"Yes, I can. You're my best friend, and I'm not going to sit around watching while you spiral into a black hole."

I held up a hand to stop her, but she ignored me and grabbed her phone.

"I'll call Jason and see if he's got any recommendations." Suki put one hand over her heart and warbled a couple of off-key lines from "I Will Always Love You."

"I don't think..."

"Don't worry—I've got this."

That's exactly what I was afraid of.

Chapter 8

SUKI WENT TO the deli to pick up sandwiches while I minded the shop. The piece of paper she'd given me before she left grew sweaty in my palms as I folded it and unfolded it again, and even the thought of the chocolate cookies she'd inevitably bring back couldn't snap me out of my worry.

Blackwood Security.

Two words and a phone number. Jason's recommendation for a bodyguard, although he'd warned they didn't come cheap.

"Call them," Suki had instructed before she left. "If you don't, I will."

If Suki had her way, I'd end up with a team of men in black surrounding me and probably a sniper stationed on the rooftop opposite for good measure. Although at least then I might get more than two hours' sleep. Last night, I'd checked the front door was locked six times and rattled every window twice for good measure. I reached for my phone. One call. How hard could it be?

Too hard. I put the phone down again. Hiring outside help would not only drain my finances, but it'd mean giving in. I didn't want that asshole of a burglar to have the satisfaction of knowing how much he'd scared me. And he had. I quaked every time I closed my eyes in bed, even if I hated to admit it.

But then there was the insurance money. I'd never expected to get a penny after Rose died, and she'd want me to put it to good use. Surely this counted? Paying cash to save my sanity, not that Rose thought I had much in the first place. To call or not to call? Without her final gift, I wouldn't even have dreamed of dialling.

As I reached for my coffee, my fifth double espresso of the day, my hand trembled. What choice did I have? Suki was right. I couldn't carry on like this.

After two rings, an efficient-sounding lady answered the phone.

"Blackwood Security, how can I help?"

I almost hung up, but I took a deep breath and forced myself to speak. "Uh, someone gave me your number to call about hiring a bodyguard. How much do they cost?"

"If you wait a few seconds, I'll put you through to a member of our customer care team. They can give you a quote."

A minute passed, then two. By the time another nice lady greeted me, I'd been forced to dab at my eyes with a tissue and take deep, calming breaths. I was a wreck, wasn't I? At her urging, I spent five minutes detailing the woes of my life, and she expressed sympathy in all the right places.

"So, you're looking for someone to keep an eye on you in the evenings? And overnight?"

"Ideally, yes." I figured I'd be okay at the shop in the day. Suki would scratch the asshole's eyes out.

"Well, we can certainly assist with that. Our executive protection team are the best in the business. Every member goes through our proprietary in-house training program and spends their first six months working under supervision."

"How much would that cost?"

"I'll just see who we have available." She clicked a few keys, then named a figure that made me wince.

"Uh, I can't afford that much."

"I'm able to offer a discretionary ten percent discount to new clients, but I'm afraid I can't go any lower than that."

Even at that rate, I'd go through all the life insurance money in less than two months. "I'm sorry for wasting your time."

Her voice softened. "I hope you manage to get everything sorted out."

Suki bounded in just as I put down the phone. "Did you call them? What did they say?"

"Yes, I called, but it's too expensive. Over a thousand pounds a day."

Her smile disappeared. "A thousand pounds? That's crazy."

I shrugged. "A bit, but I suppose they're putting themselves in the line of fire, aren't they? I'd want danger money too for doing that job."

Suki dropped the paper carrier bags of food on the table. "There must be something we can do." She stared down at the crumpled piece of paper. "Blackwood Security. Why does that sound familiar?"

She'd got halfway through unwrapping her sandwich before she snapped her fingers. "I've got it! There's a girl in my yoga class whose fiancé works there. I'm sure of it. And I think I've got her number somewhere."

"What are you going to do?"

"Call and ask if she can get us a staff discount."

Suki never hesitated to ask for favours, and people usually obliged even though her forwardness sometimes got embarrassing. She'd once got us tickets to a movie premiere by asking a friend who worked at the theatre, and I'd had to physically restrain her from reaching out to grab Mark Wahlberg as we walked down the red carpet. And me? I was too shy to blag so outrageously, but that didn't stop me from getting my hopes up as she dialled.

A minute later, she hung up the phone with a triumphant grin. "Olivia's coming over at five. She's sure we can sort something out."

As closing time approached, I fidgeted constantly, glancing at my watch every three seconds until a pretty blonde walked through the door. From the way Suki leapt forward to hug her, I figured it must be Olivia.

"I finally did that headstand," she squealed.

"Yay you! I still haven't managed wheel properly."

Ah, they were talking yoga. I'd tried a couple of classes last year, until I pulled a muscle in my thigh and couldn't walk for a fortnight afterwards. Whoever said exercise was good for you obviously hadn't tried ashtanga.

The bell tinkled again as a dark-haired guy followed Olivia in, the resigned expression on his face one that I'd seen on so many men who crossed the threshold. I looked up, and I mean up, taking in his two-day stubble and vivid blue eyes. Was that her fiancé?

Once Suki let go of Olivia, she stepped over to me

on shiny electric-blue kitten heels that added the perfect hint of colour to her black-and-grey dress.

"I'm Olivia Porter, and this is Nye Holmes."

I shook her dainty hand, trying to hide my chipped black nail varnish while I admired her perfect manicure. Nye engulfed my hand next, assessing me with a cold gaze as he did so. He may have been hot, but he gave me chills.

"So, what's happened?" Olivia asked. "Suki mentioned you'd had problems with a burglar?"

For the second time that day, I rehashed the story. It got easier each time I told it, or maybe I just grew ever more numb to the horror. Because by the end, even Olivia wiped a tear away.

"You poor thing." She turned to Nye. "We have to help her."

He shifted from foot to foot, and I knew his answer before he even opened his mouth. "I can't just provide a free bodyguard, babe. Executive protection isn't even my department, and I know their schedule's rammed right now."

"We can't leave Lily at the mercy of some madman." She sidled a little closer and ramped up her smile. "And when I had the same problem, you didn't charge me for your services."

He sighed and slung an arm around her waist. "That's because I wanted to marry you, Liv."

"You didn't know that at the start."

"Yes, I did."

"Oh." Her cheeks turned a little pink, something that reminded me of Rose. She used to blush at anything. "Still, we need to help."

He fell silent, and his mouth set in a thin line. This

was all going to be a waste of time, wasn't it? I'd dared to get my hopes up, but I'd be shaking in bed again tonight.

Olivia tried a kiss on Nye's cheek. "Please?"

I saw Suki cross her fingers behind her back and did the same with mine. Olivia went quiet too, and her gaze wandered around the shop. After a few seconds, she stood on tiptoe and whispered in Nye's ear. I didn't hear what she said, but his gaze hooded, and then his forehead crinkled.

After an unbearably long minute, he spoke again. "There's a guy on the EP team who's renovating his house at the moment. He's spent a few nights sleeping in the office lately as it was pretty much uninhabitable. I could ask if he'd mind staying at Lily's instead. You have a spare room?"

I nodded. It was still a bit messy as we'd shoved some of the broken stuff in there, but I could clear it up.

"Would that work for you?"

I bobbed my head again, and Nye turned to Olivia. "Good enough?"

She nodded and grinned.

"In that case, I need to make a phone call." He stepped out onto the pavement, leaving the three of us inside.

"Uh, I'm going to need to take one of those." Olivia pointed at a "Chat Noir" corset, made from black velvet with a sweetheart neckline.

Suki plucked it from the hanger and gave it to her. "You want the matching panties?"

She glanced sideways at Nye, still talking on the other side of the glass. "Er, yes please."

While Suki wrapped up the outfit I was sure just bought me the services of one of Blackwood's finest, a sense of relief coursed through me. I hadn't realised quite how scared I'd been of returning home at night, but it felt as if the weight of Mount Everest had been lifted from my shoulders.

Nye finished his conversation and stepped through the door as Suki handed one of our cream paper bags with its distinctive black lily logo over to Olivia.

"It's sorted. My colleague's called Max Tian, and he'll be with you about seven when he's finished his shift. What's your address?"

I scribbled it down for him, barely able to read my own scrawl, and handed it over. He squinted then read it back to me.

"When he comes, you ask for his ID, yeah? He'll carry a card like this one." He slid his own out of his wallet. It held his name, photo, and Blackwood Security's company details.

"Okay."

"You have a door viewer? Or a chain?"

"I've got both now."

"Good. Don't let him in until he's confirmed his identity. He's an inch shorter than me, black hair, part-Chinese."

I nodded, feeling a little overwhelmed.

"You need a lift home?"

"I'll be okay."

Suki was having none of it. "Yes, she needs a lift home. I'll finish up here."

I'd expected we'd go in whatever car Nye drove, or maybe a black cab, but five minutes later, a chauffeur whisked us through the busy streets of London. I'd never been in such an expensive car before. Under different circumstances, I'd have enjoyed the ride in the black Mercedes with its tinted windows and squashy leather seats. As it was, I stared blankly out at the passing streets while Nye fiddled with his phone and Olivia sat quietly. When we neared Paddington, she reached over and squeezed my hand.

"Something similar happened to me a while back, and I promise you it does get better."

"It feels like I've got this wall in front of me, and no matter what I do, I can't get past it."

"You're not alone. We'll give you a boost." She handed over a card with her phone number on it. "Call me if you need anything, or even if you just want to chat."

The car pulled up outside my building, and I stared up at its grey façade. "Thank you for everything."

"It's no problem." Then she winked. "Have fun with Max."

CHAPTER 9

NYE INSISTED ON walking me up to my flat, and only after he'd checked each room did he allow me out of my tiny vestibule. I'd begun to get used to his foreboding presence now, and I had to admit that having him there made me feel safer.

After I'd thanked him once more and secured the door behind him, I had a quick tidy up then settled down to wait for Max. A cup of tea seemed like a good idea, but when I'd made it, I stared into space until it went cold. I tried taking a sip but spat it back into the cup.

"Ugh."

I repeated the process, only to get distracted again. Why Rose? What was the man looking for? And why couldn't I just bloody remember what happened that night?

At five past seven, a knock made me jump, even though I'd been expecting it, and I tipped the cup over. Tea ran across the table and dripped onto the carpet. Great. Another few quid off my security deposit.

"Hang on a second." I blotted up the mess as best I could then hurried to the door, remembering Nye's instructions at the last minute and pressing my eye to the peephole.

"Can I see your ID?"

The man already had it in his hand and held it up next to his face. Yes, Max Tian. The picture matched. I put him at about twenty-six, only his eyes were those of a man much older. His grey suit made him look like he was heading for an evening out, not a visit to my slightly worse-for-wear abode.

I opened the door, remembering too late about the chain when it stuck at a couple of inches. Dammit, I already looked dumb and I'd barely opened my mouth yet. I pushed the door closed, took the chain off, and had another go.

Max stepped inside and dumped a duffel bag on the floor before turning to close the door himself. The chain rattled as he secured it again.

"You must be Lily?"

"Yes."

"Max." He didn't bother to offer his hand.

"Thanks for coming."

"No problem. I owed Nye a favour," he added, leaving me with little doubt he'd come out of obligation rather than choice.

"Uh, your room's that one." I pointed at the first door to the left. At least I'd managed to change the sheets before embarking on my tea-related disasters.

He picked up his bag and strode in there, then closed the door behind him. Hey, this wasn't awkward at all. I shuffled backwards, relieved to get away. Max gave off dangerous vibes, even more than Nye, and his presence was akin to having a tiger on the loose. At least he'd caged himself.

Relieved yet on edge, I headed for the sofa again, armed with a vague plan to distract myself by watching a movie. Should I try another cup of tea first? Or perhaps hot chocolate? Yes, that was a better idea. I was rummaging through the cupboard for marshmallows when I felt warm breath on my neck and leapt a foot in the air.

I clutched at my chest as I realised Max was standing two feet away. He'd changed into a pair of jeans and a white T-shirt tight enough to show off his muscled chest.

"You scared the crap out of me!"

"Sorry." He didn't sound sorry. "What's for dinner?" Without waiting for an answer, he opened the fridge and grimaced.

"I don't have food, exactly, but I've got three kinds of wine and I might have a box of cereal somewhere."

He rolled his eyes. "What the hell do you usually eat?"

I sagged back against the cupboard. "Lately? Not a lot." Which was why I'd put on a pair of drawstring pyjama pants and cinched the waist up. Not much else fitted. "I could order pizza if you're hungry?"

"Too many carbs." He opened the cupboard next to the fridge and raised an eyebrow.

"What? I like Turkish delight."

He hauled out half a dozen boxes and dumped them on the counter. "Don't worry, I believe you."

"Uh, I'll go out and get some groceries. There's a Sainsbury's around the corner."

He looked at me as though I'd gone quite mad. "Nye said you were in danger. You don't just swan off to the supermarket."

I put my hands on my hips. Sure, he was doing me a favour, but his attitude was starting to grate already and he'd barely been there for five minutes. He complained about the food, but he objected to me buying more? Prick.

"Well, what do you suggest, then?"

A thin stream of air escaped from one corner of his lips. "*We* go to the supermarket."

"Fine." I snatched a jacket from the coat rack in the hallway and shoved my arms into the sleeves. "Let's go."

He looked down at my feet and raised an eyebrow. "Like that?"

Too late, I realised I still had my slippers on. Even in London, Bugs Bunny would raise eyebrows, and the soles weren't designed for outdoors. Max's eyes burned into my back as I swapped them out for a pair of Ugg boots and arranged my tartan PJ bottoms over the top.

"Now I'm ready."

He took a deep breath and disappeared into his room, emerging seconds later in a leather jacket. Then he started lecturing. Honestly, it was like being back at school.

"Outside, you walk right in front of me. If I tell you to get down, you crouch. You don't kneel, and you don't go flat. I need you ready to run if necessary. Got it?"

"Yep."

"When I tell you to do something, you do it. No hesitation. And keep your wits about you. Can you run in those boots?"

It was my turn to roll my eyes. "Yes, sir."

"I'm being serious." He folded his arms, blocking the door.

"You don't think that's overkill?"

His glare told me his answer.

"Okay, okay. Got it."

I saluted his back with a grimace as he turned to unlock the door, but I swear he knew, because when he turned back, his mouth was set in a hard line. Did he even know how to smile?

"After you," he said, stepping back just enough to let me past.

Nope. No smiles. He still looked pissed with me and life in general. Marvellous.

Max stuck close as I set off on the five-minute walk to the supermarket, his dark aura hovering behind me like a malevolent shadow. I was glad to get under the bright lights of the store, and the shoppers milling around gave me a sense of security. Max may have been appointed my protector, but he scared me.

I grabbed a basket and headed for the comfort of the bakery aisle. Times like this called for donuts, but Max looked disgusted as I picked up two packets.

"They're on buy one, get one free," I said, as if that justified everything.

"I bet the salad is too."

"Salad doesn't have pink-and-yellow sprinkles." I selected a box of chocolate chip cookies and added them to my collection. Let him scowl as much as he liked.

In a nod to real food, I decided on a tray of spaghetti carbonara, while Max chose chicken breasts and a big bag of green stuff. No wonder he looked permanently miserable if that was all he ate.

At least the checkout girl agreed with my purchases. "Ooh, these donuts are really nice. I ate two this afternoon."

Only two? Boy, she must have great willpower. Having starved myself for weeks, my mouth watered like the floodgates had been opened. "Thanks for the recommendation."

She packed the bag while I paid with my credit card, and then she went to hand it to Max.

He shook his head. "She's carrying."

I'd always thought Suki had perfected her death stare over the years, but the checkout girl's certainly rivalled it. She passed the bag to me, her expression asking, *What are you doing with this asshole?*

"Thanks."

Mortified as I was, I wanted to get out of there as fast as possible.

As I marched towards the door, Max decided to grace me with an explanation. "When I'm working, I need to keep my hands free."

"You embarrassed me."

"In those trousers? I didn't think that would be possible."

I stopped, and he bumped into me. "Look, it's clear you don't want to be here. Why don't you just go home? I'll manage by myself."

He closed his eyes for half a second, and then his face softened a fraction. "Sorry, that was uncalled for. I've had a bad day, and I shouldn't have taken it out on you."

Wow, an apology. "I don't like this situation any more than you do."

"I understand that. I'll think before I speak next time." He held out a hand, waving me on. "We should get going. It's not good to stand around in one place."

I set off again, clutching the bag against my chest. Max unsettled me, and I didn't know what to make of him. I pictured Rose in my head. What would she do in this situation? I imagined asking her.

"You do whatever you need to do to stay safe." That's what she'd say.

We were halfway home when I got an indication of what it meant to have a bodyguard. A drunk guy stumbled towards me, clutching a can of lager, and before I could blink, Max's arm snaked around my waist and pulled me out of his path. The stranger stared up at Max's stony expression and tripped over his own feet in an attempt to get away. Only when he'd gone did Max release me.

"Uh, thanks." My stomach felt as if it'd been clamped in a vice, although the effect killed a few of my butterflies.

"No problem."

We made it home without further incident, and like Nye did earlier, Max made me wait in the vestibule while he checked the apartment.

"It's clear." He took the bag from me. "Now we can eat."

I'd assumed he'd expect me to cook, but to my surprise, he turned on the oven and took over. Good thing, really, because last time I'd tried chicken, it came out smoking.

"You need any help?" I asked.

"No."

Alrighty then. I retreated to the lounge with the first packet of donuts and a bottle of wine. It was easier not to be near Max, anyway. Donuts weren't rude. Donuts cheered me up.

Half an hour later, he laid out cutlery on the dining table then wedged a piece of cardboard under the wobbly leg. "Dinner in five."

I usually ate in front of the TV, but as he'd gone to all the effort of setting the table, the least I could do was join him. His own plate was a poster child for healthy eating, and he hadn't been able to resist adding salad to mine as well. Too bad I was already full from the four donuts I'd just eaten. I stirred my spaghetti, trying to look enthusiastic over the meal.

"So, why did you have such a bad day?" I asked. Anything to break the silence.

"Celebrity client. When I refused to carry her shopping, she whacked me over the head with her handbag."

I burst out laughing, which Max didn't find amusing judging by his scowl.

"I'm not surprised if you spoke to her the way you spoke to me."

"I'm not paid to be polite. I'm paid to keep people alive."

"But if you employed a little more tact, you might avoid future handbag-related incidents."

"I'll bear that in mind."

I made another attempt at conversation. "How long have you been a bodyguard?"

"Four years."

"Is it a hard profession to get into?"

"Yes."

He wasn't making this easy. "If you could be a farmyard animal, which would you pick?"

"What kind of question is that?"

"One designed to get you to say a whole sentence."

"Oh." He bit one corner of his lip as he thought, and that tiny gesture made him seem more human. "I guess I'd be a wolf."

"How many wolves have you seen on farms?"

He paused mid-chew, thinking again. "Okay, a dog."

"I'm not sure they count either."

"Sheepdogs."

Fair enough. "Why a dog?"

"They're not part of the human food chain. What about you?"

We had totally different thought processes. "A pig. They get to eat and sleep all day." I dropped my fork, too full for more spaghetti. "You want a donut?"

He didn't, and as soon as he finished eating, he retired to his room. It had barely gone nine o'clock. Wow. Life as a bodyguard really rocked.

Unsurprisingly, since I took ages to drop off, Max got up before me. When I walked into the lounge, rubbing my eyes, he already had his suit on.

"You want coffee?" I asked, stumbling towards the kitchen.

"I don't drink caffeine."

"How?"

He shrugged. "Just don't. It makes me sluggish."

Seriously? Right now, I couldn't function without it. The only saving grace in the break-in was that the burglar steered clear of my espresso machine. I selected a Colombian roast coffee pod, shoved it into the slot, and set it going.

"Are you having breakfast?" I asked.

"I'll get something at the office."

"Are you on celeb duty again today?"

"She flew back to LA yesterday. Bitch is someone else's problem now." I thought I detected a faint "thank fuck" afterwards.

"So, what will you do today?"

"Prep work for next week's job. Meetings."

"What do you have to do for prep work?"

"Check out locations and routes to and from them. Form evacuation plans. Research known enemies and their associates."

"Who will you be guarding?"

"Can't say. It's confidential."

"Oh."

"A politician. At least he doesn't carry a handbag."

Was that Max's attempt at a joke? I tried a tiny smile, which was met by a flicker of his lips.

"Are you coming back this evening?" After my comment yesterday, I wasn't sure.

"I'll be done around seven again. I'll bring food with me. You don't answer the door to anyone else, right?"

"I won't."

"You need a lift to work?" He looked at his watch. "I'm leaving in twenty minutes."

The chance to avoid rush hour on the Tube? I'd do anything for that, even ride with Max. "Yes, please. Just give me a minute to change."

I still had the same pyjamas on. That was one advantage of being lazy—it saved time getting ready for bed.

Today, I went with a maroon leather corset and matching velvet pencil skirt. I particularly liked the button details—I'd sewn a row of them all the way down one side of the skirt, cream in colour, and each one bore a tiny skull in the centre. A juxtaposition of pretty and macabre—my perfect style.

I peered out the window and frost twinkled on the railings around the fire escape, so I pulled on my sheepskin boots again. They hadn't been cheap to buy, but without a doubt, they'd been one of my best investments.

Max's eyes bugged out when I emerged from my room. "What the fuck are you wearing? I thought you were going to work?"

"I am."

"At a fetish club?"

That was it. I marched up to him and jabbed him in the chest. It was like poking a safe. "No, Mr. High and Mighty, I do not work in a fetish club. I own a clothes shop, and this is what we sell."

"Is Liv Porter one of your customers?"

I thought back to the corset Suki gave her. "Maybe."

Max laughed, and honestly, it changed his face. "So the rumours are true. I heard she bribed Nye with kink if he convinced me to provide my services and threatened to withhold bedroom fun if he didn't."

"Needs must."

"You women fight dirty." His lips curved into a smile. "I like that."

CHAPTER 10

"HOW WAS LAST night?" Suki asked. "Was that Max who dropped you off?"

"Last night was...interesting. And yes, it was Max." Apparently, Blackwood had its own car service.

"What do you mean, interesting? What's he like?"

I recounted the story of our trip to Sainsbury's, then his antics at dinner. It sounded even worse the second time around.

"He seems like an asshole."

"I thought so too at first. But there were times he didn't act so bad. Like when he offered me a lift this morning."

She finished making the coffee then handed me a cup. "I guess he's right, though. As long as he keeps you safe, the rest doesn't matter too much."

"He seems to know what he's doing." I recalled his quick reactions when the drunk walked past, and I'd certainly slept better last night than any other night since Rose was murdered. "What are our plans for today?"

"Six internet orders came in since we closed yesterday, and I've got Susan, Brenda, and Cindy working on them. We need another Chat Noir to replace Olivia's, plus I sold a ruffle skirt. And I've got a meeting at three about hats."

"I'll get started on the Chat Noir." It was starting to feel as though things were getting back to normal, something I desperately needed.

And apart from Jason's call mid-morning, it could have been any day two months ago.

"Just thought I'd check in. Did you have any luck with Blackwood?"

"Yes and no. A regular bodyguard cost too much, but a guy called Nye did me a deal and I've got a part-time person staying overnight."

"Nye Holmes?"

"Yes. You know him?"

"He's a legend. He's got a solve rate the Met can only dream of. How the hell did you get him to do you a deal?"

"Suki knows his fiancée, and she asked him nicely."

His chuckle was followed by an, "Aah. That explains a lot."

"Do you know Max Tian as well?"

"Max? That's who you've got staying with you?"

"Yes. He seems a little grumpy."

Jason's chuckle morphed into a full-blown laugh. "That man has worse mood swings than a woman with PMT, but he knows what he's doing."

"I noticed that. Both things."

"Good luck putting up with him."

"I'm going to need it." I hesitated. "Is there anything new with the case?"

"I'm sorry, Lily. Believe me, I'm working on it."

When he hung up, I concentrated on sewing, and before I knew it, it had gone six. Suki worked late too, full of excitement over her hat deal. Apparently, we'd be showcasing a new designer, and Suki was tweaking some of our own products to match.

"Are you almost done?" I asked her. "I need to get home to let Max in."

"Almost. You head off. I'll lock up."

I gave her a quick hug. "See you tomorrow."

What mood would Max be in when he got back tonight? At least he'd promised to bring food, which meant I wouldn't have to face the cashier at the supermarket again. Although it also meant I wouldn't be able to buy more donuts. Thank goodness I'd picked up that extra packet yesterday, and the biscuits Suki brought at lunchtime had helped with my sugar fix for the day.

A fine mist hung in the air as I scurried to Piccadilly Circus Tube station, and by the time I got out at Paddington, it had turned into full-on rain. Thankfully, I'd picked up an umbrella before I left Black Lily, so I huddled under it for the five-minute walk home, all the time praying Max hadn't arrived early. I couldn't imagine him being impressed if he had to wait outside.

Luckily, there was no sign of him, and I carefully put the chain back on the door once I'd got inside. What time was it now? Five to seven according to the clock on the kitchen wall. Time for a cup of tea. I shivered as I waited for the kettle to boil. Why was it so cold in here? The thermostat was set to twenty-three, and the radiator in the lounge was boiling.

I'd had this problem in my last flat, when an airlock in the heating system caused half the radiators to stay cold. How good were Max's DIY skills? I stifled a laugh, as I could well imagine his face if I asked him to bring his toolbox tomorrow.

"I don't carry toolboxes." I mimicked his grumpy

voice as I went through to the bedroom to swap out my corset for a jumper. "My job is to keep you alive, not do plumbing."

I'd got halfway to my wardrobe when a cool breeze raised the hairs on the back of my neck. Then the rope tightened around the front of it before I realised what was happening.

Time stood still for a second or two, my mind blank, black. Empty. But as I choked, my subconscious exploded as if it was trying to fit all its thoughts into the time it had left.

This was a joke. It had to be.

Was I asleep? Having a nightmare?

How did he get in?

Who was he?

Why?

And finally, was this how Rose felt?

The man jerked the rope and pressed into my back as my heart took off from a standing start to hammer at my ribcage. Only his grip kept me upright as my knees buckled.

Please, don't let it end like this.

The stink of his breath washed over me, and his voice came out in a harsh whisper. "I didn't want it to be this way, but I can't let you remember."

Adrenaline kicked in, and I tried to elbow him in the ribs, but he simply adjusted his grip, leather gloves pressing against the side of my neck as he gave me my first taste of death. He didn't feel bulky, but I was no match for his wiry strength, especially with him so close behind me. Tendrils of darkness closed around my mind as I pulled at his arms, but he didn't flinch. One fingernail snagged in the thick material of his sweater and tore clean off, sending a searing pain up my arm that on any other day would have made me scream and curse. But I welcomed it, the pain, because that meant I wasn't dead yet. Although with every passing millisecond, my consciousness ebbed further away.

Then I heard a faint knock at the door.

Max!

With the last bit of strength I had, I raised both my feet, twisted, and pushed off the wall beside me. The man stumbled backwards, loosening the rope enough for me to suck in one ragged breath. "Help me!" I tried to scream, but the pressure meant it came out as more of a squeak.

"Lily?" Max's voice floated through the door.

The glass lamp crashed off my nightstand as my attacker regained his balance, then the world started to dim again. A muffled thump came from the direction of the lounge. Was Max trying to break in? The memory of Spike floated through my mind, assuring me that this new door was far tougher than the old one, and I would have laughed if I'd been able to breathe. Wasn't that ironic? I was about to die because he'd improved my security.

Just as the edges of my vision disappeared, a splintering crash came from the lounge, and I fell. Was this it? Was I dead? I thought there was supposed to be a bright light to walk towards? All I saw was darkness, darkness everywhere, and I couldn't help feeling cheated.

And where was Rose?

"Lily? Lily, can you hear me?"

That wasn't Rose. Her voice sounded sweet and musical, whereas this was the deep voice of a man. My attacker? Was he still here? Goosebumps prickled my skin, and my eyes popped open only to find Max kneeling beside me.

"Thank fuck," he muttered.

Then I was in the air, cradled in his arms as he lifted me like I weighed nothing. I clung on tight as he sat on the bed with me on his lap, barely with it as he made a phone call.

"Just walked in on an attempted murder. I need backup. Perp took off down the fire escape."

He slid the phone back into his pocket and turned his attention to me. "Are you hurt? Can you breathe okay?"

I tried to speak, but my throat burned in agony. I managed to nod.

"Yes? To which?"

I raised a hand and felt the mangled flesh where the coarse rope had bitten into my skin. Where my fingers touched, fire raced through me. Max gently clasped my hand in his and moved it away. "Don't touch, it'll be sore. Can you get enough air?"

I nodded again, and his eyes softened a little.

"Don't...leave me," I choked out.

"I'm not going anywhere."

He tightened his arms around me as I wept against his chest, both for Rose and my own life, which I might have clung onto by a thread, but was surely over as I knew it. The man was never going to let me go, was he? He thought I held the key to his identity, even though I didn't know how to unlock the door.

I understood now what I didn't before. We'd entered a race. My memory against his murderous tendencies. Only one of us could win, but who would it be?

CHAPTER 11

WHEN I BEGAN shivering, Max wrapped a blanket around my shoulders and carried me through to the lounge. As he settled me on the sofa, I glimpsed the gaping hole where my front door once stood. Turned out it lived up to Spike's billing, but Max had knocked down the entire door frame and part of the wall too.

"Sh-sh-should we call the police?" I asked.

"Cavalry's already on its way." He strode to the window and peered out just as the first siren pierced the night air. Footsteps sounded on the stairs within seconds, and two men wearing black uniforms burst in. Not police. Blackwood Security?

"Guy went down the fire escape." Max pointed at my bedroom. "Is the dog coming?"

"Yeah, it's left headquarters. Cops just pulled up too. We'll head outside, see if anyone saw anything."

Sure enough, the police ran in a minute later, two constables in hi-vis jackets, and Max sent them outside to search as well. "Any sign of the ambulance?" he asked before they left.

"Almost here."

My flat soon swarmed with people. The quiet bustle was at odds with my heart, which hammered in my chest like a carpenter on acid. Could anyone else hear it? To me, it sounded a hundred decibels. But nobody put their fingers in their ears as paramedics jostled for space with police, and half a dozen men in the same black uniforms as the first pair hovered on the periphery.

"Are they your colleagues?" I asked Max.

He nodded. Figured—they all wore the same grumpy look. It must have been included as part of that six-month proprietary training program the customer care lady told me about. The medics descended on me like vultures, prodding at my neck until I shrank back into Max.

He glared at them. "She's had enough. Leave her alone."

"But she's hurt."

"Leave her alone."

The paramedics backed off, and for once I was grateful Max had an attitude problem. And even more grateful his ire wasn't directed at me this time.

A cheerful-looking spaniel arrived, led by another grumpy ninja. I reached out and got rewarded with a slobbery tongue as the sweet little furball panted all over the place. After a couple of minutes, the police let it sniff the rope that nearly killed me, and then it set off outside.

"Tracking dog," Max said.

I'd gathered as much. Bridges arrived, together with a sobbing Suki, who squashed next to me on the couch and gave me a hug. They were followed by Nye, a forensics team, and a blonde woman who looked as if she'd got lost on the way to the opera. Who attended a crime scene in a cocktail dress?

"You okay, mate?" Nye reached out and squeezed Max's shoulder, and he winced.

"I'm fine."

"Did you take the door down?"

"Yeah."

Nye called the nearest paramedic. "You need to check this guy."

"I said I'm fine."

The blonde woman marched over, pursing perfectly painted red lips. "Shirt off. Now."

Max sighed and did as he was told. Wow. I wished I could order a man to undress with that sort of authority. But I barely looked at Max's pecs, firm though they were, just gasped at the mass of bruises already covering his shoulder and upper arm. "You did that on the door?"

He shrugged, then winced again.

"Needs an X-ray," the blonde woman said.

"It's not broken."

"You don't know that. You're going to A&E."

Max narrowed his eyes at her. "Why are you even here?"

"I was on my way to some party when I heard the call come in over the radio. This sounded more interesting. Anyway, stop changing the subject. Hospital."

"But—"

"Please, Max," I said. "I hate that you got hurt helping me."

The woman turned her attention in my direction, regarding me through piercing violet eyes. I felt like I was getting an X-ray right then. "You need a proper check-up too. You can go together."

"I'm okay now."

She raised an eyebrow and gave me a look that said,

Don't mess with me.

"We'll go, okay?" Max cut in. "We'll go."

"Can I at least change first?" I'd been stuck in my corset since seven thirty, and it wasn't helping the breathing situation any.

"If you want. The police'll want your clothes, though. Evidence." She beckoned over a lady in a white jumpsuit. "Lily needs to change."

"How does she know my name?" I whispered to Max.

"She knows everything."

The forensics lady looked as if she wanted to argue but then thought better of it. I guess no one took on the blonde. I trailed the policewoman into my bedroom, and she pushed the door closed. Cool air blew in from the broken window, making me shiver, not just from the temperature but from the thought of how easily the man got into my home. Spike may have fixed a lock to the frame, but the glass had shattered like my broken soul.

"Please only touch the wardrobe and avoid disturbing anything. I'll turn my back until you're dressed again."

She looked away, and I quickly pulled underwear, a pair of jeans, a T-shirt, and a warm jumper off the shelves. I sneezed as I released the ribbons on the corset, unable to feel the tiny moment of elation I usually did when I escaped my bindings. Another sneeze came as I did up my bra, then another while I put on my socks. What the hell was wrong with me? I only sneezed like that when I was around vanilla scented candles or lilies, and I didn't have either in the flat. Did I?

I spun around, my brain taking in what my gaze had only skated over before. The vase of white lilies sitting on my chest of drawers, all ready for a funeral. My funeral.

My knees buckled.

When I came to, Max was crouching at my side while Suki fanned me with a copy of *Cosmopolitan*. I blinked a few times then shrunk away, trying to cover myself when I realised I was giving all the men in the room an eyeful.

"What happened?" Suki asked.

I pointed a shaking finger at the vase.

"Flowers?" Max asked.

"Oh shit," Suki said. Somebody brought a blanket, and she draped it over me. "Those aren't yours, are they?" She turned to Max. "Lily's allergic to lilies."

The four of us stared at the vase before the forensics lady came to her senses.

"You think the man who assaulted you brought them?" she asked.

"He must have. I don't know how else they would have got there."

"They weren't here when I checked the room last night," Max confirmed.

"But why? Why bring flowers if he planned to kill me?" I sneezed again. "I need to get out of here."

"Because he's a sick freak," Suki muttered, passing my T-shirt. She sent Max out into the lounge while I finished getting dressed, and by the time we got out of the bedroom, Max, Nye, and Bridges were deep in discussion.

"She's sure the lilies aren't hers?" Bridges asked.

"I think she'd know." Did I detect a hint of sarcasm

in Max's voice?

I stepped up beside him. "They're definitely not mine. I never have them in the house. They make me ill, just like roses made Rose sick."

Bridges's eyes widened. "Oh shit."

"It's not really that bad. I only sneeze, and it stops after I move away."

"That's not what I meant. Rose had a vase of roses in her bedroom the night she died. Pink ones. I remember them from the scene, and they were still there when we packed her stuff up last week."

My legs wobbled again, but this time Max's arm shot out and caught me. Okay, maybe he was useful to have around.

"He brought us both flowers?"

Jason's mouth set in a grim line. "It certainly looks that way. I'll send someone to the storage unit to fetch them. Maybe they'll find a fingerprint." He closed his eyes. "Dammit, we should have picked up on this before."

I reached out and squeezed his hand. "Don't blame yourself. Not many people knew she was allergic to roses. And I doubt you'll find a fingerprint. He was wearing gloves tonight."

"Do you remember anything else about him?"

I closed my eyes, my mind protesting at having to relive the experience, but I knew I needed to. "His voice. He only whispered, but he sounded English."

"What did he say?"

I repeated his words. "He's not going to stop, is he?"

Max's arm tightened around my waist. "Yes, he is."

"Anything more?" Jason asked.

"His breath smelled bad. Like he'd been eating garlic."

He scribbled more notes in his pad.

"And he was big. Taller than Max, I think, but not so muscly. When I pushed him back across the room, he didn't feel heavy. And..." Something came back to me, and I heaved. "Let me go."

Max released me, and I ran for the bathroom, barely making it before I threw up the remains of my lunch.

Suki followed me in and passed me a handful of tissues. "What? What happened?"

I slumped back against the wall, noting the shadow of Bridges in the doorway. "When he pressed up against me, I felt him. He was hard. The sick freak was turned on by what he was doing."

"Which would fit with the semen we found at your sister's place," Bridges said.

I leaned over and retched again, but this time only bile came up. Suki glared at him.

"Could you try to be a little less blunt?"

"Sorry."

When I'd calmed down a bit, Suki led me back out to the couch. Bridges opened his mouth, presumably to ask more questions, but before he could speak, the blonde woman strode back in. The black sequins on her dress glittered under the harsh lights brought in by the forensics team.

"Why are you still here?" she asked Max.

"I'm staying with Lily."

"The question was for both of you." She beckoned to one of the paramedics still hanging around. "These two need to go to the hospital."

I groaned. I'd spent quite enough time there recently, and I didn't relish the thought of going back.

"Better to get it over with," Max whispered. "She won't give up." Then he eyed up the woman. "Are you having any luck out there?"

"Not yet. It's too wet for the dog to track properly, so we're onto canvassing now. Dude was last seen heading for Edgeware Road, and you know how busy that gets in the evening."

"Keep me posted."

"Will do."

Even though I'd been walking around for almost an hour, the paramedics insisted on strapping me to a stretcher. I guess it made them feel useful. A particularly enthusiastic pair tried to do Max as well, but he cracked his knuckles when they walked towards him and they soon backed off.

Minutes later, we headed for King's College Hospital once more, blue lights flashing. Max looked thoroughly cheesed off with the whole thing.

"It's for your own good," I told him.

"So they tell me." He sighed. "I just hate hospitals, that's all."

"Why?"

"I spent too much time in one as a child."

He turned his back on me, and it was clear he didn't want to elaborate. We lapsed into silence, disturbed only by the racing engine and the occasional *whoop* of the siren. The driver seemed to be enjoying himself, at least.

The doctors separated us when we got inside the hospital, wheeling me into a cubicle while Max got whisked off for X-rays. A nurse bathed my neck with antiseptic while I clutched at the sheets. Hell, that stung.

"From the state of this, you're lucky to be here tonight," she told me.

"I know." And if Max had turned up five minutes later, I'd have been relaxing in the morgue instead.

"Do the police know who did it?"

I shook my head. "They're looking." But I knew they wouldn't find him, not with the head start he got. The best I could hope for was a clue left behind. Would the flowers help? He must have bought them from somewhere, and the vases. The one with the lilies certainly didn't belong to me.

The nurse dabbed salve onto my neck as I heard the man's voice again, his whispered promise to kill me. What if I simply drove to the airport and hopped on the next plane? I could be in Tahiti by morning. Well, apart from the lack of cash and the fact that my passport was still hidden in the bottom of a shoebox in my wardrobe. And, of course, I wanted justice for Rose.

No, no matter how tempting, I couldn't run away. I needed to stay and see this through to its bitter end.

CHAPTER 12

THE DOCTORS WANTED me to stay overnight for observation, just in case I'd hit my head, but I insisted on leaving. The clinical efficiency of hospitals freaked me out. Although where I'd go, I had no idea. With my own home playing host to the Met's investigators as well as half of Blackwood Security, it seemed Suki's flat was the only option.

"Can I borrow your phone? I left mine behind in my flat." I asked Max, who'd got out before me and sat waiting on one of the hard plastic chairs in reception. His left arm was in a padded foam sling, and he didn't look happy about it. Then again, what was new?

"Why?"

"To call Suki. I need to borrow her couch again."

"How secure is her place?"

"Um..." I'd never really thought about it.

"What floor?"

"Ground."

"She have a burglar alarm?"

"No."

"Then you're not staying there."

I put my hands on my hips and faced him. "So, where else am I supposed to sleep? In case you didn't notice, my apartment no longer has a door."

Another fun discussion I needed to have with my

landlord. Could he charge extra on top of my security deposit?

"With me."

Oh no. No way. He had to be kidding. "Nye said your house was a building site."

Not to mention the fact that Max wasn't exactly enamoured with me. The thought of us being stuck together on his home turf made me feel ever so slightly sick.

"It's got ceilings now. And double glazing, steel doors, security shutters, CCTV, and a centrally monitored alarm system."

Okay, I'll admit those features did sound attractive, but it also still had Max in it. And grateful though I was that he'd saved my life, I wasn't about to move into his half-finished house.

The double doors at the front of the hospital whooshed open, and we stepped out into the cold night air. I couldn't help shivering a little. As I tucked my hands into my pockets, Max ripped the sling off and dumped it in the nearest bin, then glanced over at the empty taxi rank.

"I'll call for a car."

"I'm not going home with you."

He smiled, and I wanted to slap him.

"Yes, you are."

"I'm not." And I needed a phone. I spotted a teenager leaning against a nearby street light and plastered on a smile. "Could I possibly borrow your phone? Just for a second?"

He eyed up Max beside me, who looked like a bull about to charge, then handed it over. "Here, lady. Keep it." He turned and ran off.

"Shit. Did I just accidentally mug someone?"

Max chuckled. "Sure looks that way."

"That was all your fault."

He held his hands up. "I didn't do anything."

"You didn't need to. You were just...you."

"Was that an insult?"

I thought about it. "I'm not sure."

He laughed harder, and dammit, he almost looked cute.

"Shut up. I need to call Suki."

Only when she answered, things didn't go quite according to plan.

"Can I stay with you tonight?" I asked.

"Uh, well, I won't exactly be at home."

"What? Where are you going?"

"Jason doesn't think it's safe for me to sleep there tonight, what with being mixed up in all this, so he's invited me to stay at his place."

I thought back to the scene in my flat, how they'd arrived together so soon after Max. No way could Jason have gone to Suki's home on the other side of London, picked her up, then got back to Paddington in such a short time.

"You were with him earlier, weren't you?"

A long pause gave me my answer. "I really like him, Lily," she whispered.

On any other day, I'd have been thrilled for both of them, but her admission left me with a pit of dread in my stomach.

"I'm glad," I lied.

"I can give you the key to my flat? Or ask Jason if you can stay with us? He's got a sofa bed."

"It's okay. Max offered me a room for the night."

Relief sounded in her voice, tinged with a hint of worry. "You're sure you'll be okay?"

No. "I'll be fine."

I hung up, and I knew from Max's smug expression he'd worked out my problem. "Fine, you win."

His smile got broader.

"Stop grinning. And can you help me get this phone back to its owner?"

"No, and yes."

Why did he have to be so bloody infuriating?

Whatever I'd been expecting from Max's home, it wasn't the large, neo-Georgian detached on the outskirts of Holland Park we pulled up to half an hour later.

Whoa. "This is yours?"

"No, I like to stop off at random houses on my way home. It adds variety to my day."

For a moment, I wondered if he was serious, but then I caught the sparkle in his eyes. Ah, so he did have a sense of humour lurking somewhere. He just kept it well hidden. I was about to make a witty retort when I remembered I was mad at him and folded my arms.

The driver of the Mercedes that had picked us up at the hospital opened my door, and I stepped out into the light drizzle. Max followed and punched a code into a keypad next to the gates. They swung open on silent hinges, and a security light blinked on, allowing me to see the detail of the house.

It was the kind of place I'd dreamed of living in since I was a little girl. The houses I'd made out of cardboard boxes and sticky tape and scraps of fabric for my collection of dolls bore more than a passing similarity. Huge windows, high ceilings, light and airy rooms. I'd always loved the period, and the symmetry in buildings of that age appealed to my inner sense of order.

Although the builder's skip sitting on what should have been the front lawn spoiled the effect a little. The rest of the garden sported a mess of mud and plant carcasses in an insult to horticulture, plus a pile of bricks that wouldn't have been out of place in the Tate Modern. Max led me past it all and up to the portico where two columns topped by decorative cornices flanked the front door.

"Have you lived here long?"

"Almost a year." He peered into an iris scanner, and there was a muffled *thunk* as bolts in the door shot back. Boy, that was some security system. "It's a work in progress."

The door swung open, and I realised what he meant. When he flicked the lights on, a bare hall stretched out in front of us. And when I said bare, I meant bare—no furniture, no curtains, no carpet, no paint. Not even a light shade. Just bare boards and plaster. The theme continued throughout downstairs.

"This'll be the lounge." He waved toward a door on the right, its only contents a blow-up sofa and a giant plasma-screen TV.

"And the dining room." Also empty.

"The study."

That one had a folding table, a plastic lawn chair, and a laptop.

"The gym."

Okay, I'd worked out where he spent most of his time. The floor was covered in padded mats, with a pile of weights in one corner and a punch bag hanging in the centre. Mirrors hung floor to ceiling on the entire far wall. I caught sight of my reflection and grimaced. From a distance, I looked as if someone had tied me to the back of a car and dragged me around the M25, and I doubted the close-up would be an improvement.

"And here's the kitchen."

Hallelujah! Some proper furniture, and the man had taste, I'd give him that. White units topped with grey marble went beautifully with the polished wooden floor, and the steel appliances were a chef's dream. Too bad I couldn't cook to save my life.

"I'm doing one room at a time," he explained. "The only way I could afford this house in this area was to buy a wreck and fix it up myself."

"You did all this?"

He shrugged. "Yeah."

"It's amazing."

I'd never seen his shy smile before, but he looked almost normal when he wore it. Not quite so robotic. "I'm glad you like it."

I had a worrying thought. "What about upstairs? What state is that in?"

"You can have my room. It's the only one with furniture."

"Where will you sleep?"

"The gym, probably."

"You can't do that." He was being sweet. I didn't know how to deal with him when he did sweet.

He raised one cocky eyebrow. "It wasn't a suggestion."

Great, he was back to being an asshole. Normal service: resumed. "Is there a bathroom? Tell me there's a bathroom."

"My en-suite's finished."

Oh, thank goodness.

I tried to stop it, but my mouth opened in a yawn of its own accord. All the talk of bed reminded me how tired I felt. I covered it with a hand. "Sorry."

"I'll show you where to go. Do you want anything to eat first? Drink?"

"Do you have gin or donuts?"

"What do you think?"

"In that case, I'll just go to bed."

The king-size bed still smelled of Max, a combination of man-musk and expensive aftershave, although I couldn't say I minded. It lulled me into a sense of safety, and despite the horrors of the evening, I fell asleep quickly and didn't wake up until...what time was it? I glanced at my watch but the face was cracked, the hands stopped at seven last night. Another casualty of the horror.

And Max didn't appear to have a clock upstairs.

I'd slept in my clothes, so I tiptoed along the bare boards of the landing, stopping to peer into each room as I passed. Even today, nosiness won out. Max hadn't been kidding—they were all empty except the one next to his, which held a drop cloth, a ladder, and a variety of paint pots. The acrid aroma of fresh gloss encouraged my headache, and I quickly closed that door again.

Max was already awake—hardly surprising as the kitchen clock said it was gone ten. He'd moved the laptop onto the breakfast bar, where he sat typing beside a mug of something that smelled disgusting.

"I'm late for work. Can you tell me where I am so I can call a cab?"

He glanced up at me. "No."

"Sorry?"

"You're not going to work. Not after the night you've had."

"You can't tell me what to do."

"Just did." He carried on typing.

Did he seriously...? A pulse pounded in my temple as I balled my fists up. "You can't order me to stay."

"True." He blew out a long breath, as if his exasperation was my fault. "What if I asked nicely?"

Max was, without a doubt, the most infuriating man I'd ever met. And considering I once went on a date with a man who "forgot" his wallet and expected me to pay not only for our cinema tickets, but also his steak dinner and the speeding ticket he got on the way home, that was saying something.

"I have to go. Suki's on her own in the shop and that's not fair."

"She understands."

"You don't know that."

"Yes, I do. I already spoke to her this morning, and I've sorted out someone to help her. She likes clothes."

He'd what? Was there any part of my life he wasn't going to meddle in? Once again, I didn't know whether to be thankful or pissed off. "Who?"

"Someone my boss knows."

"Who's your boss? Nye?" Although didn't Nye say

he worked in a different department?

"You met her last night."

Her? "The blonde dictator in the cocktail dress?"

He burst out laughing. "She'd take that as a compliment."

"Can I at least speak to Suki?"

He slid his phone out of his pocket, punched in the PIN code, and passed it over. "Sure."

I typed in Suki's number from memory and wandered out into the hallway. Although I had nothing to hide, if I talked about Max I'd prefer he didn't listen in on the conversation.

The phone rang three times, and then Suki picked up, sounding far more cheerful than I felt. "Hello?"

"It's me."

"Whose phone are you on?"

"Max's."

"How are you? I wanted to call you last night, but Jason spoke to Max, and he said you'd gone to bed."

"I could barely keep my eyes open when we got back from the hospital."

"So, what's he like? Where does he live?"

"Shouldn't that be my question?"

She gave a coy giggle, and I knew she was in trouble. Usually, Suki was only too happy to dish the dirt, everything from cringe-worthy chat-up lines to absurd suggestions in the bedroom. "He's got a flat in Islington. It's nice. You mind if I stay with him again tonight? You'll be with Max, right?"

"I don't think I have a choice."

"Lily, I'm so sorry, I didn't think. I can cancel if you want?"

"No, I didn't mean it like that. I meant Max won't

give me a choice. He's got me locked up in a fortress in Holland Park."

"Holland Park?" She gave a low whistle. "Well, I can think of worse places."

"I'm serious. I'm a bloody prisoner. He said I'm not allowed to go to work today."

"And I agree with him. Someone nearly strangled you last night, for crying out loud. Besides, I have a new assistant."

Oh, wonderful. Another cheerleader for Team Max. "He mentioned that. Who is she?"

"A girl called Tia. She's already redone the window display, and now she's manning the till. Honestly, we're fine here. She says she's free for the next couple of weeks."

Great. It looked as if I really was stuck with a man I couldn't decide whether to worship or slap. I forced myself to unclench my teeth. *Deep breaths, Lily, deep breaths.* Max wasn't all bad. He may have been irritating as hell, but he was sworn to protect me, like some errant knight of old. I couldn't help giggling at the thought of him astride a big black charger, lance in hand. See? All I needed to do was stay positive.

Upbeat.

Optimistic.

Then this nightmare would be over before I knew it.

CHAPTER 13

AFTER ACCIDENTALLY ENDING up in the study, I found my way back to the kitchen and returned Max's phone. He'd started eating half a melon, and his healthiness made me crave sugar.

"Do you have any cereal?"

"There's muesli in the cupboard beside the oven."

How did I guess? "What about proper cereal? Frosties or Coco Pops?"

"You mean empty calories?"

"Exactly."

"Nothing like that."

I opened the fridge and perused the contents. Salad, fruit, vegetables, eggs, chicken. Not an artificial colour, flavour, or preservative in sight. How could anyone live this way? He didn't even have wine.

"Ugh."

"If it matters that much to you, we can go out and get some junk food."

"Don't you have to work today?"

"Yes. I'm looking after you."

I raised an eyebrow. "I mean proper work, as opposed to babysitting."

"You've been bumped up the schedule. Congratulations."

"What do you mean?"

"My boss doesn't like it when women nearly get murdered. Ergo, you're now my full-time client."

He sounded so pompous I almost laughed. Almost. "But I can't afford that."

"It's a freebie. Despite what people say, the boss does have a heart."

I recalled the hard-faced woman I'd met last night. Yes, it *was* hard to believe. She'd ordered those men around and not one of them had argued, and even the cops had seemed nervous of her.

"Are you serious?"

"Always."

Well, that much was true.

"I should thank her."

"She's already flown back to the States."

"Maybe I could send her a gift? Do you think she'd like a corset?"

"I'm sure her husband would love it, same as any other red-blooded male."

"Even you?"

He cut his eyes in my direction. "Even me, Lily. Even me."

Why did that make my heart beat faster?

Starving after throwing up everything I ate yesterday, I gave in and went with the muesli. With skimmed milk. Double ugh. Since Max's attention was back on his computer, I walked over to the window, holding the bowl in one hand as I looked out at the jungle behind the house. Brambles covered everything except a wonky fir tree in the centre, where a squirrel hopped precariously from branch to branch. Was it searching for food? I thought of offering it some of the muesli, but I figured even a rodent wouldn't be that desperate.

"I spoke to Jason," Max said.

"Any news?"

"We didn't get the guy. But the cops have picked up the roses from the storage unit and sent them for testing."

"I'm surprised they were still there."

"Jase said he wasn't sure whether to bin them or not, so he just shoved the whole vaseful in the box when he cleared out the bedroom."

"I hope they find a fingerprint."

"So do I. Or they might be able to trace the shop where the vase was sold. They've sent the rope for testing as well."

"I'm surprised he left it behind."

"The bastard dropped it on the fire escape."

I shuddered again, thinking of my close call. The burn around my neck. That fetid breath.

"Are you cold? Do you want me to turn the heating up? I finished installing the radiators last week."

"No, I'm okay."

And could Max stop being so damn sweet? It unnerved me.

Breakfast may have tasted like fancy cardboard, but I felt some strength return as I finished the last spoonful. And with that came self-awareness and the realisation that I smelled pretty bad.

"Can I use your shower?"

"Sure."

"Do you have spare towels?"

He didn't even look at me. "In the cupboard next to the shower."

"And panties? Can I borrow a pair of yours?"

"I'm not sure they'd fit." I caught him trying to hide his smile. Gotcha.

"Can I pick some stuff up from my flat? You know, if I've got to stay here another night?"

He closed the lid of his computer and leaned on his elbows. "It's sealed off now. We'll have to go shopping."

"We? Can't I go by myself?"

"Which part of this whole bodyguard thing don't you get?"

Great. Just great. When I thought my life couldn't get any worse, I had to go shopping for undies with The Incredible Hulk. Then I thought of another snag. "My credit card's in my flat as well."

"Then I guess we're using mine."

"I'll pay you back."

"Whatever."

As with the kitchen, the shower was an over-specced luxury. Jets hit me from every direction, a veritable waterfall cascaded from the head at the top, and Max bought his toiletries from Bulgari. No wonder he always smelled so good. Not that I'd been sniffing him. No siree.

The body wash stung as I gently sponged my neck, which had mostly scabbed over while I slept. Once I'd wrapped myself in a giant towel, I examined the mess. If anything, the red welts looked worse now the bruising had come out. Although if Max hadn't been there... The temperature in the bathroom dropped a few notches, and I shivered.

Back in the bedroom, I put on the same grubby clothes, wishing I'd thought to bring a polo neck. All I could do was arrange my hair to cover the angry-looking collar as best I could and hope people ignored it.

Except when I got downstairs, Max was waiting in the hallway and held out a scarf. Plain black cashmere.

"I thought you might need this. You know, to hide the rope marks."

Another tick in the non-asshole column. If he wasn't careful, I'd be changing my mind about him. "Thanks. That's kind of you."

"Didn't want people staring, wondering if I did it."

Okay, erase that. He was just a selfish git. I pulled on my coat as he shrugged into a slim rucksack.

"What's that for?" I asked.

"So I can carry your stuff and still keep my hands free."

Oh, shit. More nice. Was I going to be in trouble here?

Rather than take the Tube, which Max proclaimed to be an assassin's dream, we glided through the streets in the black Mercedes again.

"Where are we going?" Max asked.

Given that I was having to borrow his money, and I didn't have much of my own left in any case, I figured I'd better go for economy rather than style. "Price-Mart on Oxford Street?"

"I don't do Price-Mart and I don't do Oxford Street."

Two more ticks in the asshole column.

Although he did redeem himself slightly. I'd never bought underwear from Rigby & Peller before, but I had to admit the experience was a lot more pleasant than elbowing teenagers aside in the fight for the last zebra-print bra. Of course, when I saw the prices, I understood why.

"I can only afford one set from here," I hissed as the assistant rummaged through boxes.

Max shrugged, his default action, it seemed, for everything. "You're not buying it, I am. So get plenty because we're not coming back again tomorrow."

"You can't buy me underwear."

"Why?"

"Because...you're my bodyguard and it's weird."

"What if it was socks?"

"I guess socks would be okay."

"They're both pretty much as essential as each other, wouldn't you say?"

"Well, yes, but—"

"Unless you want to go commando, which I can't say I'd object to either."

Tick, tick, tick.

Once he'd paid, Max tried to wedge the pretty boxes in his backpack, but that was sacrilegious so I took them off him. "I think I can carry my own underwear."

He shrugged. "Whatever."

Boy, someone really needed to buy him a thesaurus. He herded me back to the car, only for it to drive a hundred yards down the road and deposit us outside Harvey Nichols. Seriously?

The personal shopper was on us almost before we got through the door.

"Welcome back, Mr. Tian. How can I help you today?"

He shopped here often enough for the staff to know his name? The pretty blonde smiled up at him, but he jerked a thumb in my direction.

"Not me, her."

The girl's smile dropped for a second as she turned to me, but she soon ratcheted it up to full beam again. "How can I help?"

"I need some clothes. Just the basics."

"Well, you've certainly come to the right place. You're a size eight?"

"That's right."

Max stood guard outside the fitting room door as my new best friend, Bethany, carted outfits back and forth. No matter what Max said, I had every intention of paying him back as soon as I could afford it, so I carefully selected a capsule wardrobe rather than splurging extravagantly. Even so, it still filled six bags.

"How are we going to carry it all? I won't manage on my own."

Max beamed at Bethany, who blushed. "Can you courier it as usual?"

"Of course, sir."

Silly me. Problem solved.

"What else do you need?" he asked.

"Toiletries and make-up."

"You don't need make-up."

Should I take that as a compliment or another one of Max's irritating vetoes? "I do. I have to wear red lipstick and smokey eyeshadow to fit the look of the shop."

"But you're not there at the moment."

"I can't stay away forever. If I don't make more stock, we won't have anything to sell."

"Can't you pick up what you need and make things at my house?"

"I suppose." Why did he have to be so bloody logical?

"So, that leaves toiletries."

"And where do you usually buy those? Harrods?"

"Boots, actually."

Hurrah—a normal shop at last. We got back into the car and drove two hundred yards in the opposite direction, then Max hovered at the end of the feminine products aisle while I selected boxes of tampons. It was the only time I'd seen him look uncomfortable. He shoved them, plus the other assorted bottles I'd picked up, into his backpack and made a hasty exit from the store.

"Can we get some lunch now?" Trying on clothes had made me inexplicably ravenous.

"What do you want? And don't say McDonald's."

"Whatever I say will be wrong. Why don't you just pick somewhere?"

"I know a Japanese place nearby where the security's adequate."

By that point, I was so hungry I'd have eaten a kebab. "Japanese is fine."

When he said nearby, he meant in the next street, so we avoided a car ride at least. The maître d' welcomed him by name and settled us at a table near the back. Max took the seat against the wall and kept his beady eyes on the door.

"Where are the menus?" I whispered.

"No need for those. They'll choose for us."

"What if we hate it?"

"They'll bring something else."

"Are you always like this?"

"Like what?"

"Like an asshole." I checked off the points on my fingers. "You're too much of a snob to set foot in Price-Mart or go to Oxford Street. You only shop in hideously expensive places. And you can't be bothered to order properly, so you'll just have people cook more stuff if they don't correctly guess what you might want to eat."

A crease appeared between his eyebrows. "One. I don't shop in cheap places because I don't agree with their methods for making the clothes. I have no desire to support child labour. Two. If I choose well-made clothes that suit me, which Bethany helps me to do, I can get away with only shopping a couple of times a year. Three. If I ask the waiter to bring what's good, I discover new foods and I get what's in season and fresh."

"Oh." It seemed I might have misjudged him a bit. "I'm sorry. I must sound like such a bitch."

Another of his famous shrugs. "You've been under a lot of stress lately. It stops you thinking things through. And you're right—I can be an asshole."

"I'll try and be nicer, I promise. And I never thanked you properly for what you did last night."

"I was only doing my job."

"But still..."

"Don't think about it. If you dwell on it, he wins."

His words were similar to Bridges's, and they were both right. I tried to force my mind onto a different topic. "Do you eat here a lot?"

"Once a month or so."

"What's your favourite kind of food?"

"Pizza."

I loved a good deep pan too, especially if it came freshly delivered with all the toppings, extra cheese, and a pint of ice cream for dessert. But hang on? Max ate pizza?

"I thought you said you didn't eat carbs?"

"I don't overload on carbs often. What do you like?"

"I've got a sweet tooth, so anything with chocolate or sugar. But for normal food, I like Chinese. Do you think we could have that one day?"

"If I have Chinese, I go to Chinatown, but that'll have to wait. I can't take you there until after the cops catch the guy. It's too crowded."

"After? But when he's caught, I won't need you anymore."

He stayed silent for a second. "Yeah. Right. Look, if you really want Chinese, I'll cook it for you."

"You can cook? I mean, something more than salad?"

He bit his lip, as if he was trying to work out how much to say. "My parents ran a Chinese restaurant. I grew up helping in the kitchen."

"Around here? Do they still run it?" I couldn't help noticing he'd used the past tense.

"In Manchester. And I don't know. I haven't spoken to my family in a decade."

"Why not?"

"I don't talk about it."

Thankfully, the waiter saved us from any more awkwardness by bringing the first dishes over, and I found Max was right. If I'd seen a menu, I'd have stuck with the same safe old choices, but now I discovered a taste for crunchy tofu salad with su-miso sauce. And edamame beans. I'd always thought they looked like overachieving peas, but they were strangely addictive.

"Have you eaten enough?" Max asked.

I tried to burp discreetly and adjusted my belt out a notch. "Yes, plenty. Thank you."

"Time to pick up your work stuff, then."

I gave Suki a call on the way over so she wouldn't get a shock when we walked through the door, and it wasn't long before we arrived. Suki was waiting just inside with a hug for me, while a young brunette sprinted across the shop floor and threw herself at Max. He picked her up and gave her a squeeze—most un-Max like.

He caught me staring. "Lily, this is Tia. Tia, Lily."

She hugged me as well, catching me by surprise. "Shit, your neck looks nasty. Is Max being much of an asshole?"

"No, he's been lovely."

She burst out laughing. "You're lying. Max is always an asshole. But a sweet asshole." She faced him. "Aren't you?"

He shuffled from foot to foot like a sulky teenager. "Whatever."

She let fly with another peal of laughter. "Anyway, thanks for letting me help in the shop. It's awesome fun. I'd love to be a fashion designer someday."

"It's me who should be thanking you."

"I was only sitting around doing nothing. My boyfriend works with him." She pointed at Max. "And he's out all day. There's only so much shopping I can do."

"We started putting the pieces that need hand-finishing in boxes," Suki said. "There should be enough to keep you busy for a week or so."

"Thanks. There's a car outside."

"We'll help you to load up."

Max made me wait at the back of the shop while Tia and Suki helped the driver carry my things, and then we were off back to Holland Park. That had to go down in my short history as the craziest twenty-four hours I'd ever lived through, even beating my old school friend Debbie's hen weekend in Edinburgh, the one where she tried to strip a real policeman and got arrested.

"How are you feeling?" Max asked.

I answered honestly. "Tired."

That one word sent me to sleep. I didn't remember the journey back, or how I got into the house, or how I ended up in bed. By the time I woke, the stars were out and the building was quiet, and I drifted off again, thinking not of Rose, not of the nightmare I was trapped in, but of the man living through it with me.

Chapter 14

I SMELLED EVEN worse the next morning, seeing as it was my third day in the same clothes and I'd slept in them. Again.

Before I did anything, I needed a shower, no hardship in this place. My bags of shopping had magically appeared in Max's room, and I rummaged through until I found the pair of jeans I'd bought. Soft denim, beautifully cut—Max was right about Bethany's skills.

I'd forgotten to buy a blow-dryer, and I couldn't imagine Max owning one, so I clipped my wet hair back and went downstairs. Yesterday, Max had been sitting quietly at the counter when I got up, but today he paced the kitchen, speaking into a headset.

"So you'll keep me updated, yeah?... No, no plans to go out today... Gimme a call if you need anything from Blackwood... Okay... I'll see what resources we've got available."

"What's happened?" I asked the instant he got off the phone.

"Sit down."

"What? Why?"

"Because I don't want to have to catch you again."

A lump rose in my throat as I perched on one of the stools at the breakfast bar. Max leaned against the counter next to me.

"The cops found a body. About an hour ago."

"Whose body?" I put two and two together and made seventeen. "Suki? Please say it wasn't Suki." I gripped the edge of the marble with my already chilled fingertips.

"Not Suki. Heather. Heather Barker. A window cleaner saw her lying on her bed at eight this morning."

I felt desperately sorry for the girl, but what did that have to do with me? "I don't get it."

"She was strangled, and her best friend's ninety percent sure that the pot of heather on her dressing table didn't belong to her."

The edges of the room began to blur, and Max gently pushed my head between my knees until I stopped feeling giddy. Sick to my stomach, yes, but not giddy. I clutched at him for support as I sat up again.

"They think it was the same man, don't they?"

He nodded. "That's the theory they're working on. Jason picked up the case and saw the similarities."

Max hesitated, not for long, but enough for me to notice.

"What aren't you telling me?"

"Shit." He closed his eyes for a second, and his top teeth dug into his bottom lip. "It was worse. Much worse. This time, the guy was angry."

"H-h-how angry?"

"You don't want to know."

"Tell me, dammit. I'm not some porcelain doll you have to keep in bubble wrap."

His look said he disagreed, but he told me anyway. Then I wished he hadn't. "He raped her and sawed halfway through her neck with the rope."

Without Max to hold on to, I'd have fallen clean off the stool. Why was it every time I got a bit of strength back, every time I had a good day, that murdering bastard stole it from me? After yesterday with Max, I'd felt able to face things, but now I wanted to curl up into a ball and rock.

Max wiped my tears away with a thumb, then handed me a tissue. "I don't like it when you cry."

"I can't help it. That poor, poor girl. It should have been me."

"It shouldn't have been either of you."

The tissue soon soaked through as I sobbed all over Max. He stroked my back, a little awkwardly it seemed, but I needed his warmth. He was my safe place.

"I'm sorry," I sniffled after I'd pulled myself together a little. "I'm useless."

"Not useless. You're just...sensitive, I guess. And that's not a bad thing. There are too many people in the world who don't feel enough."

A couple of days ago, I'd have said he was one of them, but now I wasn't so sure.

"I'd rather not feel at all right now." It hurt too much. "What happens next?"

"We stay here while the police do their job."

"Can't I do anything to help?"

"No."

"But Blackwood's spending all this time and money, and I'm...I'm..."

That horrible sting of tears came again, and I pressed the heels of both hands against my eyes to hold them in.

"We do pro bono stuff every so often, and the guys at the office want this man caught as much as you do.

Every victim is someone's daughter. Someone's sister."

A dark shadow flitted through his eyes, chased by an abrupt subject change. What was that about?

"You want breakfast? I got someone to bring Frosties." He pointed at a box on the side.

My heart skipped a little at the sight. He'd done that for me? Bought food that he so obviously hated? "Thank you, but I feel too sick to eat at the moment."

"You shouldn't sit and think about it. Why don't you watch a movie or something? It might take your mind off things."

"I should work. That might help."

"I put your boxes in the study. You can use the table in there."

He'd set it up with a desk lamp for me, and even found a cushion for the chair. Another tick in the "sweet" column. I got settled, and he brought me a cup of coffee, black and strong, just the way I liked it.

"You bought coffee as well?"

He shrugged. "If the boss doesn't get her coffee, she's a bitch by ten. Didn't want to take the chance you'd be the same."

Asshole. "I suppose I should say thank you."

"I'll be in the gym. Find me if you want anything."

Try as I might, I couldn't concentrate. Once I'd embroidered half a skull upside down on a pair of silk knickers, I gave up and went to fetch more coffee. Coffee helped with everything.

I'd got halfway to the kitchen when I heard a rhythmic thumping coming from the gym. Max? What on earth was he doing in there? I crept towards the door, grateful my socks didn't make a noise on the wooden boards, and peeped into the room.

His back was to me as he attacked the punch bag with vicious kicks that shook the mountings on the ceiling. He followed those up with a series of jabs, sweat pouring down his bare spine. His sheer power combined with his speed scared me just to watch, but I couldn't tear my eyes away. Then, in the middle of a spin kick, he saw me watching and stopped. Just like that. Stopped. Leg still extended, in perfect balance. With immense control, he lowered his foot to the floor.

"Is something wrong?"

I shook my head. "I just kept getting distracted." And his naked torso didn't help matters. I motioned at the heavy bag, still swinging slowly. "Have you been doing that long?"

He looked up at the clock. "About an hour."

"I meant in general. When did you learn?"

"I started six years ago."

"Are you, like, a black belt?"

"I've never taken those kind of lessons."

"What do you mean, those kind of lessons?"

"The ones where you piss around on the mat in a church hall one evening a week and get a rainbow of colours to prove you turned up."

Tell me what you think, why don't you? "So, where did you learn to fight?"

"Partly on the street. Partly in a gym where they assess your progress by how often you get knocked out."

"Wasn't that dangerous?"

"The world's dangerous."

Didn't I know it? But the question was, how dangerous was the man standing in front of me?

An hour later, Max had showered and dressed, and looked more like a chef than a fighting machine as he chopped up spinach in the kitchen. Even so, I couldn't stop thinking about what I now knew lay underneath that shirt. The man had abs that would put any self-respecting pin-up boy to shame.

Tuna and avocado salad wasn't my favourite lunch, but I picked at it and ate half, mostly out of guilt because Max had made it. Max shovelled his in, and as he chewed the last mouthful, his phone rang. Jason's name flashed up on the screen.

Max gave me a sideways glance, then left the room to take the call. I knew he was only trying to protect me, but I hated being left out of the loop. By the time he came back, I was already imagining the worst.

"Did he hurt someone else?"

"No."

"Then what did Bridges want?"

"Just an update. They found out Heather used one of the same online dating sites as your sister, so they're pushing that angle again."

"I warned her about that. I begged her to be more careful."

"Thousands of people use them every year, and nothing bad happens. You can't blame the internet for a man's sadistic tendencies."

"But it made things easier for him."

"We don't know that for sure yet."

I walked back and forth, recalling Rose's stories of dates gone wrong. One man turned up wearing an electronic tag and claimed it was a fashion accessory. I'd pleaded with her to give up with the casual hook-ups then. If one criminal could use that method to meet women, who knew how many more of them did?

Max's hand darted out and grabbed me. "Stop with the pacing. It won't help."

"It makes me feel better. Nothing else has helped."

"Let's sit down and put a movie on. We can watch whatever you want."

"I won't be able to concentrate." Plus the idea of watching a film seemed so normal when this week had been anything but.

"Try."

"Do you have any wine?"

"Will it help you keep still?"

"Yes."

He sighed. "Then I've got wine."

Between them, Max and a large glass of red kept me seated through the first two Harry Potter films. I must have seen them a dozen times, but I didn't care. Today, I couldn't bring myself to watch anything that involved realism. By the end of Chamber of Secrets, I felt more relaxed, but my back ached from sitting on a blow-up sofa that sagged in the middle. I stood up to stretch, trying to work the kinks out.

"Feeling better?"

"A bit. Except my back hurts."

"You don't want to watch part three, then?" Max had done his best to stay awake, but I caught him yawning a couple of times.

"Could we eat first?" My appetite had returned with

a vengeance.

"You want pizza?"

"What about your diet?"

He shrugged. "It's a pizza day."

I flashed him a quick smile. "I'll have everything except anchovies."

A piping-hot pizza soon arrived and cheered me up a little. Extra cheese and pepperoni worked better than antidepressants any day. I wasn't sure Max's thin crust with all the vegetables would have the same effect on him, but he seemed happy enough.

"Are you ready for another movie now? Or do you want to go to bed?" he asked after he'd taken the empty boxes out to the bin.

It was only eight o'clock. "Another movie."

"I don't think I've ever watched this much TV in one day," he said as we settled back on the sofa.

"I'm not surprised with only this to sit on."

"A new sofa's on my list of things to buy."

And he'd probably be closer to doing it if he hadn't spent a fortune on my clothes yesterday. I reached over and squeezed his hand.

"What was that for?" He twitched and stared down as if I'd scalded him.

"Thank you for being so kind to me. You don't have to be."

"I'm just doing—"

I held up my palm to stop him. "Don't tell me it's your job. It's more than that."

I half expected him to deny it, but he didn't. Instead, he focused on the screen and rolled the opening credits.

This time, it was me who struggled to keep my eyes

open. At one point, I keeled over entirely, then shot awake as my head landed on Max's well-muscled thigh. I tried to get up, but he held me there.

"Stay, if it's comfortable."

Oh, it was. He stroked my hair in the way Mum used to do when I was a little girl, root to tip, twirling the ends.

"You're blonde?" he whispered.

Dammit, my roots needed doing again. "Yes."

"Why do you dye it dark? It's too harsh for your features."

"For work. It goes better with the clothes."

"How did you get into that scene? If I hadn't seen the shop, I'd never have pictured you as a goth."

"After my mum got sick, I went through a bad phase. I wanted to fit in with a group, any group, and that seemed the easiest. I couldn't afford to buy the outfits, so I made them myself out of old clothes I found in charity shops. Then people started asking me to make them stuff too. Black Lily Designs got born by accident. By the time I realised it wasn't my thing, it was too late to stop."

His fingers were magic. They massaged my scalp, hitting all the right spots. I had to bite my lip to keep from moaning. If Max ever got sick of working as a bodyguard, he could get a job in one of those high-end spas.

"So, are you into the subculture? The music?"

"I keep up to date with trends because of the business, and elements of it interest me. But at heart, I'm a poseur. Why?"

"I'm just curious. I want to know more about you, Lily."

My eyes were closing, lulled into sleep by his touch. "I'm not the interesting one, Max. You are."

CHAPTER 15

IN THE MORNING, I found I'd been teleported to bed again. Was it weird that Max kept carrying me like that? Maybe, but I secretly kind of liked it.

I threw on some clothes, and when I got halfway downstairs, the aroma of coffee drifted up at me. I'd never smelled instant quite that rich. Surely he hadn't...

He had.

"You bought a coffee machine?"

"Boss phoned. She said I shouldn't be giving you instant, so she sent that." He pointed at a hideously complicated-looking contraption in the middle of his counter and grimaced. "It's taken me six goes to make a cup."

"I'm not surprised."

I examined it, only for it to start beeping at me. It put my little Nespresso machine to shame. The instruction book alone was half an inch thick.

"Apparently it's the best type," Max informed me.

And his boss had even sent a selection of coffee. Colombian, Blue Mountain, Ethiopian, and Kona. And espresso cups. Those were new too.

"Something else I need to thank her for."

I was building up so many favours owing I'd spend the rest of my life fulfilling them. Still, coffee first. I sipped at the cup Max made, surprised to find it almost drinkable.

"Do you have any sugar?" I asked.

"No."

"There's nothing sweet in this house at all?"

His lips curved up in an enigmatic smile, then straightened. "Only honey."

Would honey work in coffee? There was one way to find out. I added a generous spoonful and stirred as Max looked on curiously.

"Not bad," was my verdict. "Have you got any paracetamol?"

"What's wrong?"

"I can feel a headache starting."

He fished a packet of pills out of a cupboard and handed them over. "Why don't you go back to bed?"

"I'll be okay."

It took another hour for me to admit defeat, and by then the niggle at the base of my skull had turned into a full-on migraine. A tiny army gnawed away at my brain, like the leafcutter ants I saw in a documentary a couple of weeks back when I couldn't sleep. I hadn't had such a bad headache in years, but the stress of the last few weeks had finally tipped me over the edge. I spent the rest of the day in bed, only waking briefly in the evening when Max brought me a glass of juice and more pills.

By the next morning, Monday, my head felt clearer, and I was ready to face the world again. At least, I thought so until I got downstairs, dressed in a pair of jeans and one of the floaty tops Bethany had picked out for me.

Max slid a double espresso across the counter as I walked into the kitchen. "Uh, you need to sit down."

Oh no. "What now? Did something else happen?"

"Yes."

I shuffled over to the stool of doom. Maybe I should just strap the damn thing to my backside and be done with it.

"Do you want the bad news or the other bad news?"

"Is there any good news?"

He pointed at the coffee machine.

"Fine, just tell me."

"Jason went through the open case files and found Dahlia Heath got murdered in June."

Three months before Rose. I took a deep breath and fought to keep my emotions under control. "Did she have flowers?"

"In the crime scene photos, there's a vase of dahlias on her nightstand."

"And they weren't hers?"

"We don't know yet. The police are going to start reinterviewing everyone connected with that case today."

"And what's the other bad news?" As if the revelation of another death, even an older one, wasn't horrific enough.

"The cops sprang a leak, and the press found out." He spun his laptop around to face me, and sure enough, the story was front and centre on a tabloid website. I'd always hated Monday mornings, but this one had to go on record as the worst ever.

HAS THE FLORIST KILLED AGAIN?

According to a source in the Metropolitan Police, a task force was formed yesterday to investigate a suspected serial killer in London's midst. The man, dubbed "The Florist" by insiders, has been implicated in the murders of two women in London and the attempted killing of a third.

The flower fetishist's first known victim was twenty-six-year-old Rose Matthews, a vivacious personal assistant from South London who was found dead in her flat at the end of August. It's believed the man waited several weeks before attacking Rose's younger sister, Lily, who escaped his clutches, swiftly followed by twenty-seven-year-old Heather Barker, who wasn't so lucky.

One theory put forward is that The Florist may be selecting his victims from online dating websites, although this has not been confirmed.

More details to follow...

The article included three photos: Rose posing at her work Christmas party last year, Heather, a pretty redhead, holding up a glass of wine as she grinned for the camera, and me. I wanted to scream when I saw it. The photos of the other two girls were simple, candid shots, but for me, they'd selected one from Black Lily's online catalogue, and there I was on the national news in a leather corset, with only a spray of black lilies hiding the rest from the viewer's imagination.

I made the mistake of scrolling down to the comments section, where the occasional "My name's Carnation, should I be worried?" was interspersed with a hundred seedy lines of "Phwoar" and "I'd do her."

"They've made me look like a cheap whore."

"Did they get the picture from your company website?"

"Yes, but now it's completely out of context." And they'd cropped Suki out. She'd been standing next to me in a leather pencil skirt and velvet bra.

"Even so, we'd have a hard time arguing that case since it's in the public domain."

Why did he have to be so bloody sensible about it? "It's like being attacked all over again."

He wrapped his arms around me and held me close. "I know, and you'll get through it. I promise. I'll keep you safe."

At that moment, as his heart beat steadily against mine, I believed him.

"It's for you."

Max held his phone out, stopping me in my tracks as I wandered aimlessly around the kitchen. It must have been my hundredth circuit.

"Who is it?"

"Suki."

I held his mobile to my ear with a feeling of dread. "It's me."

"Have you seen the news?" she squealed.

"Max showed me."

"It's gone mental here. The press is camped out all the way down the street."

"I'm so, so sorry."

"Why? We couldn't have bought this publicity. Tia's up front in a black wig selling stuff like crazy, and three of the journalists have promised to do features on the clothes. We've hardly got anything left, and the website's crashed twice. Brenda's roped her needlepoint club into helping with the orders. They're all set up at the community centre."

At least someone was happy with the situation, and I couldn't lie—the extra money would be useful. "But have you seen the photo of me they're using?"

"It's a good one, isn't it? You look hot."

"I wish they'd picked one of me in normal clothes."

"Those are your normal clothes. If you're not in leather, you've got your pyjamas on."

Okay, so she had a point. Apart from this week, obviously. I didn't seem capable of changing into pyjamas and putting myself to bed at the moment. "I don't like all this attention. It's as if we're profiting from Rose's death."

"And if she could see us, she'd be screaming with bloody delight. Some good might as well come out of this."

How I wished I shared Suki's attitude. I struggled to see the good in any part of this situation. "I suppose."

"Gotta go. Tia's waving me over."

"Speak to you soon."

"You bet."

I passed the phone back to Max, unsure how I felt about the latest development.

"You want to talk about it?" He moved behind me. Close behind me.

"Not really."

"You want me to take your mind off it?" Warm breath washed over me, sweet like the strawberry smoothie he'd just drunk.

Tension crackled in the gap between our bodies,

prickling every one of my nerve endings. Did he feel it too? I twisted around, my lips one tiny inch from his. His expression remained unchanged, his face impassive. Only his eyes, the pupils wider than usual, gave a hint he was affected.

"How?"

He stepped back. "I've got the ingredients for Chinese. How about we cook?"

Relief battled disappointment within me before calling a truce. I'd live to fight another day. "I'd like that."

When Max said Chinese, I imagined egg fried rice and a chicken dish. He made the entire menu, it seemed, and he didn't even use a recipe book. Chicken, vegetables, beef, little dumplings, and three kinds of noodles. The speed he chopped things up at made me fear for his fingers, but two hours later, he hadn't lost any blood and we'd ended up with enough food to feed the entire street.

"Were you planning to invite the neighbours over?" I asked.

"I don't do visitors."

"Apart from me."

"Apart from you." He surveyed the rows of dishes. "Maybe I did get a bit carried away."

I helped to carry the dishes over to the breakfast bar, seeing as he still didn't have a dining table, then picked up a pair of chopsticks.

"Did you hear any more from Bridges?"

"I thought you didn't want to talk about this?"

"I don't, but at the same time I need to know."

He leaned his chopsticks against the edge of his bowl. "Jason emailed me. Dahlia lived alone, and the only relative they could trace was an aunt in Australia. Her parents died in a car crash a few years back."

"That's awful." I considered for a second. "But at least they didn't have to go to their daughter's funeral."

He nodded. "Dahlia's landlord cleared the flat after she died, and he doesn't remember the flowers or the vase, but they're retesting her clothes for DNA. They did find a dark brown pubic hair on her sheets."

"And it wasn't hers?"

"Dahlia was blonde. And they found a similar-coloured hair in Heather's room. But they also found blonde and light brown as well."

I recalled Heather's ginger locks from the photo in the paper. "Heather was a redhead, wasn't she?"

"That's right. They've sent everything off to the lab, but that usually takes weeks to come back."

"But girls are dying. Can't they hurry it up?"

"That's where pressure from the press could come in useful."

At least they were good for something other than embarrassing me. "Do you really think it's a serial killer?"

"Certainly the same man attacked you and Rose."

"And the others?"

"If I were a gambling man, I'd put my money on yes."

"What about the break-ins?"

"I don't know. They don't fit with the rest of it. If it was only Rose's flat that got broken into, I'd say it was just some opportunistic scumbag. But yours as well? I don't believe in coincidences like that."

Neither did I. The way my gut clenched when I thought about it told me it was all connected.

"Did Jason say anything else?"

"Not yet."

"You promise you'll tell me what happens? I don't want to find out from the papers."

"I'll tell you. Now, eat before it gets cold."

I got through four helpings, and every mouthful tasted delicious. And three glasses of chilled white wine, Sauvignon Blanc with a smoky undertone. That was delicious too. As was the man sitting opposite me. Nope. Scratch that last bit. I absolutely did not just have that thought.

"You want to watch TV? A movie?" Max asked after he'd cleared the dishes away while I spent ten minutes staring into space.

"I don't think I could take another evening on that sofa." My back was still cricked from the night before, and the shiny plastic left me all sweaty. Inflatable furniture may have been cheap, but there was a good reason for that.

"You can watch upstairs. The TV pops up from the end of the bed."

Ooh, I hadn't noticed that. "But what about you?"

"What about me?"

"What will you do?"

He shrugged. "I'll find something."

That was hardly fair. "I'll only watch a movie if you do too."

"That's up to you. You can just go to sleep if you prefer." He popped a dishwasher tablet into the machine and turned it on.

"Pleeeease. I don't want to be on my own."

"If I agree, will you stop pouting?"

Was I? Oops. "Okay."

"Fine."

I wobbled my way up the stairs, clutching the bannister for support. Those glasses had been pretty big. By contrast, the bed seemed smaller than I remembered when Max flopped down next to me.

"How do you make the TV happen?"

He rolled to the side and took the remote out of the drawer in the nightstand. "Just press the grey button at the top."

A large screen rose slowly from the footboard, and I clapped my hands in glee. "Clever."

"What do you want to watch?"

I hiccupped a couple of times then got my breath back. "Anything you like. Except foreign films. They make me all confused."

"With the amount of wine you drank, I doubt you'll find the English ones any easier to understand."

"Did you just insult me?"

He rolled his eyes.

"Don't do that." I reached out and poked him.

"What?"

"That thing with your eyes."

He did it again, only this time he smiled, but before I could prod him once more, he grabbed my hand and held it close to his chest. Okay, that was better than poking. I could live with that.

The film started, and I had to admit Max was right. Five minutes in, I had no idea what was going on. So I took the only sensible option and fell asleep.

The world outside was dark when I woke, and the film

had long since finished, replaced by a late-night shopping channel where a perma-tanned host raved about the benefits of an electrical foot file. It took a few seconds for me to realise Max still lay next to me, his breathing slow and rhythmical.

I took the opportunity to study him in the glow from the television. Relaxed, he looked a couple of years younger, and even more heart-stoppingly sexy than usual. There, I said it. Happy now? He may have been grumpy, rude at times, and had an annoying habit of ordering me around, but I liked him. He had a good heart, and with my hand still trapped in his against it, I couldn't go anywhere. Not that I wanted to.

I snuggled closer, careful not to wake him, then settled into sleep again. Every heartbeat reminded me I was safe here. Safe behind the security shutters and the steel doors. Safe while the CCTV watched the perimeter. Safe with Max.

But was my heart?

CHAPTER 16

WHEN I WOKE on Tuesday morning, I was alone. The only indications Max had been there were the remote on the nightstand and a dent in the duvet on the other side of the bed. But he'd settled another blanket over me before he left, a fleecy grey one that felt like a warm hug, reinforcing my view that his outer wolf disguised a pussycat.

A soft knock startled me, and I stared at the closed door. "Max?"

"Can I come in?"

"Yes."

He pushed the door open, revealing the Max I'd first seen—sharply dressed in a made-to-measure suit and wearing an intense expression. A maroon tie hung loose around his neck, softening the look.

"Are you going somewhere?"

"The office. I've got meetings I can't avoid. There's a car with two of Blackwood's men parked on the drive, so you're not alone."

"How long will you be?"

"I'll be back early evening." He drew a phone out of his pocket and placed it next to me. "I've programmed my number in. Speed-dial one."

"Thank you."

"I'll see if I can get your phone back as well."

"The one in my flat was only a pay-as-you-go. The police took my normal phone ages ago in case there were any clues in Rose's messages."

He reached over and rested a hand on my shoulder, giving it a gentle squeeze. "You'll be okay today?"

"I'll be fine."

"You want me to pick anything up?"

"Chocolate?"

I sounded so pathetic, even to my own ears, that I wasn't surprised when he laughed.

"I'll see what I can do."

Once he'd gone, I took a shower and then wandered around the house, taking a better look after my whistle-stop tour on arrival. He'd kept most of the period features—big fireplaces, picture rails, decorative moulding. I envisioned the place full of furniture with a roaring fire in the lounge. Yes, one day it would be stunning. Would he let me visit? I'd love to see the results when he'd finished.

In the kitchen, I made myself a coffee and ate a bowl of Frosties. Then I got curious and poured a glass of the green stuff Max drank in the mornings. Did it taste as bad as it smelled? Yes. The answer was most definitely yes. I forced half of it down then tipped the rest into the sink. There was only so much healthiness I could take.

Speaking of healthy, what did Max have planned for dinner? Besides the pile of plastic tubs filled with last night's leftovers, the fridge was stacked with organic veg, chicken breasts, and fish. Hmm. Perhaps I could cook? That would save him a job when he got in.

The phone he gave me came with internet, and I resorted to Google. Something low carb, that was what

I needed. I spent half an hour searching for the perfect recipe, one that he had all the ingredients for, before settling on salmon burgers. They looked so straightforward even I could manage them, and the recipe reckoned they only took thirty minutes. That gave me the rest of the morning to watch daytime television—a talk show hosted by a woman with big teeth and a programme on house renovation—something I hadn't done for ages. See, I still knew how to relax.

By the time I woke up, it was almost four o'clock. Dammit! *Okay, don't panic.* I still had time.

I propped the phone on the counter then got the food processor out of the cupboard. It looked a lot more complicated than Suki's. Hers only had three buttons, while Max's had more functions than the space shuttle.

First, I weighed out five hundred grams of salmon, then roughly chopped a bunch of parsley, two spring onions, and some lemon zest, and put the whole lot in the processor. Once I'd fished all the bits of shell out of the egg, I was good to go.

I pushed the button, and nothing happened. Ah, I'd forgotten to switch it on. No problem. I tried again, and with an almighty roar, salmon, egg, parsley, onion, and lemon sprayed all over me and the kitchen. Some even got as far as the hallway.

I looked in horror at the lid, which had flown off and landed behind the kettle, then groaned. This...this was why I ordered pizza so often.

Max's voice came from the doorway. "What the fuck is that awful smell."

Oh no. Talk about bad timing. "Er, I had a bit of an accident."

He stepped around a lump of salmon and picked a piece of spring onion out of my hair. "As accidents go, it's impressive."

"I'm so sorry. I thought I'd make dinner, and it all went wrong, and now there's mess everywhere and I'm a terrible cook and I've ruined everything." I gulped back tears. The events of the last few weeks had turned me into a snivelling wreck. I never used to be this emotional.

Max tucked a lock of hair behind my ear then wiped his fingers on a tea towel. "Go and have a shower. I'll sort out the mess."

"I'll help."

"Get in the shower, or I'll put you in there myself."

Was he serious? A vision of Max carrying me up the stairs bridal style flitted through my mind. Or would he throw me over his shoulder? For a second, I was tempted to find out, but then I thought of the mess I'd make of his suit. "Okay, I'll go."

I traipsed out of the kitchen, and the sound of Max's laughter followed me upstairs as I rued having brought yet another disaster into his life. What had he done to deserve me?

When I walked back into the kitchen, there was no sign of the explosion, and Max was shaping the last of eight salmon burgers on a baking tray. Did I really take that long in the shower?

"I found your recipe. These need to chill for fifteen minutes before we cook them."

"I'm sorry."

"Don't be. I haven't seen anything so funny in years. Oh, don't look at me like that. I hate it when you look at me like that." He fished around in his rucksack and held out a couple of boxes. "I brought you chocolate and Turkish delight."

"You remembered?"

"Your cupboard was full of the stuff. I figured you liked it."

"I love it." Without thinking, I gave him a hug, then realised what I'd done. I tried to pull away, but he wrapped me up in his arms.

"Be happy, Lily. Please."

"You make me happy," I whispered.

He let go abruptly. Too abruptly. I'd scared him off.

"I'd better make the salad." He turned his back on me and walked to the fridge.

Dammit.

Salmon burgers à la Max were delicious, unsurprisingly. The awkward silence? Not so good.

"How was work?"

"Okay."

"Did you speak to Bridges?"

"Yeah."

"What did he say?"

"They haven't made much progress."

It was like being back where we started, with me asking questions and Max avoiding the answers. Okay. Fine. Time to resort to other tactics. "If you could be a fruit, which one would you pick?"

He raised an eyebrow. "Banana."

"Why?"

"Do you really need to ask?"

My gaze dropped downwards, and I forced my eyes back up to his face, trying to block the dirty thoughts that filled my mind. "Uh..."

Before I could answer, he ticked off points on his fingers. "Bananas are low in fat, low in sugar, high in fibre, they contain potassium, which is good for your heart, and they come in convenient packaging. Taste all right too."

Whew, I'd got out of that one. Down, girl. I decided to try another question, one that didn't involve dubiously shaped objects. "If you could be a Hollywood actor, which one would you be?"

"Does it matter?"

"No, but I want you to stop acting like a robot and talk to me."

"Sorry." He dropped his cutlery. "Look, I don't do well with...what you said earlier. You shouldn't say things like that."

Finally! We were getting somewhere. "Why?"

"Because it's not true."

"Yes, it is."

"You might think it is, for an hour, or a day, but this isn't a natural situation we're living in. Sooner or later, you'll realise your mistake."

"What if there's no mistake?" Who was Max to tell me how I felt?

"I can't make anyone happy. I don't have it in me."

"Who did this to you?"

"Did what?"

"Lowered your self-esteem so much you don't believe in yourself anymore?"

"I believe in myself," he whispered. "I'm good at my job."

"Life's not just a job, Max."

He pushed his chair back and stood up.

"Don't walk away. You can't run from every difficult discussion."

He kept walking.

I scraped the remains of dinner into the bin then sat back at the table with my head in my hands. Why? Why did I always have to ruin things?

In the quiet of the house, I heard the distant sound of Max hitting the punch bag, the fast *thud, thud, thud* as he beat his frustrations into submission. I should have gone upstairs. I should have, but I didn't. My feet carried me to the gym, and I sat on the floor as Max's feet flew.

"What do you want?" he asked without stopping.

You. "I want you to speak to me. What happened? What made you like this?"

"Fine. You want to know? I'll fucking tell you."

Thud. Thunk.

"I went to a shitty school in a shitty part of Manchester."

Smack. Smack. Smack.

"The English kids hated me because I was half-Chinese, and the Chinese kids hated me because I was half-English."

Thud. Thud.

"From the age of eight, I worked in the kitchen at my parents' restaurant. They spent their whole lives telling me I didn't chop vegetables fast enough, or cook well enough, or clean thoroughly enough."

His comments about child labour made sense now, and my heart ached for the little boy he'd been. How could parents do that to their own flesh and blood?

"The only good thing in my life was my sister, then she got leukaemia and nearly died. My parents wouldn't even take me to visit her in the hospital. I had to steal money for the bus fares to start with."

Thud. Thud. Thud.

"Then there was an incident, and she hasn't spoken to me in eleven years, seven months, and four days." He turned to face me. "That enough? Or do you want me to bleed more?"

He wasn't kidding. He hadn't bandaged his hands, and blood streamed down his knuckles, matching the tears dripping down my cheeks.

"Max, stop it. Stop hurting yourself."

"I don't know how to," he whispered.

I took a step forward, hesitant. Then another when he didn't move away. "Let me show you."

His shoulders slumped as he let me guide him out of the gym. Defeated. In the kitchen, he stood quietly at the sink while I washed the blood off his hands then applied antibacterial cream and bandages. By the time I'd finished, his shutters had come down again. Almost. This time, I detected a tiny chink of light at the bottom.

"You need to get some sleep." I tried to lead him upstairs, but he shook his head. "Why not? You stayed with me last night."

"And I shouldn't have."

"Please? I hate thinking of you on the floor in the gym."

"I've stayed in worse places."

"Like where?"

"Shop doorways. Park benches. A couple of squats."

I gasped. "You were homeless?"

He shrugged. "For a while."

I thought I'd run out of tears, but another trickled down my cheek. Max brushed it away. Wrong. All wrong. I should be comforting him, not the other way around.

"The bed's plenty big enough."

He shook his head again. "Step too far, Lily."

He backed away, and I knew I'd lost him, at least for today.

Now it wasn't just Rose's killer giving me sleepless nights. The man who made my heart ache just from looking at him had joined in the game.

CHAPTER **17**

"ARE YOU HOME today? Or do you have more meetings?" I asked.

"Home."

So far, we'd got through juice and cereal, with coffee for me and weird fruit tea for Max, all without mentioning last night. I didn't know where to start, and Max clearly wasn't about to. No, his eyes flitted between his laptop and his phone as he sipped, and I fixed my gaze on the squirrel hopping around in the old fir tree.

I should have been happy to have Max's company. When he was near, I breathed a little easier, and it had nothing to do with my lack of corset. With Max around, the tension that had been buzzing through my body since I woke up in hospital after Rose's murder dialled down a notch, from painful to merely uncomfortable. But at the same time, some space to think would have been nice.

"You want to watch Netflix? They've just added a load more movies," Max asked.

I groaned without meaning to. "Sorry. I just can't take another day on that couch. Not without visiting a chiropractor, anyway."

"I've ordered a new one, but it won't be here until next week."

"You did?"

"I don't like seeing you uncomfortable."

See? Sweet. But that still left a few days. What else could we do in this huge, empty house? I glanced over at him, but his attention had been taken by a crow perched on a branch above the squirrel. I knew what I'd like to do today, but no way was I about to go there again and risk another blow-up, not when Max was mostly back to his old self. *Keep your distance, Lily.* I could hardly lie upstairs by myself, because that seemed kind of rude, and I knew I wouldn't be able to concentrate on sewing. So that left...

"Painting."

"Huh?"

"Why don't we paint?" I thought about the pile of paint pots in the otherwise empty bedroom next to his.

"Like landscapes?"

"No, silly. The walls."

"I didn't bring you here to work."

"But I'm bored. Please? It'll give me something to do and help you out at the same time. It's perfect."

Judging by his troubled expression, brows knitted, he didn't share my enthusiasm. "Are you sure?"

"Totally." I leapt up and went to grab his hand, then thought better of it and beckoned him instead. "Come on."

It turned out my painting skills were on a par with my cookery. Max had done half a wall by the time I'd poured paint into my tray, and when I started my bit, it went all blotchy. Luckily, I'd borrowed an old T-shirt because I wasn't much better.

"Is there a secret to this?" I turned to ask. Then stopped. "Uh, I think I'm stuck." Literally. Stuck. When I'd whipped my head around, my hair caught on the roller, and now the strands were glued fast. "Could you help?"

Once he'd stopped laughing and helped me to get the emulsion out of my hair, we both decided it would be a better idea for me to gloss the skirting boards. Max had already put the undercoat on a few weeks back.

"This is actually quite relaxing," I said a while later. I'd done three of the four sides while Max had moved on to painting the feature wall in dark red.

"I don't mind the painting part. It's buying the stuff I hate."

"You've picked nice colours. The off-white goes nicely with the burgundy."

"You think? I panicked when the assistant started talking about tints, so I just grabbed the first one off the shelf. Did you know there are over fifty shades of white?"

"Better than fifty shades of grey."

He grinned for a second. "I don't know about that."

Then his smile was gone. Did I imagine it? My mind ran riot as I painted the last of the wood, trying to keep my lines straight. Max in his suit, that tie hanging around his neck. What else could he do with it?

"Lunch?" he asked, and I jumped.

"Sounds good." At least he hadn't done me a prescribed food list or attempted to force-feed me eight times a day.

Nope, he simply prepared a salad and served it up with the box of chocolates I forgot to eat yesterday. I'd take Max over Christian any day. And at least today, things were getting back to normal. Or what passed for normal where Max and I were concerned.

"So, what's next? More painting?"

"I don't have any more paint."

"Can't we buy some? If you've got a couch arriving next week, we should paint the lounge beforehand."

"I can do it after."

"Please? I'm sick of being stuck here, and I doubt The Florist's going to come after me in a DIY store." I sidled up to him. "And he wouldn't get near me with you there, anyway."

Max looked down at me and pushed a few strands of hair away from my face. "Okay, Lily. You win. We'll go shopping."

Score. "What colour is the couch?"

"Chocolate brown."

It turned out Max had his own car, a black SUV tucked away in the garage beside the house. Before long, we'd driven the few miles to B&Q, found a trolley, and located the paint aisle. Max was right. The array was bewildering.

"There are actually fifty-eight shades of white." I knew that because I'd counted. "But only thirty-seven shades of grey." Why did I feel short-changed?

"Would you hurry up and pick something?"

"How about cream?"

"Just put it in the trolley."

"And we need something else for the chimney breast. A darker colour." I perused the shelves. "None of these are quite right." I wandered down the aisle. "How about wallpaper?"

He trailed after me with the grim yet resigned

expression of a man walking to the gallows. "Wallpaper? I've never hung wallpaper."

"It's only gluing stuff to the wall. How difficult can it be? And look! This one's perfect." It really was. A russet pattern of scrolling leaves, fleur-de-lis, and elegant Latin script on a worn metallic stucco background. "You've got to get it."

"If I buy it, can we go?"

"Yes." At least after we'd bought brushes, wallpaper paste, something to cut the paper with, and a table to work on.

And then, of course, we had to put it up. Max groaned when I suggested it. "Can't we leave it until tomorrow?"

"We're on a roll. Sorry. No pun intended."

"I should have gone to the office."

"Nonsense. This is much more fun."

Between Max's mostly good mood and the concentration needed to decorate neatly, I'd barely thought about The Florist all day. But I should have known the respite was too good to last. Max was halfway up the ladder with the last sheet of pasty wallpaper in his hands when his phone rang.

"Fuck."

"Leave it. They can call back."

"I can't. That's the phone I have to answer. Can you get it?"

"Where is it?"

"In my back pocket." He reversed down a couple of steps to let me reach.

I fished it out, resisting the urge to give him a quick grope while I was at it. Damn, the man had glutes. "Hello?"

"Lily?"

"Yes?"

"It's Nye. Is Max there?"

"He's hanging wallpaper."

A series of guffaws followed. "Sorry, I shouldn't laugh, but it's hard to imagine Max being domesticated."

"Did you want something important?"

"Yeah. The old lady who lives opposite your flat called the police again. She heard someone in the hallway. They're on their way."

I stiffened as Max finished with the sheet of paper and took the phone. "What?" He listened for a moment. "Keep me posted."

I still hadn't moved when he put his arm around me. "He won't get you. I promise."

"Why has he gone back?"

"We don't even know it's him. Your neighbour's bound to be on edge after all that's happened. Come on, let's get you a drink."

I thought he meant a glass of water, but he poured me a generous measure of wine. I was halfway through it when Nye called back, and this time Max put him on speaker.

"He didn't get in, but Jason reckons there are pry marks around the edge of Spike's security shutter. Seems our perp went at it with a crowbar."

"Same man, do you think?"

"Lady said he wore a hood again. I'd guess at yes."

"Then there's still something in there he wants."

"But what?" I asked. "I can't think of anything I own that's worth stealing."

All my jewellery, all my knick-knacks, they were

only valuable to me. On eBay, even my favourite necklaces would only make a few pounds, and my laptop was so old I crossed my fingers every time I pressed the On button.

Nye fell silent for a few seconds before he spoke. "Assuming this is all one man, he tried Rose's first. So I'm betting it's something of hers, and he thinks you might have it. Did she give you anything recently?"

I racked my brains. "Only a few clothes. And some make-up."

"The police have released the scene now. I think we should go through the remaining rooms in your flat— the ones he didn't touch. If there's something there, we want to get to it first."

Finally—something I could do to help. "Then let's go and look."

I spent most of the night watching TV, unable to sleep. The news depressed me, so I switched to the shopping channel, and by the time Max brought me coffee at 6:00 a.m., I was almost sold on the idea of a new workout routine. Almost, but not quite. Today, even getting out of bed was a struggle. The prospect of trawling through the mess in my flat didn't seem nearly so attractive at that time in the morning.

"We need to leave in half an hour," he said. "Nye's sending someone to help search while I watch the door."

I covered my mouth as I yawned. "Mmm."

"Or do you want to stay here?"

"No, I'm coming. If anything's out of place, I'm

more likely to spot it than a stranger." I held my hands out. "Give me the cup."

I fell asleep in the car as it crawled through the busy rush-hour streets, and I only flickered my eyes open when Max nudged me. "Are we here?"

"Right outside. Are you ready for this?"

No. "Yes."

If Max was Mr. January and Nye was Mr. February, then the guy leaning against the wall outside my flat must have been Mr. March. If I got out of this hell alive, I planned to apply for a job at Blackwood. Preferably as the girl who measured the staff up for uniforms. If those three were anything to go by, working in that office would be the closest thing to heaven on earth.

Mr. March thumped Max on the back then held out his hand to me. "Zander Graves."

I took a second to study him. While Max had a dangerous air about him, Zander could have stepped from the pages of the Abercrombie & Fitch catalogue. "Lily Matthews. Thanks for coming."

His mouth set in a hard line. "We all want to see this bastard caught. Do you have any idea what we're looking for?"

"None at all."

He took a deep breath. "Guess we'd better get started, then."

Max unlocked the three padlocks on the security door, and I couldn't miss the jagged edges of the metal where someone had tried to get in. Slowly, the door swung open, revealing my dark flat.

"Spike put grilles over the windows too," Max said, flicking the lights on.

The place was as I'd last seen it apart from the

powdery residue clinging to every surface from the police's search for fingerprints. Ugly. Messy. Depressing. The only two rooms the man hadn't touched were the kitchen and bathroom, and the bathroom barely had anything in it unless you counted the bumper pack of loo rolls I'd bought on special offer. Even so, I went through the vanity unit while Zander prodded around in the cistern.

"I didn't put anything in there."

"Your sister might have when she visited."

"Why? Why wouldn't she tell me if she had something to hide?"

"Can't help you with that, I'm afraid."

After finding nothing but the tube of expensive moisturiser I thought I'd lost back in the summer, we moved on to the kitchen.

"Ugh. Do people really eat this stuff?" Zander pulled my collection of Turkish delight out of the cupboard and put it on the counter.

"I love it."

"You know it's mostly sugar?"

"That's why I love it."

He shook his head and carried on tearing the room apart, peering into every box and packet as though it might hold the answer to life. Which in a way, it could.

And we found...nothing.

"Whatever he's looking for, I'm going to suggest it's not here," Zander said.

"Have you tried the cooker hood?" Max called from the other room.

"Yes. And the gaps underneath the drawers."

Zander rinsed his dusty hands and dried them on a tea towel while I stared at the shambles. Now that my hopes for finding a clue had vanished into the ether, the thought of tidying everything was too daunting for words. How I longed to be able to walk away from the place and never look back.

"Do you want coffee?" I offered. Anything to put off the next step.

"Wouldn't say no. I'll start putting the stuff back while you make it."

Oh, thank heavens. I found a stray carton of long-life orange juice as well and took a glass out to Max.

"It was all a waste of time," I said.

He gave my arm a friendly squeeze. "No, it wasn't. At least we know there's nothing here now. Otherwise, we'd have kept wondering."

"I suppose."

"Do you want to bring anything back with you? I can get Zander to help carry it down to the car."

Well, since we were there... I packed a suitcase with extra clothes, a few books, and my laptop, and found another bag for the half-finished clothing projects in the spare room, those that hadn't been ruined by my unwelcome visitor. Apart from a dented cover, my sewing machine had survived, so Zander loaded that up as well.

"Thanks, mate," Max said. "You need a lift back to the office?"

"Quicker to take the Tube at this time of day. See you soon. Bye, Lily."

I waved as he strode down the street, tucking his overcoat around him.

"Now what?" I asked Max. I'd had such high hopes for this morning, and now they'd been dashed. I wanted to stuff myself with an entire box of Turkish delight and cry myself to sleep.

"We go home and wait. Something's got to break."

As long as it wasn't another woman's neck. "If only there was a way to unlock my mind. There must be something in there from that night at Rose's. Maybe I should give myself another bang on the head and see if that shakes something loose?"

"Bit drastic." He opened the car door for me, looking thoughtful, then climbed behind the wheel. "But have you thought about hypnosis?"

CHAPTER 18

"HYPNOSIS? DO YOU think that could help?" I'd seen those shysters on TV, making members of the audience cluck like chickens. "I always thought they were from the same mould as fortune tellers—a bit of a scam."

Max started the car engine and pulled out into traffic. "Maybe. And I'm not talking a stage hypnotist. Nobody's gonna make you bark like a dog."

"So what do they do?"

"Forensic hypnosis is more of a conversation in controlled conditions, but there are pros and cons. It could help you remember, but then the police might not be able to use you as a witness."

"But I can't remember anything, anyway. What have we got to lose?"

"You can't remember anything from Rose's, but I meant for his second visit. You're the key witness there."

A memory of that night jerked through me, the man's whispered voice in my ear. I closed my eyes and forced myself to calm down. "So it's a gamble? I remember and we might win, or I don't and he wins?"

"Yes."

I hated the odds on that. The thought of The Florist getting away with what he'd done sickened me.

"Can we speak to Bridges and see what he thinks?"

"I'll call him."

On the journey, I considered the risks and the possible rewards, if you could call them that. I'd already had nightmares about The Florist strangling me, and if it turned out I saw him kill Rose? I'd have to live with that for the rest of my life, no matter how short it might be.

But what if hypnosis was the key? What if it helped to catch the man? I could get justice for Rose, and Dahlia, and Heather, and stop The Florist from killing again.

I had to try it, didn't I?

And when Max spoke to Jason as we sat in the thick London traffic, he agreed. As they'd got my written statement for the second attack already, he considered the possibility of getting a new lead outweighed the downsides.

"If we wanted Lily to testify, we'd need someone for her to testify against, and we've not had much luck with that."

"No new leads at all?"

"A couple. But we're having a hard time making anything stick."

"Can Blackwood help?"

"I've already spoken to Nye, and he's digging. Firstly, we've got a guy called Derek Kramer. Lives in West London. Forty years old, moved back in with his mother after he got divorced, and works at the local garden centre."

"How did you find him?"

"He was one of the guys in Lily's phone. You know, the messages Rose sent her? Only back then he called himself Drake and claimed he was thirty. And when he messaged Heather on a different dating site, he'd morphed into Darius. It took the cyber-crime guys ages to track him down."

Max tapped his fingers on the steering wheel, looking far from relaxed. "How likely does he look?"

"His mother's given him an alibi for all three murders, plus the attempt on Lily's life and the two break-ins. But I sat in on her interview, and I reckon she's lying."

I thought back. A man pretending to be younger. "I remember Rose talking about him, or someone similar. They went out to a bar. She said he must have used a really old photo of himself, and when he ran his hand up her leg, she nipped to the loo and escaped out the fire exit."

"Really? That's useful information. Anything else?"

"No. It was ages ago, and she only mentioned it in passing."

"And the second lead?" Max asked.

"A guy Rose worked with. Steve Macklin. A witness said they had dinner a couple of times, but in his initial interview, he denied ever seeing her socially. We brought him in again yesterday, and he claims he lied because he panicked. Says he was worried we'd try to frame him."

"Wouldn't be the first time I've heard that line."

Steve... Steve... "Steve in the HR department?" I asked.

Bridges's voice came out of the built-in speakers. "That's the guy. Why? Do you know him?"

"I spoke to him at Rose's funeral." My heart did a little skip. "And he's got my address. He wrote to me about Rose's life insurance."

"Life insurance?" Max asked.

"Apparently. I didn't even realise she had a policy, but I understand she got it through work."

"And what about you?"

"I don't have any."

"But if you died, who would inherit the money from Rose?"

"Uh, I hadn't thought about it. My mum, I guess. I don't have anyone else left. But it's only sixty thousand pounds."

A huge sum to me, but would somebody really resort to murder over it?

"People have killed for far less, Lily," Bridges said. "And what would happen to your business? That's got to be worth something."

"It hasn't been doing so well the last few months with all the...distractions."

"But the brand name alone is an asset. Who would get that?"

"Suki."

"Shit."

I knew exactly what he was thinking. His new girlfriend had just been added to the list of suspects.

"But it couldn't have been Suki. The person who attacked me was a man."

Max reached over and squeezed my hand. "There's always the possibility of an accomplice, Lily."

"It's not Suki. She's my best friend. You're looking in the wrong place there, trust me."

Silence.

I hated silence.

"Look," I said. "Are we doing this hypnosis thing or not?"

"You have a preferred hypnotist?" Max asked Bridges.

"Nye knows someone good. Can you record the session?"

"I'll make sure we do."

Max spoke to Nye and made arrangements for the hypnotist to meet us the next day, two o'clock at the Blackwood offices. Normally, I'd have been brimming with curiosity to see where Max worked, but that was tempered with apprehension. I wanted to get the visit over with, and at the same time, I wanted it to be a lifetime away.

When we got back, Max locked us in the garage so we could unload everything through the internal door. The study looked a little more homely once I'd arranged my things in there, only I had to keep reminding myself this house wasn't my home. But where was home? Certainly not the flat we'd just left, with all its bad memories and grim reminders of death.

Wouldn't you like to stay here? my subconscious whispered. *Big, airy rooms, a dreamy kitchen, and a man who makes Nick Bateman look a bit ugly?*

"Shut up," I hissed.

"What was that?" Max asked as he wandered in with a stray box of material.

"Nothing. I just cleared my throat."

"Do you need a drink?"

"Thanks, but I'm okay."

"Do you need pizza?"

"I like the way you want pizza, so you try to blame it on me."

"I can make salad if you prefer."

"No, I need pizza. Topped with fries and onion

rings, with a side order of chicken wings and a pint of ice cream."

He rolled his eyes but wandered off holding his phone as I began the countdown to the dreaded hypnosis session.

Less than twenty-four hours to go.

"Are you still sure about this?" Max asked as he led me across the underground car park to a lift in the far corner.

"No, but I'm doing it anyway. Will you stay?"

"Yes, I'll stay."

His grip tightened on my hand as the doors slid open, but he dropped it when we reached the ground floor. Why? Was he ashamed of me?

The blonde receptionist looked up expectantly, and Max gave my name. As with everything else in the building, she was perfect and posh. Her sleek French twist and manicured fingernails complimented the shiny black-tiled floor and cream sofas arranged around a pair of glass coffee tables.

No wonder Blackwood charged a lot—someone had to pay for the fancy coffee machine set up for visitors and blondie's designer outfit.

Once I had my visitor's badge clipped on, Max buzzed us through a set of double doors on the far side of the atrium and led me through an open-plan office full of glass and pale wood.

"Where do you sit?" I asked.

He pointed to the far corner, where an unoccupied desk showed no signs of use. Others had photos, plants, maybe a favourite coffee mug, but Max's space was devoid of any personality. I'd once thought the man was too, but now I knew better.

"In here." He pushed open the door to a conference room where a grey leather couch at one end had been set up with a video camera pointing at it.

A tentacle of fear tightened around my chest while others slithered through my veins, cold and slick. I perched on the edge of the sofa while Max pulled out a chair, not sitting on it but waiting. It wasn't long before Nye came in, followed by a kind-looking man whose grey hair curled around his collar.

"This is Dirk Hohenaur. Dirk, this is Lily."

Dirk's handshake might have been limp, but his voice was smooth as a chilled glass of cider on a summer's day.

"Good to meet you, Lily," he said. Slightly Germanic, although the Queen's English dominated now.

"Where do we start?"

"If you lie back and get comfortable, then we'll begin."

I slid my shoes off then swung my feet up on the couch. Dirk made me concentrate on different parts of my body, tensing, then relaxing, then...nothing.

Nothing until I woke up in Max's arms, crying. "What happened?"

I knew from his face, and Nye's beyond him, that the news wasn't good.

"You did your best, Lily."

"But it wasn't good enough, was it?"

I stared out the window the whole way back to Holland Park, unseeing. Somewhere out there was the man who killed my sister, only I wouldn't tell myself who he was. According to Dirk, I'd blocked it out, probably permanently. I'd remembered a little more after my Tube journey—walking up to the flat, unlocking the door, and going inside—but nothing of any use. I didn't remember seeing Rose or the man who threw me off the balcony.

"Don't punish yourself, Lily." Max sat next to me in the Mercedes, belted in.

"I can't help it. I feel like I've failed Rose."

He slid a hand across and uncurled my fingers from where they gripped the edge of my jacket. "You haven't. She'd be proud of you for everything you've done."

"You don't know that. You never even met her."

"But I know you, Lily. I know you."

"We've got a plan," Jason said to me the next morning. He leaned back against Max's breakfast bar, taking advantage of the new coffee machine.

"I'm glad someone has. I'm all out of plans." And sleep. And good humour.

"We're going to put out a press release saying you've been hypnotised and you don't remember anything."

"Great. So then the whole world will find out how useless I am."

Max pulled me tighter against his chest and I sagged backwards, letting him take my weight. He had his arm around my waist while I sat on a stool, as if he could protect me from any more revelations.

"On the contrary," Jason said. "The public will

understand how hard you've tried to help, and The Florist will realise you're not a threat to him anymore."

"You think he might give up on me?"

"That's what we hope."

"How will we know?"

"Well, that's the thing. We won't."

Over the next two weeks, Max and I settled into a routine. I'd offered to go home, a suggestion that was met with a scowl and a "no." That was it. No elaboration, no justification. Just "no."

And no, I didn't argue. Because apart from his occasional tendency to be an asshole, something I found happening less and less often, Max made a good housemate. The sofa arrived, as did a carpet fitter, and the lounge started to look more like a lounge and less like a building site.

I began to enjoy our evenings a little too much. Those hours spent lying with my head on a cushion in Max's lap after a homemade meal and a delicious glass of wine. We'd wake up in the early hours, necks cricked and backs aching, but it didn't stop us from doing it again the next night. Or the one after that.

Despite Max's dislike of visitors, he let me invite Suki and Bridges around after work one Tuesday to have dinner. This time when Max cooked Chinese, the portions were about right. Thankfully, no more had come of the stupid notion that Suki could somehow be involved in the murders, so there wasn't any awkwardness to deal with.

"How's the case going?" I asked before dinner.

I almost didn't want to know, and I certainly didn't want to talk about it while we ate.

"Kramer's mother lied about at least three of his alibis." Bridges ticked them off on his fingers. "One, she was out at a church supper. Two, she'd gone to visit a friend in hospital. Three, she was in the pub—a neighbour saw her."

"Is he cooperating?" Max asked.

"Is he heck. We brought him in for an interview this morning, and he spent three hours yelling at the top of his voice that he didn't do anything."

"And what's the likelihood that he did?"

"We haven't been able to prove our suspicions yet. The judge knocked back our request for a DNA sample and told us we need to find more evidence first."

"Normally, I'd offer Blackwood's services, but if you're trying to get a semen sample to prove he's had a vasectomy, that could be tricky."

"Exactly. So far, we've only got his ex-wife's word on the matter. They had two kids, and she wanted a third, but it never happened. Apparently, they usually got freaky with the lights off, but one day she noticed a scar near his scrotum. He swore it was from an accident in the gym, but she didn't believe that. Said he was kind of cagey."

"She reckons he got the snip in secret?"

"Indeed she does. And speaking of vasectomies, Steve Macklin's ex-girlfriend says he's had one, and the HR manager at Medicorp confirmed that he took time off to recover from a minor operation two years ago."

Everyone's ears pricked up at that.

"Are you bringing him in?"

"Planning to. I'll let you know when I've got more."

Conversation over dinner turned to more pleasant subjects, and although Suki and Bridges did most of the talking, Max was no longer as closed off as when we first met. What had brought about the change? I kind of hoped I'd had something to do with it, because I liked this new, more sociable version of him.

While the men chatted over one last beer, a rare break from healthiness for Max, I took Suki on a quick tour.

"This place is a bloody palace." She let out a low whistle after seeing Max's bedroom. "And you're sleeping in here alone?"

"Yes."

"Why?"

"I don't think he likes me in that way."

"Oh, don't be ridiculous. He looks at you like you're the fairy on top of the Christmas tree. And Jason said he's never gone all dopey over a woman before."

"He isn't dopey."

"See, you like him."

"Okay, I like him." I dropped my voice. "He slept next to me on the bed once, but nothing happened, and when I asked if he wanted to do it again, he said he didn't."

"Probably he was just confused. You need to make things really, really clear to him."

"I'm not sure about that."

"Well, I am."

I couldn't think about it, not when I'd be alone with him in the house in a few minutes and I might be tempted to do something stupid. A change of subject was needed.

"How are things with you and Jason?"

She giggled. Giggled! Suki never giggled over a man. Oh, this was bad.

"I really like him. I've been staying with him most nights, and normally by this point in a relationship I'd be plotting my escape, but every day I take more stuff to his place and he doesn't seem to mind. Is that crazy?"

I'd seen the way he looked at her. "No, it's not. Maybe you've finally found the man you're meant to be with?"

She took one last glance around the room. "Maybe you have too?"

CHAPTER 19

LIVING IN LIMBO was a strange feeling. Like walking on a tightrope with the knowledge I absolutely would fall off at the end, probably into the second circle of hell. Because that was how going home would feel.

Between us, Max and I had painted the whole of downstairs, installed fancy light fittings, and made a start on tiling the master bathroom. I'd only ever lived in rented accommodation before, and there my DIY efforts had extended to calling the landlord to let him know what was broken.

If someone had suggested I might enjoy looking at paint swatches or comparing the properties of tiling grout, I'd have laughed them right out of their straitjacket. But there I was again, in B&Q, measuring shower trays against the floor plan of the bathroom I'd carefully drawn out on graph paper.

"What about this one?" Max asked, pointing at a double-width enclosure.

"If you get that, you won't be able to fit a bath in as well."

"I don't take baths. I only take showers."

"But if you ever have a girlfriend live there with you, she'll want a bath. Trust me."

"Do you like baths?"

"Yes. With bubbles and candles and music. And a

good book."

"Then I'll get a bath. But candles are a fire hazard."

Sweet. Asshole.

It may have been limbo, but I'd take him whatever way I could get him.

Then it all got turned upside down.

Max's phone rang the following Saturday night while we were curled up on the new sofa, watching a program on bats. Max liked documentaries, and I'd learned to live with them.

He picked up, and I heard Jason's excitement from a few feet away. "We've made an arrest."

Max clicked the phone onto speaker and put the phone between us. "Who? The Florist?"

"Yep."

Max's shoulders relaxed, and mine should have too, but with the news came the realisation the countdown had just ended and I no longer had an excuse to stay.

"Who? Kramer?"

"No, Macklin. Being honest, I always thought he was the less likely of the two suspects, especially when he cooperated with the investigation. Kramer was so damned evasive I figured he had to be hiding something. Perhaps he still is, but that doesn't change the evidence against Macklin."

"What else have you found?"

"We held one fact back from everyone. You guys too, I'm afraid."

Max stayed silent, but he narrowed his eyes at the phone.

"Come on," Bridges said. "You can't deny you guys have done the same to us on occasion."

"Yes, but you know this one's personal for me."

Personal? Since when?

"Sorry, mate."

"Go on, then. What did you withhold?"

"Each of the murder victims had a lock of hair missing. We found them in Steve's bedside table, along with photos of all the girls."

Bile rose in my throat, and I ran to the kitchen. Dinner came up in the sink before I could stop it.

"Shit," I muttered as the sight of second-hand pizza made me heave again.

Max twisted my hair back and gripped it in one hand as he reached for the roll of paper towel with the other.

"It's okay, Lily."

"Nothing's okay."

"I know we can't bring Rose back, but at least they've got the fucker who killed her."

Tears dripped down my face as he wiped my mouth, splashing onto the counter and then the floor as he led me back to the lounge.

"Sit, Lily."

I slumped onto the sofa and sank back into the cushions; the sofa Max had bought because he wanted me to be comfortable.

"It's over."

"Yes," he said softly.

"I can go back to work. You can go back to work."

"Yes."

"You must be happy."

"I'm happy you can live your life without having to look over your shoulder."

"But Rose can't." Another waterfall poured down my cheeks.

"Come here."

I shuffled over to him, squeaking on the leather, and he wrapped me up in his arms as I sobbed my heart out with him for the last time.

I'd finally fallen off the bloody tightrope.

Max must have carried me up to bed again. The curtains were still open, and the lights of passing traffic flickered across the ceiling, accompanied by a soft hum each time a car went past. I'd grown used to this place, and the thought of leaving it hurt far more than it should. No, not it. Him. Leaving him.

I rolled over to look at the time. Half past midnight. The witching hour. My glass of wine from earlier sat next to the new alarm clock, condensation dripping down the stem in the glow of the red numbers. Max must have thought I needed it. He was probably right. I sat up and took a sip. Okay, gulp.

What would I do next week when I was alone in my apartment again? Sit by myself in the dark? Hell, I didn't even have a proper door right now. And no matter how many grilles and shutters and steel bars Spike had installed, I wouldn't feel safe. Not alone. Not without Max.

Did he know how I felt? Not just my fear, but my love? Because that was what bubbled up inside me when I sat with him in the evenings, and when we ate breakfast in the mornings, and when we just...were.

I thought back to Suki's words from Tuesday. Maybe I *did* need to make things really, really clear to Max. After all, what was left for me to lose? Only my dignity, and I had precious little of that left, anyway.

And Rose? What would Rose say? She'd be freaking ecstatic that I'd found a man I liked enough to get naked with. I could just picture her now, squealing as she rushed around searching for lipstick and a waxing kit. When had I last tidied up down there? Definitely this week sometime, so at least I wouldn't do The Florist's job for him and die of embarrassment.

I rolled out of bed and snuck into the third bedroom, which was where I'd moved my work things while we painted the study. I needed help, and I needed it fast before I chickened out.

One chance. I had one chance to make my case.

CHAPTER 20

I TOOK ANOTHER swig of wine, or liquid courage as I preferred to think of it, and pulled the laces on my corset tighter. I'd lost my mind, clearly. Actually no, I hadn't lost it. I knew exactly where it was—one floor down with the man stretched out on the couch.

What did I have in the way of knickers? I rummaged through the "finished" pile until I came across a pair of "Unwrap Me" silk briefs, dusky pink with maroon spots and satin ribbon ties at either side. Not the most practical for wearing under clothing, but that's not what I designed them for. No, these babies were only made to be taken off. I slid them on then adjusted the bows until they sat just right.

The only pair of heels I had were plain black stilettos, so those would have to do. Terrified over what I was about to do, I slid them on and teetered to the door. With one last desperate glance at the dregs in my wine glass, I walked towards the stairs.

I knew the way now, even in the dark. My heels clicked on the wooden stairs as I crept down to the ground floor. We'd picked out the new carpet for them together, classic cream, but unless tonight went the way I hoped, I wouldn't be here to see it installed.

One chance.

Except when I got to the lounge, the only sign of

Max was a wrinkled blanket and a half-empty glass of whisky. Whisky? Max didn't drink whisky. The occasional glass of wine and a rare beer, but never whisky. I sniffed to make sure, but there was no mistaking it.

On tiptoes, I crept through the house, pausing when I heard him in the gym.

Thud. Thud. Thud.

I stood in the doorway, watching as he pounded the bag like a man possessed. What had set him off? Sweat glistened on his back in moonlight that reflected off every mirror, and all he wore was a pair of black satin gym shorts. I watched for half a minute, captivated by his smooth movements until he turned and saw me.

"Is everything okay?" He blinked a couple of times as he took in my appearance. "What happened to your pyjamas?"

Oh bloody hell, this really was the most stupid idea I'd ever had, wasn't it? "I—" It came out as a croak, and I cleared my throat. "I wanted to ask you something."

"What?"

Now or never, Lily. "Will you sleep with me tonight?"

"We've been through that."

"I mean..." I tried again. "I mean, will you *sleep* with me?"

He let out a long sigh, which was hardly the reaction I'd been hoping for. Only the fact that I was slightly tipsy and wearing four-inch heels stopped me from running out of the room. He took a step closer, and I rued doing the damn corset up so tight. I could barely breathe.

"I'm not the kind of man you want, Lily."

"Let me be the judge of that."

"There's too much you don't know about me."

I reached out a hand and placed it on his chest, surprised to find his pulse hammering as fast as mine. "I know you have a good heart."

Another step forward, and he'd closed the remaining distance between us. The heat radiating from his body seared my already sweaty skin.

"Fuck." He closed his eyes for a long second. "Are you sure about this?"

I nodded.

"I need to hear you say it."

"Yes, I'm sure." Mostly.

He peeled my hand from his chest and grasped it tightly. On legs as wobbly as a baby fawn's, I followed him over to the wall of mirrors, where he positioned me in front of him under the reflection of the full moon.

"You want me to stop, you tell me. Do you understand?"

"Yes. I understand."

I thought he'd be in a hurry, but he swept my hair to one side and slowly trailed a finger down my neck.

"You're beautiful, and don't let anyone tell you otherwise." His lips followed his finger, soft, feathery kisses that left goosebumps in their wake. His other hand rested on the top of my thigh as he paused to watch us in the mirror.

The intensity of his gaze made me look away, but when I did, he gently grasped my chin and turned me back. "Look at yourself. You see the way your eyes widen when you're aroused? The way your cheeks flush? That's what makes a woman sexy. Not make-up or fancy clothes."

No, I'd never looked at myself that way before. Indeed, I'd gone out of my way to avoid it. My previous fumbles in the dark had left me wanting, not wanton.

His right hand crept higher, and he tugged at the ribbon. A second later, the knickers slithered down my leg. Max stepped to the side, his hand moving to one globe of my ass, then further. A finger slipped between my cheeks, pausing to press on a place no man had ever been. "One day, Lily, but not tonight," he whispered, before it continued its downwards journey.

Freaking hell. He'd barely touched me and I was ready to come. The first delicious flutters of an orgasm stirred in my belly, and I clenched my thighs together.

"Wait, sweet Lily. Good things come to those who wait." He knew. He fucking knew.

Another kiss, and he tipped me forward from the waist. Just an inch or two, but it gave him access. That finger pushed inside me, probing and stroking, hitting my G-spot without the slightest hesitation. Did Max have a PhD in female anatomy? I gasped, watching my reflection, shocked by the state of myself but unable to turn away.

Then he withdrew.

"What are—"

"On your knees."

"Huh?"

He nuzzled my neck for a brief moment before repeating it. "Get. On. Your. Knees."

I should have felt humiliated. I should have felt degraded. But from the way my juices flooded down my thighs, my libido disagreed with me. I dropped to the floor.

Max crouched behind me. "Lean forward. Hands in

front of you."

"Are you serious?"

"You know you want to." He chuckled. The bastard chuckled.

But the worst of it was, he was right. In the mirror, his shorts bulged, and I couldn't wait to get my hands and my mouth on what was inside. I hit the mat.

"Stay there. Don't move." One fluid movement and he was on his feet.

Wait. What? "Where are you going?"

Rather than answer, he moved away silently, and from the corner of my eye, I saw him disappear out of the gym.

That asshole! How could he leave me here like this? I had a good mind to follow and ask him exactly that, but I couldn't. My legs wouldn't move. Instead, I faced the mirror again, puffed out my chest, and sucked in my stomach. Better. Thank goodness for the corset. If he planned on this being a regular occurrence, I'd need to start using the gym for its intended purpose.

Time ticked by, one minute then two, before his form darkened the doorway once more. I didn't hear his footsteps as he made his way back to my side. How did he do that? How did he move so quietly?

This time, he knelt behind me.

"Good girl. I'm surprised you did as you were told."

"So am I."

That earned me a laugh. But it didn't last long as he leaned over the top of me, pressing his chest into my back and his cock into my ass. It nestled between my butt cheeks like a small tree.

Holy hell.

"Turn your head," he instructed, and as I did his

lips captured mine in a searing kiss. I forgot who I was and where I was as his tongue tangled with mine, but all too soon he pulled back. I watched his reflection as he tugged his shorts down, his cock springing free. Okay, I was having a rethink on the mirrors. They weren't so bad. The rip of foil broke the silence as he unwrapped a condom, and with one movement, he rolled it on.

"Still sure?"

I gritted my teeth. If he didn't get on with it, I was about to have a lust-induced heart attack. "Yes, I'm bloody sure."

He angled his hips and gently pushed inside, grasping my hip bones with strong hands. I gasped as he hit places never touched before. Suki had spent years trying to convince me to buy a bigger vibrator, and now I realised what I'd been missing. Hot damn.

Max leaned forward, fluttering soft kisses over the back of my neck and shoulders, but I needed more. Sod the foreplay. I pushed back into him, searching for the friction I desperately needed, but he tsk-tsk-tsked and held my hips still.

"Patience, Lily."

"I've been patient, Max. For weeks and weeks. Will you just get on with it?"

"Lucky I like your smart mouth."

He wound my hair around one fist and used it to twist me to the side so he could kiss me again. A lot of heat, a bit of tongue, and a bite to my bottom lip that made me squirm as the delicious pain travelled all the way to my core.

"Well, I like your cock. Use it."

He laughed and tugged my hair harder so I arched

my back, but at least he began to move.

I watched our reflections as he thrust into me, leaning forward on one hand as he pounded harder. I tried to hold back as my breath got shorter, my stomach tighter, until eventually I couldn't take it any longer. *Time to give in. Why fight it?* I closed my eyes and moaned long and low, then opened them just in time to see Max's face relax as he came too.

Only his arm around my waist stopped me from sprawling on the floor. My own limbs had turned to jelly. Vodka jelly, like those vicious little shots that Suki and I may have indulged in on the odd occasion. Of course, Max had no such issue as he helped me to my feet.

"You good?"

"I'm fucking fantastic. So are you."

His smile grew broader as he swept me off my feet and cradled me in his arms. "Let's get you upstairs. I want to find out what else you're hiding under this wicked piece of temptation."

As he climbed the steps, I couldn't help wondering what else he had in store. "Do you always have to be like that? In control?"

Dark, yet delectable. Pushy, yet perfect.

"Not always, but I like it. So do you."

Fair enough. He had me there. In fact, he could have me anywhere.

CHAPTER 21

I WOKE THE next morning with the unfamiliar sensation of a man's arm over my stomach and a pleasant ache between my legs.

I twisted to look at Max, still asleep and breathing softly beside me. No wonder. He must have been exhausted after the amount of effort he put in last night. I couldn't resist giving him a gentle kiss on the lips, and his eyes flickered open.

"Good morning," I whispered.

"For once it is."

His waking voice was hoarse, low, and bloody sexy. I shuffled a little closer, pressing myself against him.

"Do you have anything important to do today?"

"You."

You know, sometimes I adored his monosyllabic answers.

True to his word, he did me once, twice, three times. By then we were both starving, and I think Max was empty.

"I'll make us some lunch," he said, propped up on one elbow next to me.

"Not salad. I need more than salad."

He dipped his head and kissed me deeply. "I'll think of something."

With a new day came a new Max. A smilier,

touchier Max. Touchy in the sense that every time he moved past me in the kitchen, he brushed against me, or stopped to caress me and press his lips to mine. It might have made lunch take longer, but I wouldn't have changed a thing.

And he cooked pancakes. I hadn't eaten pancakes for ages. Max's came with cream cheese and salad while he smothered mine in chocolate sauce and maple syrup. I didn't even know he had maple syrup in the cupboard.

"Good?" he asked.

"Amashing." I tried again without my mouth full. "Amazing."

Rather than sitting opposite me today, he'd moved his stool onto the same side, and he rested his free hand on my thigh as he ate. I'd never been so...so...lost for a man before. He'd filled me completely, in every sense of the word, and I couldn't get enough of him.

"What do you want to do this afternoon?" He put his fork down, finished.

"Can we go out?"

He nodded.

"Without you acting as my bodyguard? Just Max and Lily?"

His answering smile told me all I needed to know. "Where do you want to go?"

"I don't care. Let's hop on the Tube and see where it takes us."

It took us to Southbank, and we spent a pleasant hour wandering around, looking at the tourist attractions. I bought a couple of second-hand books from a stall by the river, and we paused to watch a group of kids skateboarding in the undercroft of the

Southbank Centre.

Max may have eased up on the rules and carried my shopping, but he kept one arm firmly around my waist, and his gaze darted everywhere. As we walked past the London Aquarium, I stood on tiptoe and kissed him on the cheek.

"What was that for?"

"For being you."

That earned me a kiss back.

"Do you fancy visiting the aquarium someday?" I asked.

"Love to."

Wow, enthusiasm. "You like fish?"

"Not unless they come grilled."

I shoved him in the chest. "Don't be an asshole."

"I wasn't planning to look at the fish."

Oh, now we were back to sweet, and I couldn't resist wrapping both arms around his neck and going in for a proper kiss.

But our special moment was interrupted by a lanky youth, jogging backwards in front of us as he snapped photos on his mobile.

"Hey, it's you. Miss Black Lily. I've seen your picture in all the papers. Can I get a photo together?"

Max didn't even hesitate, just grabbed the phone and tossed it in the river.

"Oi, man! You can't do that!"

Max took a step forward. "Take another picture of my girlfriend and you'll go in after it." He kept staring until the kid gulped and moved out of the way. My hero.

"Girlfriend?"

"What else would you call this?" He pointed

between us.

I thought about it for a few seconds. "Girlfriend works."

He smiled, adjusted his arm around my waist, and carried on walking.

We'd had the whole of Sunday together, but alas, Monday came far too quickly. And with Monday came work.

"Will you be in the office all day?" I asked Max as he buttoned his shirt. Such a shame, but at least I'd get to unbutton it later.

"Not sure. I don't know whether I've been fully added back into the rota yet."

"What hours do you usually work?"

"Before? All of them. Now? I'll try to cut back on the overtime. Means sorting out this place'll take longer..." He paused to give me a quick kiss. "But it'll be worth it to see you more."

"At least furnishing a second bedroom isn't so much of a priority now."

He grinned. "True."

I'd woken early and packed up the bits I needed to take back to the shop. Despite everything, I'd managed to make a few pieces over the past couple of weeks, as well as sketching a handful of new designs. And with Max dropping me off at Black Lily before he went to work, getting them there would be a lot easier than carting them on the Tube.

I finished getting dressed as Max brushed his teeth, cinching my corset tight. Like always, I left that bit until last.

"I hate the thought of other men seeing you in that all day."

"What would you suggest I wear instead?"

"I could pick you up a stylish burka."

"Nice try. You'd better learn to deal with it."

"I know. At least I get the satisfaction of peeling you out of it when you get home." He reached over and pulled the end of the tie so it popped open.

"Hey! I just did that up."

"I know that too." His eyes twinkled. Playful Max. Another of his many faces.

And when we got to Black Lily, I got helpful Max as he carried everything inside before pressing me up against the car for a searing kiss. We both ignored the whistles of passers-by as he checked out my tonsils.

"I'll call if I get away in time to pick you up, otherwise take a cab home."

Home. He'd asked me to move in with him last night, properly, and that had been the easiest decision I'd ever had to make. "I can take the Tube. It's cheaper."

"Cab. It's safer. And text me the registration number before you get in."

I still needed to get used to his constant overprotectiveness, but there were worse traits he could have. And he only did it because he cared.

"Okay, a cab. Do you want me to start dinner?"

"No."

We both burst into laughter at the same time, and I practically skipped into the shop.

Suki stood open-mouthed behind the counter. "Did I just see what I think I saw?"

"If you saw Max kiss me, then yes." I couldn't keep the smile off my face.

"Woohoo!" She grabbed me and swung me around, only to stop as a prim-faced lady wandered in. "Details later," she hissed. "All of them."

We had a run of customers, which meant I escaped the inquisition until our morning coffee break. I made us espressos while Suki tidied up the items left in the changing room, and then we took to our stools at the back, positioned where we could still see the door.

"So, what happened? I thought you said he wouldn't make a move."

"The move was mine. I don't know what came over me. Apart from wine. The wine definitely helped."

She clapped her hands. "Awesome! So what now? Is it serious?"

"I'm moving in. He's helping me fetch the rest of my stuff at the weekend."

"I'm green with bloody envy. That house is dreamy."

"Isn't it? And he's already said we can have a claw-footed bathtub."

It would have to wait a month or six until we saved up, but I intended to help with that even if Max didn't want me to. We'd already had that talk and left it at an impasse.

"So, what's he like in bed?"

I choked on a mouthful of coffee. "You can't ask that."

"Oh, come on. You're my best friend, and I tell you everything."

"Yes, but I don't always want to hear it." I'd even resorted to sticking my fingers in my ears on occasion.

"Just a hint?"

"When I pick up my stuff, I'll be leaving my vibrator behind. My landlord can stick it somewhere uncomfortable."

Her shriek caused two people on the street to stop and peer in at us strangely.

"Shhh."

"I'm so happy for you."

"Oh, don't get all gushy. It's weird."

By the end of the day, my face hurt from smiling so much and I was counting down the minutes until I could leave. It was 5:00 p.m. Only half an hour to go. Max had messaged earlier to say he'd be back by seven, and as I wasn't allowed to cook, that gave me enough time to paint my nails, shave my legs, and sort out my roots if I hurried. At least I didn't have any big decisions to make about colour. In that respect, the goth look was easy—black and black.

"Go, would you? You're making me tired just watching you," Suki said as the clock hit quarter past.

"Are you sure?"

"Out." She pointed towards the door. "Ohhh."

Zander Graves stood in the entrance, and he didn't look happy. The feeling of terror I'd experienced so many times over the past month came flooding back. "What's wrong? Where's Max?"

"Could you come with me, please, Lily? I need to speak to you." Gone was Abercrombie Zander. This was Man in Black. He looked as if he'd dressed for a funeral.

"Why are you here?"

"Max asked me to come and get you. I'll explain in the car. Now, please. We need to go."

"Just go. I'll be okay here," Suki said, although her voice shook a little.

I snatched my coat off the hook and shoved my arms into it before tightening the belt. Then, with one last backwards glance at my second home, I stumbled after Zander and got into the waiting Mercedes.

CHAPTER 22

I HALF FELL into the backseat, and Zander slid in beside me. Before I could do my seat belt up, the driver took off for a destination unknown.

"Where's Max? Why are you here and not him?"

"He's in a helicopter somewhere over the East Midlands. He asked me to pick you up."

"Why?"

Zander took a deep breath and closed his eyes. "The cops just found Poppy."

"Dead? She's dead, isn't she?" Another victim. Another life wasted by a madman. Then it hit me. "When was she killed?"

"The police and the medical examiner have narrowed it down to Wednesday evening."

"And Steve..."

I had a horrible feeling I knew what Zander was going to say.

"Steve was being questioned by the police until the early hours. Either he's not The Florist, or we've got a copycat on our hands."

"But the hair..."

"The colours matched, but as it was cut rather than pulled out, there are no root bulbs containing DNA. It's difficult to tie it back definitively. Steve's denying all knowledge of how it got into his bedroom. Of course, he could still be responsible for the first four deaths, just not Poppy."

Bridges's comments about accomplices came back to me. "Could he have been working with someone? Kramer?"

"Kramer's missing. We're looking for him and also a connection between the two of them. Another possibility is that Macklin has an accomplice who's trying to throw us off the scent."

I sagged back in the seat. Was this never going to end? How many more girls would have to die before the monster after us made a mistake? A tear trickled out the corner of my eye and I swiped it away. I didn't want to look weak in front of a virtual stranger, but Zander noticed anyway and offered me a handkerchief.

"Don't worry; it's clean. I only carry it for...well, for situations like this."

"You ride in cars with a lot of crying women?"

"It's not the first time."

The town car sped through the backstreets to Kings Cross and pulled into the underground garage Max had parked in before, the day I got hypnotised. I recognised his SUV a couple of rows over as Zander led me to the lift.

"I'll show you to Nye's office. You can wait in there until Max gets back."

"Where's Nye?"

"He's out right now."

Nye had a big squashy couch, but I couldn't sit on it. I stood instead, staring out the window at the street below as tiny people went about their business while I was trapped inside. An assistant came in with coffee and biscuits, but I felt too sick to eat.

It seemed like forever before Max walked through the door, not pausing to acknowledge anyone as he strode across the room. I threw myself into his arms the instant he reached me and we both clung on tight.

"I won't let anyone hurt you," he said, his voice muffled by my hair.

"I know, but why is this still happening?"

"Sometimes the police make mistakes. Trust me, I've already had words with Jason."

"It's not his fault."

"I know, but if he had a clue they'd got the wrong man, he should have said something on Saturday. We were out in the open yesterday." He closed his eyes. "That fucker with the camera would never have got near you if I'd been alert."

"It's not your fault either."

"Yes, it is. I shouldn't have let you out before a conviction."

"Are you kidding? I'm not staying locked up in your house for another month. Or a year. Or however long. I've got a life to live."

Max's face fell. "But I thought you liked my house. Our house."

"I love it. But not twenty-four seven."

"I don't think I'll get another month off work. Not unless I leave. But then I couldn't afford to keep the house." He kicked the door shut. "Not that the house matters. You're all that matters."

"You're overreacting. Anyway, I don't want to go gallivanting around town. I only need to work in the shop. I went through the books this morning, and even though Tia helped a lot, Black Lily isn't doing well. Suki and I need to make the samples for the new collection and do a pile of alterations for regular customers. If we let them down, they'll go elsewhere."

"I'm terrified of losing you," he whispered. "I've waited my whole life for you to come along."

"You won't lose me. You can drop me off in the morning, and if you're working late, I'll catch a cab here in the evening and wait in reception. The Florist works at night. He's not going to come into a lit shop in full view of West End pedestrians."

Max's brow furrowed, and I knew he hated the idea. But I couldn't give in. If I did, and let myself be hidden away, it would feel as if I'd gone to prison instead of that murdering piece of scum.

"Okay, but no cab. If I can't come at five thirty, I'll send a car."

I let out the breath I'd been holding. "Deal."

"Are you okay here for a few more minutes? I need to debrief today's team then phone Jason and find out what the fuck else is going on."

"I can stay as long as you want." Plus I needed to call Suki. With all the stress, I'd forgotten, and she'd be worrying as well. "Can I borrow a phone? I left my bag in the shop."

He pointed at the sleek black one on the desk.

"And I don't suppose you've got a T-shirt I can borrow? I've still got a corset on under this coat, and I hate wearing it after work."

He looked me up and down and chewed on his lip. "No, but I know where we can find something." He opened the door and beckoned me to follow him.

We took the lift up four storeys onto a floor with a higher ceiling than those downstairs. The desks were set farther apart, but few people occupied them. Those who did stared with unhidden curiosity as Max led me up a flight of stairs at the side to a row of glass-fronted offices. The first one was empty, and he pushed the door open.

"Whose office is this?"

"Dan's."

"Who's he?"

"She. Daniela. She's about your size." He opened a closet at the back and pulled out a cocktail dress. "Too fancy." Another rummage. "This?"

The black sweatshirt with the Blackwood shield on the chest looked about right. "I think that'll fit. Won't Daniela mind?"

"No. Do you want jeans?"

"I'll be okay in my skirt."

"I won't be long. You can stay up here if you prefer."

I felt awkward enough wearing another woman's clothes, let alone taking over her office, even if it was a very nice office with a posh leather chair and a fancy glass desk. "I'd rather come downstairs with you."

He held the door open for me to leave, and once we got back in the lift, he slid an arm around my back and touched his lips to mine. "I missed you."

I tried to pull his head down more, but he chuckled and straightened up. "There's CCTV in the corner."

Whoops.

Max kept his word, and in less than an hour, we were on our way. When he closed his door in the car park, I put my hand on his before he could start the engine.

"Are there cameras down here as well?"

"There's cameras everywhere in this building." He paused. "Except the bathrooms. I'm pretty sure the bathrooms are okay."

"I'll remember that tomorrow."

Max's garage at home had no such surveillance-related issues, and he kissed me until my lips stung before we even got out of the car. By the time we reached the bedroom, I'd lost most of my clothes but he was still fully dressed.

"This isn't fair."

"I don't see a problem." He unknotted his tie and let it slip through his fingers to the floor. Navy blue silk this time, with subtle dots in dark grey. Bethany's influence again? Or Max's natural sense of style? I'd bet my entire stash of Turkish delight that Max didn't own a single novelty garment—tie, socks, or worse, underpants.

"Don't drop that," I told him.

"I'll pick it up later."

I stooped to retrieve the tie and put it back into his hand.

"Why do I need this?"

Without speaking, I lay back on the bed and crossed my wrists above my head. "Maybe I like it when you tell me what to do."

His eyes darkened as he realised what I meant. "In that case, I'm never dropping a tie again." Slowly, too slowly, he unbuttoned his shirt, and I got to enjoy the view as he peeled it off and threw it into the laundry hamper. Then he knelt over me, and as he reached for my hands, it occurred to me I should be scared to be in this position, to have a man incapacitating me like this.

But this was Max. I trusted him.

And boy did he repay that trust. Three orgasms before dinner, and I only made it downstairs because he carried me.

"You need to eat something. Otherwise you won't have enough energy for later."

"What's later?"

"I have a very large collection of ties."

Oh boy. He could try them all on me if it led to the same result as earlier. They'd become my new favourite item of clothing. Hmm. Perhaps we could sell ties in the shop? A unisex line with matching lingerie...

"Earth to Lily."

"Sorry, what?"

"Are you good with omelette and salad for dinner? Or should I order something in?"

"Omelette's fine."

And quick. They were quick, right?

Max checked his phone while he cooked. "Looks like The Florist got careless."

I stiffened. "What do you mean?"

"Message from Jason. They found skin under Poppy's fingernails. It's on its way to the lab."

"You mean they might have DNA?"

"Yes. And they reckon it's the same man, not a copycat. He was shooting blanks again."

That poor, poor girl, having to suffer that at the end. "I wish I could remember."

He stopped what he was doing and gave me a hug. "Don't punish yourself for it. It's not your fault."

I sighed, long and deep. "Logically, I know that. But it still frustrates me. Did Jason say anything else?"

"The vase was there again. Small and red, with six

poppies. They're trying to trace the manufacturer and canvassing flower shops in the area."

"He could have bought them anywhere."

"That's the problem. He's so fucking slippery. One of the neighbours saw him leave this time, but he was wearing that damned hood again."

"Maybe someone else will have seen him?"

"They're going through CCTV." He dropped his arms and went back to the hob. "But enough of him. He's not ruining our evening."

"Right. I'm curious about what you can do with a belt."

CHAPTER 23

"SO, WHAT HAPPENED last night?" Suki asked.

"The police found a girl called Poppy, dead."

"You already told me that on the phone, remember? I meant with Max. Did he take your mind off things?"

"You can't ask that!"

"You're blushing, so clearly the answer's yes. Lucky you—Jason was out working all night."

At least I'd drawn the bodyguard rather than the detective, even if the circumstances were less than ideal. "Is he working tonight too?"

"He's got the early shift today, although he said he'd most likely work overtime because of The Florist." She broke into a grin. "But he's given me a key to his flat. It's not on a par with your palace, of course, but I can't believe it!"

Neither could I—Suki's previous relationships could barely be measured in hours, let alone weeks. "Cupcakes for lunch, then?"

"You bet. Is it too early for champagne?"

"Never, especially if it's one of those mini bottles. We could share it?"

"Deal."

I tried to take my mind off the case by cutting out panels for my sample corsets. Deep red leather for one, midnight velvet for another. The noise of the sewing machine stopped me from thinking, and by lunchtime, I had the first of them more or less finished.

"Can you lace me into this?" I asked Suki, holding up the dark blue piece. Over the years, I'd learned to do it myself, but it was always easier with help.

"Sure."

It didn't take long, and I stepped out under the spotlights for a better look. "I might add some cream lace. What do you think?"

"Not too much, or it'll be overpowering. How about a touch of embroidery at the bottom instead?"

I nodded. "That could work. I'll leave it on while I work on the other."

All in all, I survived the morning without being consumed by thoughts of The Florist, but it was too good to last. When Suki went out to hunt for lunch, cake, and alcohol, my phone trilled.

A male voice came through the speaker. "It's Nye."

I groaned then clapped a hand over my mouth. "Sorry."

"Don't worry. I feel like that myself every time the phone rings at the moment."

"Has anything bad happened?"

"No. I just wanted to give you an update."

I dragged a stool over so I could watch the door, unsure whether I'd need to sit down or not. Without Max around, I didn't want to take any chances. "Okay."

"We've got The Florist on CCTV, but it's grainy. The police are going door to door in case anyone else has footage. You were right about his height and build."

Nausea clutched at my throat as I recalled the man pressed up against me. His hard cock. His harsh whisper. His rancid breath. "That's it?"

"We're a little more hopeful on the vase. Yours, Rose's, and Heather's were mass-produced rubbish, but Poppy's looks a little more refined. The police have a team tracking down the manufacturer, and we're hoping they'll be able to get us a list of stockists."

"That's good. How long will it take?"

"It depends on how willing they are to cooperate. If we need to go the court-order route, a few days. Keep your fingers crossed they're willing to simply email the details without a fuss."

"I will. Do you know if Max'll be picking me up tonight?"

"I think it'll be someone else. Max has meetings all day. If it isn't Zander, I'll let you know who to expect, and remember to check their ID."

"I will."

After that depressing discussion, I needed four cupcakes to feel human again. The champagne helped too, even if I'd lost any enthusiasm for celebrating.

Soho clouded over in the afternoon, and hailstones the size of golf balls battered any pedestrians unlucky enough to be out walking. A handful sheltered in the shop until the storm passed, dripping all over the floor. We didn't sell anything, but they were full of thanks for the cups of tea we made them.

I'd hoped for a chink of blue sky, but darkness followed the grey, and the hail turned to plain old boring rain as the afternoon wore on. I tucked a faux-fur trimmed cape around my shoulders, turned the heating up a notch, and carried on sewing.

Zander turned up five minutes before closing, complete with a giant umbrella, which he held over me as we dashed to the car. Suki came too, and we dropped her at Piccadilly Circus to catch the Tube before carrying on to Blackwood.

"Is there any news?" I asked once she'd disappeared down the steps.

"The import company that sold the vases is playing ball. The police have three stockists to check first thing tomorrow."

"Anything else?"

"The DNA came back, but it doesn't match anyone in the database."

"At least if they arrest somebody else, it should be easier to confirm whether he's The Florist, right?"

He smiled, trying to convey some sort of positivity. "Absolutely."

Traffic was terrible on the way back, most likely because everybody who'd usually walk wanted to keep out of the rain.

"You mind if I drop you out the front?" Zander asked. "I'm late to pick my sister up. You can take the umbrella."

"No problem." He'd spent enough of his time running around after me as it was.

When the car stopped, I picked my way round the puddles and dashed into reception, trying not to drop too much water on the tiled floor.

"We've got an umbrella rack right over here," the receptionist said, waving one hand in its direction. "Who are you here to see?"

"Max Tian."

"Is he expecting you?"

"He should be. My name's Lily Matthews."

Her professional mask turned into a wide smile. "Oh, you're that Lily. Max isn't back yet, but I'll call

Nye's assistant. She'll take you through to the break area."

Two minutes later, a small black lady hurried through the door, wearing a smile that matched the receptionist's. "You must be Lily? I'm Janelle."

I followed her through the doors and across the big room with all the desks. Hidden behind a potted plant lay a kitchen I'd never noticed before.

"Max said you like coffee. Can I get you a cup?"

Really? He'd been talking about me? "I'd love one. Black, please."

"Coming right up."

I took a few seconds to look around. The kitchen was like the rest of the building—modern and functional. Three bowls of fruit sat on the counter, next to a box of charity Christmas cards and a stack of magazines. *Glamour, Runner's World, Guns & Ammo*. Wow. There must be some interesting people working here.

"Has Max said much else about me?" My curiosity was well and truly piqued.

"Not a lot. Just that if you want chocolate or Turkish delight, he's left boxes of both in his desk drawer. But he doesn't have to."

"Have to what?"

"Say much. I can tell by looking at him that he's crazy about you."

"How?"

"He's smiled at least twice this week."

"That often?"

She slid a cup of espresso onto the table in front of me, then took a seat opposite with her own hot chocolate. "Before, once a month was normal. But then, he didn't have the best life growing up, so it's hardly surprising."

"I know. I feel so bad for him."

"He told you?"

She seemed surprised, but I wasn't, not really. Max's walls were difficult to climb over, and if anyone tried to smash their way through, they'd probably break a hand.

I nodded. "A couple of weeks back."

"He must feel really comfortable with you then. Usually, he won't talk about his time in prison."

What?

I'd never been shot, but as Janelle's words punched into my chest, I imagined that was what it would feel like. "Prison? Did you say prison?"

Her colour dropped a couple of shades as her eyes widened. "I thought you said he told you?"

"He told me he got bullied at school and he didn't see eye to eye with his parents. You're telling me he was in jail?"

"Could you just forget I said that bit? It was ages ago, anyway."

I shoved my chair back, coffee forgotten. "What for?"

"I really don't think I should say any more."

"Where is he?"

"I don't think—"

"Where. Is. He?"

She shrank back a few inches. Was I truly that scary?

"Uh, conference room B."

I strode into the main office, breathing fire, and stomped up to the nearest employee. "Where's conference room B?"

Silently, he extended a finger to a closed door in the corner, and I marched in that direction, fighting back tears. With every step, I trembled more. Prison? Max was a criminal?

I shoved the door open without stopping to knock, and four startled faces turned to look at me, Max's included.

"Lily? Are you okay?"

"Do I look okay? Is it true? Were you in prison?"

He went paler than the freshly painted wall in the fourth bedroom at home. His home. Was it mine anymore? I had my doubts after that reaction.

On the giant screen in front of me, I recognised Max's boss, the blonde lady. She leaned forward in her high-backed chair and sighed. She looked like a bloody Bond villain—all she needed was a cat. "Technically, it was more of a young offender's institution."

"You're not helping," Nye snapped at her.

"Fine. I'll just leave that one with you." She reached out and pushed a button, and her head shrank into the middle of the screen before disappearing.

The two strangers scurried out as well, leaving me, Max, and Nye.

"You want me to go, mate?" Nye asked.

Max nodded, and Nye backed out of the room.

"Is it true?" I asked again, less powerfully this time.

"Yes."

"Why didn't you tell me?"

"I didn't know how. It's hardly something you slip into casual conversation."

"We were living in the same damn house. What part of that is casual to you?"

He sank into a chair. "I know I should have told you. I was scared you'd react...well, like this."

"What for? What were you in prison for?"

Time stood still as I waited for his answer. Theft? Assault? Drugs?

"Manslaughter."

I collapsed into the chair opposite him, and my butt squeaked down the leather. "You killed someone?"

"Yes."

"What? How?" His words, or rather word, sank in. One word that changed my entire life. One word that hurt me far more than The Florist ever could. That one word destroyed my heart, my soul, and my reason for living. "Actually, don't. I don't want to know."

"Lily—"

"Shut up! You promised to protect me from a killer when you're one yourself. How do you think that makes me feel? Did you ever plan to tell me?"

He looked at the floor and shook his head.

Well, at least that was honest. If only he'd been that forthcoming before. How could I spend my life with a man who'd not only killed somebody, but planned to withhold such a big part of himself from me? I'd have told him anything about my past. *Anything.*

And he wouldn't even make eye contact now.

With some effort, I heaved myself up and stumbled towards the door. Max tried to follow, but I held up a hand. "Don't you dare come near me. Ever! Just keep away. I never want to see you or speak to you again."

The same faces that had watched me come in looked on, impassive, as I dashed out, twisting my ankle on the steps as I half fell down them. I realised too late I'd forgotten my bag, but no way was I going back inside. No, there was only one place I could go. Suki's flat.

I looked both ways along the street—not a cab in sight, and even if there had been, I didn't have any money. I didn't have a coat either, and I was wearing three-inch bloody heels.

Welcome to my life.

Chapter 24

WATER DRIPPED OFF me in rivulets as I tailgated a neighbour into Suki's apartment building. Out of the rain, I leaned against the wall in the hallway and unstrapped my Mary Janes. Never again was I wearing heels. Never. Tomorrow I'd buy ballet pumps or better still, moccasins.

My blisters screamed as I tripped up the front steps and hammered on Suki's door. Of course, there was little chance of her being home. No, she'd be at Jason's place doing all the things that I'd never do with Max again. I wiped more tears away and grimaced at the black streaks of mascara that stained my hand. No, I wouldn't be wearing that in future either.

Deep breaths, Lily. Deep breaths. I plastered on a smile as best I could and tapped on the door opposite. A minute passed, and I tried again a little louder. That time the volume of the TV dropped a smidgen, and Agnes peered around the doorjamb. Good thing she never went out. Suki said she got her groceries and everything else delivered and knew all the local couriers by name.

"Hi, Agnes. Do you think I could borrow Suki's spare key? She's out, and she said I could stay here tonight."

"Who are you?"

"Lily. Suki's friend. You remember me? I brought you round cupcakes a couple of months back when Suki made too many."

She peered a little closer. "Ah, yes. I didn't recognise you with all that black stuff on your face. Back in my day we just wore rouge and a touch of lipstick." She shuffled backwards. "Wait a second, dear."

She headed inside, and as I waited, the shivers began. On the way over, while I was jumping at every shadow and noise behind me, I'd barely thought of Max and the horrible confrontation we'd just had, but now he was front and centre of my mind.

"I think it's this one." Agnes held out a key on a piece of pink ribbon.

"Yes, that's right. Thank you."

"Have a good evening."

Yeah, right. I shoved the key into the lock and fell inside, flipping the lights on as I went. Where was the phone? It wasn't on its charging unit in the hallway, but I found it discarded on the bed, next to a pile of Suki's underwear and an empty crisp packet.

"Suki?"

"Lily? Why are you in my flat?"

"Because I broke up with Max."

"You *what?*"

"We split up."

"Hang on, hang on. Yesterday, you'd moved in with him and started mentally decorating the rest of his house and planning the names of your kids."

"I had not! Well, not the kids part."

"I saw you at lunchtime. You had a baby name website open on your phone."

Busted. I was only wondering what went with Tian, okay? Or maybe Matthews-Tian. Arrrgh!

"I think it's safe to say that's never going to happen."

"What could he possibly have done that was so bad?"

"Killed someone."

Spluttering came down the line as Suki spat out whatever she was drinking. "Dammit, I need a tissue. Hang on a sec... What, today?"

"No, a while ago. He went to prison."

"That's crazy. Where on earth did you hear that?"

"Someone he works with told me by accident. Then I asked him and he admitted it."

"You must have misunderstood. I mean, Max is a grumpy sod, but killing someone? Hold on." Her phone clattered onto the table. "Jason. Jase! Come here, would you?"

Their voices were muffled, but still clear enough. "There's some ridiculous story going round about Max killing someone and going to jail. Did you hear it?"

A long pause. "Shit. How did you find out?"

"You mean it's true?"

He must have nodded, because the next thing I heard was Suki screeching.

"You asshole! Why the hell didn't you tell me? My best friend's been living with a murderer."

"It was a long time ago."

"Oh, well that's all right then. As long as he hasn't killed anyone recently."

"What are you doing?"

"What do you think? I'm packing."

"Can't we just talk about this?"

"You clearly don't understand my priorities here. Keeping Lily alive and happy—that's my priority. Now, get out of my way."

She picked up the phone again. "I'll be with you in half an hour. I need chocolate and wine."

That made two of us. As I raided the cupboard for a bottle of...well, anything really, guilt welled up inside me. Not only was my love life an utter shambles, I'd successfully managed to screw up Suki's too. Some friend I was.

I poured myself a generous glass of white, not caring that it was warm. I just needed something to numb myself, to help me forget that right now I should be settling down to a healthy meal of salad and fruit juice, followed by an evening of dirty sex with the man I loved. Okay, I loved him. Yesterday. But today I'd found out he wasn't the person I'd thought, and that love had turned to...hate? Did I hate Max? My head said I should, but the ache in my heart suggested otherwise. How quickly my world had been flipped upside down.

A key scraping in the lock and a bit of swearing announced Suki's arrival. She backed in, dragging a suitcase and a couple of carrier bags overflowing with clothes.

"Here, I'll give you a hand." I grabbed one of the bags and the handle broke, spilling leather and silk everywhere. Looked as if I wasn't the only one who'd been putting work samples to good use. Amazing use. I screwed my eyes shut and groaned. How could it all have gone so wrong?

"Where's the wine?"

"On the counter."

I shovelled up the clothes, carried them into the bedroom, and added them to the pile on the overstuffed armchair next to the window.

Suki wandered in, and I saw she'd rejected the glass I'd left out in favour of a bigger one. "I can't believe they didn't tell us."

"I don't want to talk about it." Bad enough having to think about it.

"Suits me. Have you eaten?"

"I can't eat."

"Well, I need to. I'll order a pizza."

Without food, the alcohol went straight to my head, and by the time Suki started munching on her stuffed-crust meat feast, I could barely stand. I gripped the windowsill, staring out at the traffic below. Perhaps I should just open the damn thing up and throw myself out? You know, save The Florist a job and put myself out of my misery to boot?

"What's the point in going on?" I slurred.

"Hey! Don't talk like that. He's only a man. There's thousands more out there." That wasn't the first time I'd heard her say those words, but she lacked her usual conviction.

"But he was...sho...sho...shweet." I dropped my glass, and it shattered on the laminate floor. "Don't worry. I'll pick it up." I wobbled towards the paper towel on the counter, only to embed the shards in my feet.

"Ouch." I hopped forward, then fell on my knees.

Suki dragged me towards the bedroom. "Leave it. Just leave it."

We both collapsed on the bed, and I picked glass out of my feet while Suki flicked on the TV.

"Let's find something better than men. Let's find..." She started snoring, and the remote slipped from her fingers.

I picked it up and found the menu. News...too depressing. *The Only Way is Essex*...too orange. Some romcom...also miserable. Finally, after hopping through the channels twice, I settled on Price-Drop TV. I really needed one of those blenders. I really needed...

"My head hurts."

Suki woke before me, and her moaning soon ensured I got no more sleep either.

"My head hurts. My feet hurt." My heart hurt.

"Did you get all the glass out?"

"I think so." I bent one foot towards my head, and my knee protested. The bottom was covered in scabs, but it looked clean. At least the alcohol I'd also trodden in would have prevented any infection. A girl's got to look on the positive side, right?

"It's eight o'clock. Do you think we could get away with going in late?" Suki asked.

"I've got a fitting at half nine."

"Dammit. I'll look for the paracetamol while you make the coffee."

My head pounded as I got dressed. I swore on my single pair of Jimmy Choos I was never going to drink again. Luckily, I'd left them at Suki's flat a while back. If they'd been at Max's, I'd have waved goodbye to them, because I didn't want to go over there to pick up my stuff. At some point, I'd have to take a trip back to my old flat, but that would mean asking Jason to ask

Nye for the key, and I didn't fancy doing that either. Thankfully, Suki and I were about the same size. I cursed under my breath. I'd need to start wearing Price-Mart again—it was all my budget would allow.

Neither of us fancied squashing on the Tube, so we shared a cab. I'd borrowed a corset and a ruffle skirt from Suki and found a pair of ballet pumps stuffed down the back of her wardrobe. I felt short but comfortable. Well, as comfortable as I could feel with seventeen Band-Aids stuck to the soles of my feet.

"Jason's texted me again," Suki said as we pulled up outside Black Lily.

"What did he say?"

"Another apology, an offer of dinner, and he said he's going to speak to someone about a vase. You know what that means?"

"Zander told me they were trying to trace where The Florist bought Poppy's vase."

"Oh. Well, let's hope they do a better job than they did last time."

Suki rolled up the shutter while I unlocked the door.

"Bloody hell, it's freezing in here," I muttered.

She walked over to the thermostat. "It's still on twenty-five."

I wandered further inside, slowly, a horrible sense of unease building in my stomach. Last time I'd felt an unexpected chill, a madman leapt out at me. I grabbed a display vase and hefted it in front of me. Wouldn't that be ironic? If I whacked The Florist with a bunch of sodding flowers?

But the back door was secure.

"The radiator's freezing," Suki called. "There must

be a problem with the boiler. I'll call the landlord."

Marvellous. On past form, he'd get back to us in a fortnight, right after we'd both frozen to death.

I offered to get lunch, but Suki insisted on going in case The Florist was lurking. Even so, I jumped every time a customer poked their head through the door, and I sighed in relief when Suki got back.

"I got Vietnamese soup. Extra spicy to keep us warm."

I grabbed a pot off her and wrapped my hands around it. "Good plan." My fingers were like ice. If this carried on, I'd need to wear gloves all day.

"Then I went to the patisserie and got donuts. And brownies. And a couple of chocolate eclairs."

See, this was why she was my best friend. Sod the salad.

It was almost the end of the day, and we'd resorted to wearing scarves and furry headbands when the bell over the door jangled. A man stood on the threshold, dressed in black, but he didn't look like one of our usual customers. I stepped a little closer as he crossed the threshold. He looked familiar. Where had I seen him before?

He shrugged out of his rucksack and put it on the floor in front of him. "Lily?"

I realised who he was. Rose's ex. Damien. I hadn't seen him in months, and it looked as though he'd spent some time in the gym. That and he'd finally got a decent haircut. A flicker of fear ran through me as I recalled the early stages of the investigation. The police hadn't arrested him, but he'd never been completely ruled out either, had he? "What do you want?"

"I was hoping to have a little chat."

CHAPTER 25

"WHAT COULD YOU possibly have to say to me?" I asked.

Damien shifted from foot to foot. "I just wanted to let you know how sorry I am. I read in the paper that Rose died, and then the police said..." He gave his head a little shake. "I'm sorry."

Seriously? "I don't see why you care now. You hurt her enough while she was alive."

Suki stomped up behind me. "Don't you realise when you're not welcome?"

"I know me and Rose didn't part on the best of terms, but I still cared about her."

"Cared enough to cheat on her with a bloody Pokémon," Suki muttered.

I appreciated her sentiment, but it wasn't helping matters. "Okay, you've come, and you've said how sorry you are. Is there anything else? Because we were just locking up."

"I was tidying the flat the other day, and I realised I'd picked up some of Rose's clothes when I cleared out my stuff. I thought you might want them back." He shrugged. "They're no use to me."

I was surprised he hadn't just thrown them in the rubbish. Maybe he did have a heart after all? "Thanks."

He pulled a bin liner out of the backpack and

passed it over. "Yeah, so I guess I'll be going. Hope they catch that bastard soon."

"Me too."

He took a woollen cap out of his pocket and tugged it down over his ears, then disappeared into the night.

Suki picked up the bag and peered inside. "Guess Rose's jeans wouldn't fit the Japanese bitch." She held up a silk scarf. "This might come in handy if we get cold tomorrow, though."

"Put it in the storeroom and let's get out of here. I'm bloody freezing."

We both needed to save a bit of money, so we hopped on the Tube to get home. In any case, it was a lot warmer down in the tunnels. Apart from my trip with Max on a rather empty Sunday, I hadn't been on those trains for ages, and I'd forgotten how unpleasant it could be. As I stood with my face wedged in a man's armpit, I rued yet another thing I'd miss about Max. He'd spoiled me with those rides to and from work.

"I'd better cook tonight, I guess," Suki said as we traipsed up the front steps into her building.

"I could have a go."

"Did you magically turn into Jamie Oliver while you were with Max?"

"He cooked. I managed to explode a salmon once."

She stopped and stared. "How did you... Actually, I'm not even going to ask. But I'm definitely cooking. Spag bol okay with you?"

"Anything's fine, but I'm still quite full from all those cakes."

"At least you ate something." She poked my ribs. "You're so skinny now. You'll lose your tits if you eat any less."

Who cared? I wasn't planning to show them to another man in a hurry, and after the episode with the press, I couldn't see myself modelling for the shop in the near future. We'd have to hire someone. Another expense.

Suki's phone buzzed, and she picked it up and tutted. "Jason again."

"Maybe you should ease up on him a bit?"

"He should have told me—us—about Max. I mean, there's no way you'd have dated him if you knew his history, right?" She stared at me. "Right?"

"No, of course not."

I thought back to the Max I'd known. He'd been a mercurial mix of sweet and moody, but never violent. But then again, I'd never been the best judge of character. I once went on eight dates with a man without realising he dealt drugs as his day job. It was only after he noticed a couple of policemen following us when we came out of the cinema then legged it down the street that I realised my error. I got questioned for twenty minutes before the police decided I was clearly too stupid to be part of his empire.

"Jason said he didn't want to cause problems, as if that was a good excuse." Suki fished around in the freezer before emerging triumphantly with a bag of mince. "I asked what Max did, exactly, but he didn't know the details. It happened while he was a juvenile, and the records are sealed."

Was that better or worse, to kill someone so young? What did that mean for him later in life? Dammit, I had to stop thinking about it. "Can we change the subject?"

"Sure. To what?"

Oh, I hated it when people asked that. "I don't know."

In response, she twisted the cork out of a bottle of red. "In that case, let's discuss the merits of a good Pinot Noir."

"So, what did Jason want last night, anyway?"

Curiosity got the better of me as we waited on the platform at Whitechapel. We'd come prepared for the day in cute but toasty overcoats, fingerless gloves, and scarves.

"His message said they'd traced the vase to one shop, but the shopkeeper's assistant didn't remember who bought it. And they got The Florist on video, but it was dusky, and he went around a corner and disappeared. Maybe into a cab or through the park there."

I sighed and tucked my hands deeper into my pockets. "Whoever The Florist is, he's smart. He's always one step ahead."

"He's also been lucky so far, but that'll run out one day."

"It hasn't shown any signs of doing so yet."

"It will." She paused, and I glanced up at the matrix display. One minute until the next train. "Jase also said Max isn't doing well."

Why did she have to tell me that? As if I wasn't feeling bad enough already. "That makes two of us."

The crowd on the platform stepped back as the

train pulled in, and a crowded carriage was no place to carry on that conversation, thank goodness. I'd ride the District line all day if it meant avoiding more awkwardness.

By the time we switched at Embankment, Suki was too busy trying to work out where the woman next to us bought her handbag to worry about Max. Today was one of the rare times I was glad her attention span rivalled that of a toddler's. A few more stops, and we reached Piccadilly Circus, ready to face the early-morning tourists on our short walk to the shop.

"At least it's not raining today," Suki said as we emerged from the station. "Can we quickly stop at the pharmacy?"

"Are you okay?"

"I'm getting a bit of a sore throat. Hope it doesn't turn into something worse."

Except it did. By mid-morning, Suki was necking back cold and flu remedy like an alcoholic at a free bar. Usually, she dealt with the landlord, but I'd got so sick of the situation that I picked up the phone myself.

And got through to his secretary. "We're freezing in here. There was ice inside the windows this morning."

She clicked a few keys. "You're on the maintenance list, but we're busy."

"If I go and buy a heater, will you discount it off the rent?"

"I can ask, but it's unlikely. We should have an engineer with you tomorrow. Day after at the latest. I've shuffled you above the people with the faulty toilet."

"I bet if you were the one sitting in a fridge, you'd do something faster."

Her voice dropped to a whisper. "I've got my jacket wrapped around my feet and a hot water bottle in my lap."

"Oh." Yep, the landlord was a total asshole, and I felt a little guilty for chewing her out. "Sorry," I mumbled, then quickly hung up.

"Anything?" Suki asked.

"What do you think?"

She sighed, and her teeth chattered again. "Could you put the kettle on?"

"You should go home. You're not in a fit state to be here, and I'm sure the customers don't want to catch whatever it is you've got." I didn't either.

"I'll be okay. I'm not leaving you on your own."

By three o'clock, she was curled up in the break room with a swath of faux fur tucked around her legs, and I'd had enough. I nipped out the front door and waved a cab down, then marched through to the back of the shop.

"Get up. You're leaving."

"I'm not."

"Yes, you are. I've got a taxi driver waiting outside."

"But what about you?"

"I'll only be here for a couple more hours, then I'll be back to make us both something to eat."

"I feel quite ill enough already," she rasped.

"Come on." I held my hand out. "Up."

I bundled her into the back of the cab and made sure she had cash to pay the driver. He didn't look too happy about riding with all the germs, but she had to get home somehow, and if I recalled my facts correctly from the pub quiz I entered with Rose a few months ago, taxi drivers were only allowed to kick a passenger out if they had bubonic plague.

Two and a half hours left. Maybe two, if things stayed quiet. I could get away with closing a little early on a Wednesday. A couple of customers came and went, including one who said she'd try things on another day when it was warmer. The rest of the time I sat on my stool, too chilly to sew, trying desperately not to dwell on Max. What was he doing right now? Working? Another celeb client with a dangerous handbag?

An hour ticked by without a single sale. Sod it, I was going home. I put the shutter halfway down to deter any more customers, then washed up the coffee cups and dealt with Suki's pile of tissues. Nice. The back door was securely locked. Now to set the alarm, and I'd be done.

I'd just reached out to the control panel when a shadowy figure ducked under the shutter, and I nearly had a heart attack.

"Lily?"

Breath whooshed out of me as I realised who it was, and I flipped the lights back on. "Andrew? What are you doing here?"

"Sorry to come so late. I've only just got out of the office, and I hoped I'd catch you. I've brought your cheque."

The cheque from Rose's life insurance. I'd almost forgotten about that. Money came somewhere below murder and heartache on my list of priorities. "Oh, that's ever so kind of you."

"Steve said he tried to post it before his unfortunate... Well, it just goes to show how little you can know a person, doesn't it? Anyway, the cheque came back. The postman scribbled a note on the envelope to say you didn't have a door." He raised an eyebrow.

"There was a bit of an accident."

"I'll say. And it's freezing in here. Are you trying to save money on the heating?"

"No, it's broken. I've been wearing gloves and a scarf all day."

He held up his hands. "Mulberry, cashmere lined. An extravagance, I thought at the time, but they've paid dividends."

I raised my own. "Price-Mart. Desperation."

He laughed. "Have you got an engineer arranged to fix it? I know a good one. He sorted my boiler out at home last winter."

"The landlord's supposed to be sending someone, but I'm not holding my breath."

"Well, let me know if you want my guy's number. Or I could speak to your landlord. Sometimes they respond better to a touch of gentle persuasion."

"Thanks, that's really kind."

His smile dropped. "Rose was a good girl, and I miss her terribly. If there's anything I can do to assist, just let me know."

No sooner had the words left his mouth than a clatter came from the back of the shop. I stiffened, staring towards the break room.

"Is somebody out there?" he asked.

"There shouldn't be. It sounded like it came from the alley."

"It's probably nothing. Perhaps a tramp?"

I nodded, but the shakes had set in, and my teeth started to chatter worse than Suki's had earlier. "Sorry,

I'm just really jumpy at the moment."

He gave me an understanding smile. "I'm sure you are. Didn't I read in the paper that you got attacked as well?"

"A few weeks back."

"Sometimes I wonder what this world's coming to. Do you want me to take a look outside and check it's safe?"

I ran my gaze over him, considering. Andrew was an older man, but tall and relatively fit. "I don't want you to get hurt."

"I'll be fine." He dropped his briefcase at his feet and picked up the pole we used to lift clothes down from the higher pegs. "Where's your back door?"

I pointed to the break room. "Through there. The key's in the lock."

Hefting the pole in his hands, he walked off, leaving me standing there among the mannequins. I eyed up the gap under the shutter at the front. At least I could escape if needs be, although what about Andrew? What if he got hurt?

What if The Florist had finally come for me again?

Chapter 26

I STOOD, POISED between fight and flight as the back door opened then closed again. Dammit! I shouldn't have let Andrew go out there by himself. What if he got hurt? What if Kramer was the real culprit and he'd come for me? Another person injured, and it would all be my fault. I eyed up my handbag, sitting on the worktable. Maybe I should grab my phone and call the police?

And say what? That I heard a random noise coming from the alley? A few pedestrians walked by outside, laughing and joking. Could I stop them and ask for help?

"Whatever it was, it's gone now." Andrew's voice sounded from the break room, and the tension seeped out of me as he continued. "I had a good look around. Perhaps it was a cat? Or an urban fox? I even checked the dumpster." He wrinkled his nose. "Smelled pretty bad in there."

"Thank you, and I'm so sorry. Can I make you a cup of tea before you go? I think we've got biscuits somewhere."

He put the pole back where it belonged and rubbed his hands together. "I wouldn't say no. I've been stuck in a series of boring meetings all afternoon, and the refreshments were dire. It left me hungry for something else."

"Hang on a sec." I wound the shutter down the rest of the way to stop any more visitors. "That's better. Do you take sugar?"

He patted his stomach. "Gave it up a few years ago. My wife complained I was getting tubby."

"How is your wife?" I asked as I pottered around with the kettle. Luckily, I'd boiled it not long ago, and Suki must have been to the minimart recently because we had a whole assortment of biccies plus a box of liqueur chocolates.

"My wife's good. Busy packing at the moment."

"Are you going on holiday?"

"Not exactly. Something longer term." Andrew took the cup of tea I held out then followed me through to the shop. "I sold the company. The new owners asked me to stay on as chairman, but I decided to go with early retirement." He mimed a golf swing. "Practise my game."

Retirement was a distant dream for me. Oh, to have enough money to not have to work every day. "Lovely. Are you moving nearby?"

"Quite the opposite. Bali. We always wanted to live somewhere hot."

"Ooh, I'm so jealous! I'd love to live there, but I can't even afford a holiday. Will you send me a postcard?"

"I think I can manage that. I'd better post it here, though, seeing as you don't have a door at home."

"I'll be moving soon, anyway. When are you leaving?"

"We're looking at the end of the month. I've got a few loose ends to tie up here, and we need to finalise our house purchase."

"At least you'll be in the sun for Christmas. Custard cream?"

As I held out the packet of biscuits, an almighty crash sounded from the back of the shop, swiftly followed by another, then another. The cup slid out of my other hand, spilling dregs of tea as it shattered on the floor below. That definitely wasn't a fox.

"What the—" Andrew started as Max appeared in the doorway.

A haggard, dishevelled Max. If I thought our time apart had been difficult for me, it seemed to have hit Max ten times harder. His face was covered in days' worth of stubble, his hair greasy. Had he even changed his clothes?

"Max? What the hell are you doing?"

He ignored me, his stare focused only on Andrew.

"Get away from her."

Andrew held his hands up. "Don't mind me. This is all quite innocent. I promise I'm not treading on your toes."

"Max, this is Rose's old boss. He just stopped round to drop something off."

"I know exactly who he is." Max's voice was hard, flat, a robotic imitation of a man. Not the man I'd come to know. And love? I thought I had, once.

"I'm just leaving. Won't be a jiffy." Andrew pushed his chair back, but before he could get to his feet, Max launched himself across the room. He had Andrew pinned against the wall by his throat before I could blink.

I beat my fists on Max's back, but he didn't show any signs of noticing. Had he lost his damn mind?

"Please, Max, stop. Please." A river of tears streamed down my cheeks as I tried to pull him away.

"How do you like it, you fucker?" he growled as Andrew's face got redder and redder.

"Please." My knees gave way, and I sank to the floor beside him, sobbing. "Why are you doing this?"

My words finally seemed to get through to him, and he looked down at me, eyes disturbingly blank. "This man killed your sister, Lily. He should pay for that."

"What are you talking about? He employed her."

"And strangled her." Max tipped his weight forward, and Andrew's limbs flailed. I glanced downwards. His feet were a couple of inches from the floor, and he had nothing to hold on to.

Was Max serious? Andrew? I could barely fathom that. Rose had worked at his company for years. I'd met him a dozen times, and he'd always been friendly. I mean, Rose had even had that crush on him when she first started working at Mediforce, although nothing ever happened between them. If he did kill her, why? And why now?

"I can't believe it," I whispered.

Max jerked his head at Andrew's briefcase, still sitting on the floor halfway along the shop. "Look inside."

"What? Why?"

"Just do it."

My heart hammered against my ribcage as I crawled over to it. It took me three goes to open the catch while Andrew choked and spluttered behind me.

"What the—" Inside, nestled in a carrier bag, lay a small crystal vase and a single black lily. My lily.

I turned back slowly, holding them in my hands.

"Why?"

Even as he struggled to breathe, Andrew laughed. "You'll...never...know."

Max pressed harder, and the older man's lips took on a bluish tinge. Coming to my senses, I rushed over and grabbed Max's arm.

"Stop!" I pulled, and Max's muscles bulged as they worked against me, but he didn't loosen his grip. "Please!"

"He doesn't deserve to live."

"But if you kill him, you'll lose your life as well." Whatever happened, I had to stop Max from doing something really, really stupid. "I don't want you to go back to prison."

"It would be worth it after what he did to you."

Andrew's breath was shallower now, and he'd stopped fighting so much. His limbs twitched with his final efforts.

"No, Max. It wouldn't. He's scum. Don't let him ruin both our lives." I scrambled to my feet and rested a hand on Max's shoulder. "Please."

My touch seemed to wake something in him, because he released the pressure on Andrew's neck, letting the man crumple to the floor. He lay there, motionless, and Max rifled through his pockets until he came up with a length of thick twine.

The rope meant for my neck.

As Max bound Andrew's hands, my knees weakened again and I dropped to the tiles, huddled between rows of skirts as if they could hide me from the evil in the world. In my own damn shop. Evil. That's what Andrew was. Pure evil.

He flopped about as he regained consciousness, and

Max grabbed a packet of stockings from a nearby rack and used them to tie up his ankles as well.

He was tightening the knots as the first sirens sounded outside.

"Lily, let the police in."

"What?"

"Raise the shutter. The police need to get in."

My legs were numb as I stumbled across the shop to do as he said. Actually, all of me was numb. From my lips to my fingers to the emotions inside me. I'd lost all feeling.

The first uniformed officers burst in, and Max backed away with his hands in the air.

"Did he hurt you, ma'am?"

"No." Not tonight, anyway.

"What happened?"

"The man on the floor came to kill me, and Max stopped him."

"Max is that man?" He pointed, and I nodded.

Meanwhile, Andrew came to his senses and started screaming bloody murder. "That freak! He just tried to kill me!" The policemen stared as Andrew flipped himself onto his back and glared at everybody. "I was sitting here drinking tea when that madman burst in and grabbed my throat."

The nearest cop turned back to me. "Is that true?"

"Yes, but—"

"So, this Max, he attacked unprovoked?"

"Not exactly, I mean—"

"Totally unprovoked! I didn't even have a chance to defend myself. Look at my neck."

Andrew tilted his head back, and we all saw the ugly red marks on his skin.

The policeman next to Max reached for his handcuffs. "Sir, put your hands behind your back."

Max did so, and I heard the ratchet as the cuffs closed around his wrists.

"No! You've got the wrong man."

"Ma'am, these are serious allegations."

I pointed at Andrew. "That's The Florist. He had a vase and a lily in his briefcase."

"Those were gifts for my wife."

Could he be telling the truth? Then I remembered the length of twine. "Plus he had rope in his pocket. Max used it to tie his hands. What kind of man carries around rope?"

Andrew narrowed his eyes at me. "I've never seen that before in my life. This Max must have brought it with him. Maybe he's The Florist?"

That lying bastard! Before I could stop myself, I sprang up, marched over, and kicked Andrew in the bollocks. "That's for my sister."

One of the policemen grabbed me before I could have another go. "Ma'am, we'll have to arrest you as well if you keep that up."

"Fine, do it."

The bell at the front of the shop jangled as reinforcements arrived, and I almost cried with relief when I spotted Jason at the back of the group with Detective Nash.

"Jason, you have to do something. Andrew's The Florist and these idiots won't listen."

He hurried over and put an arm around my shoulders. "We know. Don't worry, it'll all get sorted out."

Max spoke up, his voice hollow. "I had a man

stationed out the back here, but he's disappeared."

Jason swung into action immediately. "I'll take a look." He beckoned to two of his colleagues. "Come with me."

Max had somebody watching? I supposed that shouldn't have surprised me with his protective traits, but that...that meant he still cared, even after the way I'd walked out on him. Max cared. With a sickening feeling, I thought back to the noise I'd heard earlier, then to Andrew heading out the door with a pole in his hands. The perfect weapon. Andrew may have looked smooth in a suit, but when he grabbed me around the neck in my flat, I'd felt the power he possessed. He had the devil himself living inside him.

I took a step towards the back door, but the policeman who'd grabbed me earlier blocked my way. "Stay here, ma'am."

Seconds ticked by, but it wasn't long before Jason came back in, looking pale. "We need an ambulance."

I gasped. "You found him?"

"In the dumpster. He's got a nasty head injury."

"That was Andrew as well. We heard a noise, and he went out to investigate. He must have knocked the man out."

"I'll fucking kill him," Max growled as Jason called for medical help.

I closed my eyes and took a deep breath. "Not helping."

More commotion sounded in the street, and this time Nye strode in. Angry Nye, nothing like the friendly guy I'd met in the past.

"What the fuck are you doing, standing around?" He pointed at Andrew. "That bastard should be in jail and Max deserves a medal, not a pair of handcuffs."

"Easy, mate," Jason murmured.

"I will not go easy. One of my men's injured according to the radio traffic, another's in handcuffs, and all because your constable missed a valuable witness and your system's too slow to get a search warrant."

"I'll admit the situation's less than ideal, but I'm trying to rectify it."

"Try harder."

Nye moved to my side while Jason started barking orders at the men standing around.

"Are you okay? Did you get hurt?" Nye asked.

"No to both."

He shrugged out of his jacket and tucked it around my shoulders. "We'll get you checked out when the medics get here, just in case."

"Why is Max still in handcuffs?"

"They're just unravelling what went on. Don't worry, nothing'll happen to him."

"I thought he was going to kill Andrew," I whispered.

Nye cut his eyes over to where Max stood, head bowed. "I'm surprised he didn't."

CHAPTER 27

I DIDN'T WANT to leave Black Lily, but Nye made me.

"I'll take you back to the office. It's best you wait there."

"But what about Max?"

"Max is a big boy. He can take care of himself."

The first part, I knew all too well. The second? I wasn't so sure about that. He'd barely been in control when he attacked Andrew, and just now, when an officer led him past to the waiting police car, he wouldn't even look at me. He'd shut down.

I'd tried talking to him. "Max?"

Nothing.

"Max, are you okay?"

A brief glance. Silence.

"Ma'am, can you move out of the way, please?"

Max fixed his gaze on his shoes again, his hands braceleted behind his back as they walked by without another word.

"Not so tough now, is he?" Andrew sneered from his position behind me on the stretcher. They'd untied his wrists and cuffed them to rails on either side, and one of the police officers carefully bagged the rope for evidence. With any luck, they'd be able to match it to the first length he brought for me, the one he dropped on the fire escape outside my flat.

"He's tougher than you'll ever be. You're nothing but a coward, raping and murdering innocent women."

Andrew laughed, and carried on doing so as the paramedics wheeled him out to the ambulance. I heard his guffaws echoing even when they'd closed the doors and set off down the road to the hospital.

"He won't escape, will he?" I asked Nye. A fair question, I thought, when he'd managed to evade capture for so long.

"No chance. They sent two policemen in the ambulance with him, and we've got one of our own vehicles following."

The first ambulance, the one with the Blackwood surveillance guy, had already departed, and Nye said we should leave too. I took one final look around my shop, my last little bit of sanctuary before The Florist stole that from me as well. Now, it swarmed with policemen and medics, and even a few firemen for good measure. Would I ever feel safe there again? Would I feel safe anywhere?

Back at Blackwood, Nye parked me in his office while he disappeared into one of the conference rooms. Janelle slipped in a few minutes later, looking worried.

"I'm sorry about the other day," she said.

"Don't be. Max should have told me. I mean, you knew, and I bet Nye did, and even Jason knew. I'd have found out sooner or later." And sooner was better, even if it didn't feel like it right now. How much more painful would it have been in three months? Six?

She leaned down and patted my arm. "I should

have been more tactful. Nye's always telling me to think before I open my big mouth."

"That's not very nice."

"Well, maybe not in so many words, and besides, he's right. Can I get you anything? Coffee? Tea?"

"A box of tissues and the entire Cadbury factory?"

She chuckled and squeezed my shoulder. "I'll see what I can do."

She came back a few minutes later with supplies. "Here's the tissues. The boss's nutritionist's been on the rampage again, so I couldn't find any chocolate in the kitchen, but then I remembered the boxes in Max's drawer. Here you go."

She dropped an armful of truffles and Turkish delight, the expensive kind, and I burst into tears.

"Oh shit. I did it again, didn't I?"

Yes. Yes, she did.

Janelle beat a hasty retreat, leaving me to dry my eyes until Nye came back half an hour later. By then, I'd settled into one of the big leather chairs and discovered a remarkable fascination with an abstract painting on the far wall.

"What's happening?" I asked, dragging my eyes away from the blue-and-purple swirls.

"The Florist's under guard in hospital. Thanks to the rope and the lily, they've managed to find a judge who'll grant a search warrant now. That'll give them enough for a conviction."

"How do you know? What if it doesn't?"

"Trust me."

"I'm not sure I want to. Not after your lack of openness last time."

"Yeah, sorry about that. Look, the prison thing was

a long time ago. Max has changed since then, although we've seen the biggest difference since you came on the scene."

I took a deep breath. "What did he do?"

"I don't know, exactly. He doesn't work directly for me, so I don't have access to his personnel records." He held his hands up. "I'd tell you if I did, honestly."

"How could he get a job here with that kind of history?"

"You'd be surprised. In this industry, the people who fight crime best are often those with knowledge of its inner workings. He's not the first person we've employed with a record, and he won't be the last."

"I'm not sure that's the answer I wanted."

"It's the only one there is."

"He scared me tonight."

"He scared everyone. Including Andrew Burns, which was a good thing."

"How did he know it was him? I mean, we were sitting there drinking tea when Max burst through the door like a man possessed."

"Because I called and told him so. At that point, we needed to find you fast, and Suki said you were alone in the shop. I tried calling, but you didn't pick up. Max was nearest, and when we couldn't get an answer from Mike out the back, Max came for you."

Dammit. I was never putting my phone on silent again. Poor Mike. He'd got mixed up in this through no fault of his own as well. And from the way Andrew took him out, I had little doubt I'd have soon been next.

"But how did you know? Jason told Suki they didn't have many leads."

"Jason shared information with us. He shouldn't

really have done it, so I'd appreciate you keeping it quiet, but he was aware there are certain rules we bend that the police can't."

"Like what?"

Nye sighed. "The need for search warrants. Little things like that. Look, let me get a coffee and I'll start at the beginning. You want another cup?"

"I might as well. Anything to warm up."

A few minutes later, he returned with a cafetière and a blanket. I wrapped myself in it, wishing I wasn't still wearing a bloody corset again, while he perched on the edge of his desk and began his story.

"The police tracked down the shop that sold Poppy's vase, but the shop assistant didn't remember who bought it."

"I know that part. Jason told Suki."

He rolled his eyes. "Good to hear his breaches of confidentiality extend beyond us. Anyhow, I paid a visit as well, and the cops were right. The assistant barely remembered her own name, and they didn't have CCTV in the shop. The manager knew he'd bought the vase two days before Poppy's death because of the till data, but that was the most useful thing I got. At least until I went outside."

"What happened then?"

"I stopped to give a few quid to a homeless man a couple of doors up and asked him if he happened to see our guy. Turned out he remembered The Florist quite well. Or the tight-fisted asswipe, as he called him."

"Why, what did he do?"

"Hooded guy walked out the shop carrying a bag, and when the homeless man asked if he had any spare change, the idiot spat his gum into the cup he held out and told him to get off the street because he made the neighbourhood untidy."

"I agree with the homeless man—what an asswipe."

"Exactly. Anyway, the guy still had the paper cup and the gum, crumpled up in his trolley. Which meant we had DNA. And he also got a good look at The Florist's face when he bent down to commit his act of utter asswipery."

"So he was able to describe him?"

"Oh, it gets better. Before Davey—that's the homeless guy—before Davey's wife left him and he ended up on the streets, he studied art at college. I brought him back here and gave him lunch and a sketch pad, and he was only too happy to draw us a picture of The Florist. It was really good. I'm tempted to frame it."

I'd be tempted to burn it. If I never saw that man's face again, it would be too soon. "And it looked like Andrew?"

"One of my colleagues recognised him from the business pages of the morning paper. Andrew just did a massive deal to sell his company."

"He mentioned that while we were drinking tea. He and his wife were about to emigrate to Bali."

Nye nodded, settling back into his leather chair. "No extradition treaty. Figures."

Realisation dawned. "So once he left, he'd never have been convicted? I was one of the loose ends he said he needed to tie up." I shuddered, thinking how close I'd been to meeting my maker.

"I'd say so. We knew we were on the right lines when one of my colleagues checked his medical records and found he had a vasectomy six years ago."

"You can do that? Go through medical records?"

"You didn't hear me say that part. Or the next bit."

"What did you do?"

"Once we'd worked out he was at the office and his wife had gone to an aerobics class, I popped around to his house and took a quick look inside."

"You broke in?"

"Not broke. I picked the lock carefully."

I felt like laughing hysterically at his lip service to the law, but I could hardly complain. After all, the dead couldn't speak, could they? "And?"

"He keeps some interesting trinkets in his desk drawer."

"Like what?"

"A silver rose necklace like the one you reported missing, a lock of red hair, a keychain with a sprig of heather embedded in it, a woman's ring, and a photo of you."

"Could you pass the bin, please?"

He held it out. "Why?"

Once I'd finished throwing up the gooey remains of the Turkish delight, Nye handed me a wad of tissues. "Should I go on?"

I sat back in the chair, feeling a little faint. "You might as well. I don't think there's anything left inside me." Between them, Max and Andrew had done a good job of relieving me of both my heart and my soul.

"He also had a pen in there with his ex-business partner's name on it. Did you know he died a few years ago?"

"Rose told me about it. He was working late one evening and fell down the stairs."

"And broke his neck."

My eyes widened. "Oh my gosh. You think Andrew killed him as well?"

"It's a theory. And he's certainly gained financially from his death, after the deal to sell Mediforce. It made big bucks." He gave a low whistle. "Profitable business, medical compliance software."

Wasn't it just? So Andrew was stinking rich as well. I wanted to scream with the injustice of it all. "Now what?"

"The police will take a DNA sample, and when they match it to the skin under Poppy's fingernails, that'll connect him to one death for certain. Once they go through the house, tying him to the rest should be easy as long as they don't balls up the paperwork."

"And Steve Macklin?"

"Burns knew he'd had a vasectomy because Macklin took time off work, and we reckon he used that information to frame him. It was pure dumb luck when Macklin got pulled in for questioning while Burns was out killing Poppy. Macklin also admitted to having an alibi for two of the other incidents, although I bet girlfriend number one won't be happy to hear about girlfriend number two."

"Ouch. Did they find Kramer?"

"Trout fishing in the Lake District. Apparently, it helps him to relax. We may have taken a quick look at his medical records too. Turns out that scar really was from a gym injury—he had a tough workout and ended up with testicular torsion." Nye's hands went to his lap, presumably as a reflex action, and he grimaced. "Poor guy. The doctors had to go in and untwist things."

Yeuch. What a mess. So many lives affected by one nutcase, although if Steve was cheating on two women,

I didn't have an awful lot of sympathy.

"And what about Max? What'll happen to him? Will he get punished for hurting Andrew?"

"Doubt it. They've already let him go."

My heart did a little skip and then stood still. "Is he coming back here?"

"Don't think so. The boss is in town, and she picked him up. Nobody's heard from them since."

In part, it hurt that he'd disappeared without even speaking to me, but I also felt relief. What would I say to him? I wanted to thank him for saving me again, but I also couldn't forget his past actions.

His vanishing act gave me the space I needed to think.

CHAPTER 28

TWO WEEKS LATER, and the memories of The Florist had started to dim, not significantly, but more like a puff of cloud passing in front of the sun. One day, they'd burn themselves out—at least that was the hope I clung onto.

But Max? His light would never fade. Every time I closed my eyes, the hurt was still there, sharp as ever.

"Ready to go?" Suki asked.

"Two minutes."

Heading into December, Christmas shopping season was in full swing in London, and Saturday was always our busiest day. The reporters we'd spoken to weeks before had kept their word, and a series of features in the press meant the shop was more crowded than ever. We'd already sold out of the new white-fur-trimmed corset I'd debuted last week. Brenda had recruited another member of her needlepoint group to help permanently, taking our little team up to six.

Now all I had to do was plaster a smile on my face and pretend to be cheerful while my heart broke, every damn day.

There was no sign of Max for the first week, not even a whisper, and my calls went straight to voicemail. Nye kept me updated with happenings on the case, and he said the boss had recruited Max onto one of her special projects and he hadn't been in the office. Nobody knew when he'd be back.

Then my stuff arrived by courier at the shop. Every last thing, from the half-finished corsets to the boxes of Turkish delight from his kitchen cupboard. I cried in the toilet while Suki stacked them in the back room, and they'd stayed there ever since. They made me think of the good times, and remembering those made the bad times seem even worse.

I'd even taken a ride past the house in Holland Park one day last week, just to see if I could catch a glimpse of him, but the security shutters were down on every window. Either he'd gone away or he was holed up in darkness. I wasn't sure which would be worse. As the cab paused outside, I'd been tempted to hop out and ring the bell, but fear held me back. Fear that Max would send me away. The way he'd rejected me hurt like hell, but if he did it in person, I might as well head straight for the nearest cemetery and jump into my own grave. How could I live with an obliterated heart?

At least there was a resolution to my flat nightmare in place. Nye had arranged for the door to be replaced, and the landlord agreed that if I paid half the rent for the rest of my term up front, he'd release me from the contract. I'd been there each evening this week, going through my stuff, packing up the few bits I wanted to keep, and carting the rest to the charity shop down the road. Another couple of days and I'd be done.

My final tangible reminder of The Florist, gone. From what Jason told me, the police had a watertight case. Andrew's DNA came back a match, and they'd found his sick souvenirs right where Nye said they'd be. Confronted with the evidence, Andrew had decided to take the coward's way out and plead insanity.

"He just sits there babbling," Jason said a few days ago. "I know I'm supposed to remain professional at all times, but I really want to punch him."

"How can he be insane? He ran a successful business for years, he held meetings, he even got married. Everyone thought he was perfectly normal."

"He's not crazy, he's smart. A highly intelligent sociopath with a good lawyer is the worst kind of criminal to deal with, hands down."

"So, do you think he'll get away with it?"

"He'll get locked up all right, but I'm worried he'll go to a holiday camp rather than the hole he deserves."

And that thought made me furious. Once or twice, I'd caught myself wishing Max had pressed on his neck a little harder, for a little longer, but then I got angry for having those thoughts. Max didn't deserve to suffer for Andrew's crimes any more than he already had.

"Today's going to be a good day, I can feel it," Suki announced as we left her place. "The jewellery shop three doors up is having a pre-Christmas sale. I thought I'd buy something for the dinner tonight."

"They've got some lovely pieces. That red-and-gold necklace in their window is beautiful."

"Do you think that'd go with my dress?"

"Definitely."

After giving him the cold shoulder for almost a week, Suki had finally let Jason back into her life. It was for the best. There were only so many angst-ridden cocktail sessions I could take. And me? I'd refined my depression into one glass of red and four cubes of Turkish delight per evening.

Tonight, Jason was taking Suki to his Christmas

party, and despite the number of police officers in attendance, I had a horrible feeling it would be carnage. I'd sewn a label into the back of her outfit with my phone number on just in case she turned up somewhere she shouldn't, and I kept my fingers and toes crossed she wouldn't do anything she'd regret in the morning.

The day went quickly, helped by the party atmosphere on the street, and Suki dashed off as soon as I put the "closed" sign into the window.

"See you later," she called. "Don't wait up."

"Wasn't planning on it."

I no longer had any fear as I hopped onto the Tube back to Paddington. Max had eliminated that for me with his final act. I desperately needed to thank him, but I'd rewritten the letter I planned to send twenty times over and I still hadn't found the right words. Maybe I never would.

Heart heavy in my chest, I opened my new front door and flicked on the light. Whoever Nye got to fix it did an excellent job. Honestly, if you didn't know half the wall had been missing two weeks ago, you'd never be able to tell. I tossed my handbag onto the kitchen counter and stepped into the lounge.

Then stopped.

What was that smell?

The faint whiff of tobacco smoke drifted in from the bedroom, tickling my nose. Bloody hell! Tell me I didn't have another sodding visitor?

I grabbed the nearest heavy object, the hideous

lamp Rose had brought back for me from Magaluf the year before last, and tiptoed through to my former resting place.

"You might as well put that down," the woman said without bothering to look at me. She was out on the fire escape, puffing away.

"Who the hell are you?"

She turned, her face catching in the glow from a street lamp, and I recognised Max's boss. Only this time her hair was lighter—platinum blonde instead of the darker honey colour she'd worn before. She stubbed her cigarette out on the railing and walked inside.

"I haven't touched these things since I was fifteen. It's been a hell of a month."

"You know they'll kill you?"

"They'll have to get in line." She crumpled up the packet and threw it at the bin in the corner of the room, scoring a perfect bullseye despite the dim light.

"What are you doing here?"

"A favour."

"What kind of favour?"

"Max mentioned there were a few issues with an asshole of a lawyer and an insanity defence."

"You've spoken to Max?"

"He's not in a good place." She smiled brightly, at complete odds with her previous expression. "Mr. Burns is in a worse place."

A feeling of dread built in the pit of my stomach. "What happened?"

"We had a little chat. Max, like the rest of us, was curious why Burns did what he did. What makes a respectable figure suddenly turn into a serial killer? Is it something that's always there, lurking in the background? What does it take to flick the switch? It's always fascinated me."

"Jason said he wouldn't talk."

With one smooth movement, she hopped up to sit on the kitchen counter.

"Every man will talk. You simply need to ask the right questions."

"And you did that?"

"Sweetheart, I'm the fucking quizmaster."

I sat down on the one remaining seat in the flat, a kitchen stool I wasn't quite sure what to do with. "So why? Why did he do it?"

"Most motives in this world boil down to one of three things: sex, money, or revenge. People claim to kill for other reasons, but when you get right into the nitty-gritty, it's those three. They dress it up with ideological bullshit, but that's all it is. Bullshit."

"So, which one did Andrew kill for?"

"Two, actually. Money first, then he discovered he had a taste for the sex part."

"I feel sick."

"If you need to puke, go right ahead. I can wait." She glanced at her watch, suggesting waiting would be a hardship.

I swallowed down the bile and gritted my teeth. "I'll hold it."

"Attagirl. Well, our friend Andrew knew Mediforce had a good product when sales took off a few years ago. He celebrated the first big contract the company landed by shoving his business partner off the sixth-floor landing. Apparently, his neck made a hell of a crack when he landed."

Deep breaths. Deep breaths. Keep it down.

"So the company was his. Almost. He had a bit of a problem. When your sister started working there, it was a tiny start-up and money was tight. A couple of months he couldn't even afford to pay her salary, but she stuck by him anyway. As a thank you, the next month it happened, he paid her in share options."

I vaguely remembered those days. I'd been surviving on student loans, and Rose came around every evening for beans on toast. So many times, I'd urged her to get a different job, but she'd still been in her Andrew-is-a-god phase and wouldn't hear of it. Try as I might, I couldn't recall her mentioning share options. "Options is where you get the right to buy shares in the company at a set price, isn't it?"

"Exactly. They have to vest first, either after a certain time or a particular event. Rose's vested on the sale of the company. If she'd exercised them, she'd have owned ten percent."

"And Andrew didn't want her to have it?"

She shook her head. "He said, and I quote, some dumb blonde shouldn't get what he worked for just because he'd been in a tight spot eight years ago."

"That bastard!"

"He soon regretted the 'dumb blonde' comment, believe me."

"And then he tried to kill me because he thought I might be able to identify him?"

"Apparently you walked in right as your sister breathed her last."

I heaved myself off the stool and ran, and I barely made it to the bathroom before lunch came up. Dammit. I didn't want to look weak in front of that woman. She was like fucking tungsten.

"You know you could take lessons in tact from Janelle?" I told her, half expecting to get my head bitten off.

"You're not the first person to say that. And Janelle's got better over the years. Did you know she told the last prime minister he could do with spending more time in the gym?"

"Are you serious?"

"Yeah. He wasn't her biggest fan after that. Anyway, sorry about Rose."

"It's okay." At least I was getting the answers I needed. The closure. "Did Andrew mention Dahlia? She got killed first."

"Practice run. That's when he came up with the idea for the flower gimmick. She had a vase of dahlias in her bedroom."

My eyes widened. "He killed a woman for practice?"

"He's whacked."

"And Heather and Poppy for fun?"

"He told me, 'There's no feeling more powerful than watching the light drain from a woman's eyes, knowing I was the one to extinguish it.' Fuck it. I forgot the tact again."

I'd got used to her bluntness by now. I still hated it, but I'd gone beyond vomiting. "And what about the break-ins? Were they Andrew as well?"

"Yup. He destroyed all his paperwork for the share options, but your sister still had her option certificate. He needed it back, but he couldn't find it."

"So if she'd lived, and she found it, she'd have got some money from the sale?"

"Precisely. You know, the options most likely pass

on to her heir. You might want to look for it."

"We already tore both flats apart, and I don't remember seeing anything like that." In fact, I couldn't recall any paperwork at all. Rose ran her banking online, and her post went straight in the shredder because she was paranoid about identity theft. One of her friends had a credit card stolen and ended up paying a fortune in top-ups for a mobile phone she didn't own.

"Look again. It might be easier now you've got a clue what you're searching for. And have a word with the company's lawyer. The money's in escrow at the moment, and you don't want it to get released."

"I don't even know where to start with that."

"I'll get someone to call you on Monday. He'll help."

"Thank you." She slid down from the counter and headed for the door. Then I thought of another question. "Why did you come?"

"To give you the news about Andrew."

"I get that, but why? You don't even know me, and you're obviously busy. Why would you take the time?"

She sighed and turned back. "Max asked me to. He wanted you to have the answers."

"You've spoken to Max?"

"I don't have a choice seeing as he's camped out in my house, gracing everybody with his misery."

"He's still upset?"

"Sweetheart, you fucking slayed him when you left."

"I didn't feel great about it myself, but he kept something really big from me."

She stepped back and leaned against the counter. "Do you know why he killed the man he killed?"

"No one could tell me." But I bet she knew.

"He raped Max's sister."

I went faint and clutched the stool for support, but she wasn't done.

"Max was fifteen at the time. Fleur was fourteen. Some bastard held her down and stole her innocence, and she was so scared she wouldn't report it. Fourteen, but she looked twelve. She'd spent half her childhood being treated for leukaemia."

"What happened? Afterwards?" I whispered.

"Max hunted down the animal that did it and punched him until his brain popped." She shrugged. "I'd have done the same. Max got three years in juvie after the judge took mitigating circumstances into account. I'd have given him a fucking medal."

"Where's his sister now? Max barely mentioned her. She didn't...?"

"Paris. Max doesn't know she's there, but I keep an eye on her. After he got arrested, his parents disowned him for bringing shame upon the family. Told him never to contact any of them again."

"How could they do that? To a fifteen-year-old boy? To their own child?"

"Because the world's full of fucked-up people. Trust me, I know. I'm one of them." She gave a hollow laugh, and I didn't doubt what she said for a second.

"What happened when he got out of prison? I'm surprised he didn't look for her anyway."

"Believe me, I've done that one to death with him. His parents fucked him in the head. But you know what it really is? He's scared. Scared that if he finds Fleur, she'll reject him, so he'd rather keep her as a memory."

"So that's it? He gave in?"

"Max has self-esteem issues."

"But he shouldn't. Once you get past his outer-asshole, he's the kindest man you'll ever meet."

"Juvie didn't help him. Once he got out, he lived in the dark, and he'd have ended up back inside soon enough. But I run a charity and an acquaintance of mine referred him there, and I saw he only wanted to protect people. So I trained him as a bodyguard. He's a bloody good one when he keeps his demons under control."

She walked over to the window and stared out into the night. I used to do the same thing, hoping to see the stars, but in London, they were usually hidden from view.

"He was so angry when I first met him, but he's changed. And the biggest change came all at once after he met you."

That's what Nye said too. "I think I might have made a really big mistake."

"About time you realised that." She turned back to face me. "Take a look in the mirror. Nobody's perfect, honey. Not me, not you. See all those jagged edges? The only thing that matters in life is finding the person who slots into yours."

"Can you tell me where he is?"

She gave me a half-smile, a genuine one, and it softened her whole face. "I'll take you to him."

Chapter 29

THE BLONDE WOMAN whose name I still didn't know tore the parking ticket off the window of her Aston Martin and lowered herself into the driver's seat. I took the other side, inhaling the rich smell of leather.

"Bad luck. The wardens lurk on every corner around here."

She shrugged. "I get one most days. Sometimes two. My record is six in twenty-four hours, but I'm sure I'll beat it sooner or later." Without further ado, she mashed her foot on the accelerator and squealed away from the kerb.

"Are you trying to get a speeding ticket too?"

"Might as well go for the full set."

After a hair-raising journey through Belgravia, she pulled through a set of imposing metal gates, along a short drive, and into an underground garage. I'd thought Max's home was impressive, but this place made his look like a Wendy house.

Once she'd turned off the engine, she led me past a row of equally expensive cars to a lift in the corner, a setup reminiscent of Blackwood. "I don't know where he is, but I'd guess at the gym. That's where he's been spending most of his time."

She was right. I heard the *thunk, thunk, thunk* of fists on leather as we rounded a corner, then she opened a door and he stood in front of me, bare-chested and gorgeous.

He did a double take when he spotted us, and the woman backed away.

"Play nicely, kids."

He took a step towards me, tentative, then spoke first. "What are you doing here?"

"That woman came to see me."

"Emmy?"

So that was her name. "She went to visit Andrew."

"I know."

"Will she get into trouble?"

"No chance. She's careful." He shook his head ruefully. "More careful than me."

"What you did saved my life, and I need to thank you, and..." All the words I'd spent days thinking about fled from my mind, leaving only three. "I love you."

"What?" he whispered.

"I..." Was this a terrible idea? "Love you."

He covered the ground between us faster than I thought possible and swept me off my feet.

"Really?"

I nodded, and his smile came back, the one I'd missed seeing for so long. Then he kissed me. Long, deep, and sweet, a richness I felt from my toes to my tongue. I'd left my body and travelled skywards by the time he pulled back.

"I thought I'd lost you," he whispered, laying his forehead against mine.

"I didn't understand. About your sister. Emmy told me."

He didn't say anything, and his face stayed still until a single tear rolled down his cheek. Even though his expression was blank, pain leached from his eyes.

"You miss her, don't you?"

"She had half my heart. Then you took the rest."

A lump came into my throat, and I wrapped my arms around him as tightly as I could. "How about you have mine instead?"

He nodded solemnly. "I'll look after it. I promise."

"I know you will. Do you want to go home?"

Another nod.

"To our home?" I asked, hoping.

"I'd like that. Lily?"

"Yes?"

"I love you."

Before I could melt onto the floor, he swept me into his arms, pausing only to grab a set of car keys from a lockbox in the garage as he carried me out to the car. His driving speed rivalled Emmy's as he floored it through the London streets, but when we got home, he changed pace and gave it to me slow and sweet.

As I drifted off to sleep that night, my chest felt full for the first time in weeks. I might have handed Max my heart, but he'd given me his in return.

Max woke me up on Sunday morning with a sweet kiss, a smile, and a glass of orange juice.

"Sorry, I don't have coffee anymore. I sent it all back to you. And the coffee machine."

"We've got bigger problems than that."

"What?"

"I don't have any clothes."

He crinkled his brow in that adorable way of his.

"But you don't need any."

Not when he looked at me like that, I didn't. Hey, if the worst came to the worst, I could make something out of a bed sheet, toga-style. Or wear one of Max's shirts, crisp, white, and smelling of him.

"That's a good answer. Put the drink down and come back to bed."

He grinned at me, eyes gleaming. "I still have ties."

"That's all we need."

Today's was dark green and made from silk. I expected Max to bind my wrists again, but instead, he blindfolded me.

"Lie back and relax, sweet Lily," he instructed.

Relax? How could I relax when his tongue was stroking its way across my breasts, teasing my nipples before heading downwards? He swiped it over my most sensitive spot and I gripped the sheets, unable to stop myself from crying out. He took me to the edge, then let me step back before pushing me forward again. Just as I could take no more, I heard the rip of foil and he pushed inside me, right where I wanted him to be.

"This is home," I whispered.

"Our home."

I was deliciously exhausted when we made it downstairs for a late lunch. Rather than the toga idea, I'd borrowed Max's bathrobe—soft, grey, and fluffy, even if he didn't yet have a bath to go with it.

"I missed you so much. I missed this," I said, taking my place on the stool while Max fired up the gas.

"Same. Even if I did get breakfast made for me

every morning in Emmy's palace."

"Who cooked? Her?" Somehow, I couldn't imagine that.

"Not likely. She'd kill us all. No, she has a housekeeper."

"I'll try and learn the basics. Maybe I could take lessons?"

"You don't need to. I like cooking for you."

"I want to feel useful. You know, contribute something."

Rent too, but we'd have that discussion another day.

Max took a break and came over to cuddle me. "You do. You bring happiness, heart, and soul into this house, and that's more than enough for me."

"Did I mention I love you?"

His smile got so wide I worried it might crack his jaw. "Yes, but I'll never get sick of hearing it."

"I love you."

After lunch, we made a quick detour to the bedroom again, and then it was time to face up to the practicalities.

"I really do need some clothes. If I turn up to work tomorrow wearing the same clothes I wore yesterday, you'll be able to hear Suki's shriek in King's Cross."

"I've got earplugs."

"I'm serious." I threw a pillow at him. "At the very least, I need some underwear, and don't suggest Rigby & Peller again because they'll be closed by now. Not to mention the cost."

"Fine. We'll pick up your stuff. Where is it?"

"I've got some at Suki's, more at my flat, and the boxes you sent over are still at the shop."

"Where do you want to start?"

"Suki's, I guess. She'll be glad to have her sofa back, even if she is spending half her time with Jason." I had another thought. "I could do with picking Rose's things up from storage as well, if you don't mind having them here."

He leaned over to kiss me. "The house is as much yours as it is mine now."

Yep. I definitely loved him.

We got to Suki's flat in the early evening, but there were no signs of life. Still, she'd sent me a misspelled text message at eleven this morning to say she'd made it to Jason's, so I knew she was safe. I packed my things into carrier bags plus a borrowed suitcase, and Max carried them downstairs.

"Car's full. Do you have enough for a few days?"

"Really?" I surveyed the piles of clothes still on the couch. "I didn't realise I had so much stuff."

How had I ever managed to bring it all here on my own? Desperation had given me a strength I never knew I had, but moving house with Max gave me the security I never realised I needed.

"We can do another trip if you want to. Or come back tomorrow."

"Tomorrow's fine. Is it pizza night?"

"It's whatever night you want it to be."

Suki's shriek the next morning didn't quite reach King's

Cross, but the people in Soho certainly raised their heads. "You've got back with Max!"

"How do you know?" I hadn't even said "good morning."

"You've got this big stupid grin on your face. You only ever got that with Max. So, tell me, am I wrong?"

"You're not wrong."

"This is fantastic! Oh, it's been such a great weekend. You got back with Mr. Grumpy, and I managed to stay upright doing the conga down Brick Lane."

"I'm not sure I want to know. You got home safely, that's all that matters."

"I even got to ride in a police car."

I looked up sharply. "You didn't get arrested, did you?"

"No, it was shift change and they were going in that direction."

My phone rang before I could chastise her over misuse of public funds. Unknown number. Usually, I let those calls go straight to voicemail, but what if it was Max calling from the office?

"Hello?"

"My name's Oliver Rhodes. Emmy asked me to give you a call." His accent was American, kind of posh, confident.

"Are you the lawyer?"

"That's right. Just to let you know, I've spoken to the firm acting for Mediforce. They've agreed to hold a portion of the sale money back for three months while you look for that option certificate, in light of the situation with Mr. Burns."

"That's kind of you to organise, but I'm pretty sure

it's gone." Which was a shame. A few quid would come in handy, seeing as Rose's life insurance cheque was currently police evidence and the insurance company was dragging their heels about issuing a new one.

"You never know. People often lose things only for them to turn up in the strangest of places. The money's there in case you do locate it." He reeled off a number for me to call in that unlikely event, and I scribbled it down on the back of my sketch pad.

"Thank you."

When I hung up, I felt more frustrated than ever. Rose had died for that money, and in three months, Andrew would get it anyway.

"Suki, do you remember any papers in Rose's flat?"

"I think there was a copy of *Heat* magazine on the coffee table."

"Nothing else?"

"Sorry. Is it important?"

In the great scheme of things? Rose was gone and no amount of cash would bring her back. And I had Max now. As long as we had enough to live on, that was all that mattered.

"No, not really."

CHAPTER **30**

FINALLY, THE MOVE was complete. Another day gone, and the last of my scattered belongings were safely ensconced in the fourth bedroom. I'd stacked the boxes and bags as best I could, but the messy pile still made me groan. Who knew I'd accumulated that much stuff? But unpacking could wait. Everything could wait, because Max was home and I had a hot itch between my legs that only he knew how to scratch.

"Champagne?" Max asked, leaning against the doorjamb, more relaxed than I'd ever seen him. Not just his attire—soft jeans and a cashmere jumper—but his posture. Some of that tension he'd always carried in his shoulders had flittered away.

I looked at the bottle in his hand. "You bought Cristal?"

"The shop assistant said it was the best kind."

"Damn right it is." I'd only ever drunk it once before, when Suki got hammered and accidentally bought a bottle in a nightclub. We'd both lived on spaghetti hoops for the next month to pay for it. "But why?"

"Because you're properly moved in now, which makes this officially the best day of my life."

I'd run out of space for ticks in the "sweet" column, and only added a handful to "asshole."

"Give me a few minutes to get my breath back, and I'll make it even better."

His response was to kiss me, fast and hard. "Hurry up."

Asshole.

Two days later, I already felt as if I'd lived with Max forever.

"Would you get a move on?" he called.

"It's not my fault you don't have enough hair to blow-dry."

Tonight was Max's work Christmas party, being held at the ridiculously posh Black Diamond Hotel somewhere in Kensington. And at that moment, I envied his ability to look obscenely sexy two minutes after stepping from the shower.

He strode in, wearing his tuxedo, while I hopped around trying to do my dress up with one hand and hunt for my blingy Swarovski necklace with the other. Yes, I know I should have done it earlier, but I was busy. And that was all Max's fault.

"You look beautiful. The car'll be here in ten minutes." Not content with taking a cab, Max had hired a freaking limo.

"I'm only half in my dress. Can you help with the zip?"

"Which way? Up or down?"

I rolled my eyes at him. "It depends whether you want to go to this party."

He opted for up, and I confess to being a little disappointed. Now I just needed to find my necklace.

"Car's here," he shouted up the stairs a few minutes later.

"Almost ready." I'd resorted to rummaging through the boxes in the spare room, just in case. When did I last wear the sodding thing? From the photos on the hotel website, the ballroom at the Black Diamond called for designer outfits, sparkles, and fancy shoes, but so far, I'd only managed to find a smaller, less flashy pendant, and the left side of the bedroom looked like a tornado had swept through it.

Max's footsteps sounded on the stairs. Dammit! I'd just try one last bag before I gave up. I dumped the contents out on the floor, only to find I didn't recognise any of it. Where did it come from?

I sank to my knees as I realised it must be that bag of Rose's Damien brought back all those weeks ago. Every time I thought I was starting to get over her death, something like this brought the nightmare home again. A pair of her earrings, a snakeskin belt, a...what was this?

Hiding under a Scooby Doo T-shirt, I found an envelope, Rose's neat printing proclaiming it to be "work stuff."

No way! It couldn't be? I tore it open, in a hurry to see what she'd kept.

"Lily, we really need to go. What's that?"

"I don't know. I found it in a bag of Rose's things."

He picked up one of the sheets and started reading. "I think we've found our missing option certificate."

I leaned over his shoulder. "Really?"

"Really. Looks like we've got a reason to party tonight."

The words stared out at me. Rose, or her

representative, was entitled to buy ten shares for five hundred pounds each if Mediforce got sold. Ten shares didn't sound like much, but the purchase price did.

"I don't have five thousand pounds."

"If they're worth exercising, I'll give you the money. But we're late."

The boring necklace would have to do. Max fastened it around my neck, and I tucked the certificate back into its envelope. It had been there long enough— another few hours wouldn't hurt.

When Max told me Emmy's assistant knew how to organise a party, he wasn't kidding. The guy had flown a dance troupe in from Las Vegas, and each table had its own teppanyaki chef. We were seated with Nye and Olivia, Janelle and her girlfriend, plus Zander and a voluptuous blonde who left after the main course when he accidentally called her by the wrong name. Undeterred, he simply took out his phone and a replacement arrived in time for dessert.

Olivia giggled and rolled her eyes. "That's so Zander. He has a different girl every day of the week."

"He seems quite charming."

"Oh, he's got a silver tongue, and apparently he knows how to use it."

Max had a platinum tongue, but I wasn't about to announce that in public. Some things were better kept to myself. "I love your dress. Where did you get it?"

"Ishmael. He's just opened up a shop in London. Did you make yours? It's beautiful."

"Yes, I love making clothes."

"I'm so jealous. I can't even knit. All I can do is make cakes, but if I eat too many, I get fat."

"I'd love to be able to bake. I tried making pancakes the other day, but Max installed this hideously complicated monitoring system and when he came back from jogging, I had to explain why there was a fire engine on the drive."

And half a dozen firemen. Always the enterprising one, Suki had convinced the whole group to strip down to their T-shirts so she could take photos of them posing with their hoses.

"Oh dear. If you like, I can show you how to make simple cupcakes? I've got a foolproof recipe."

"I'm not sure it'll be Lily-proof."

"You won't know unless you try."

"Okay. I'd love to. Do they have frosting?"

"Of course."

And so that night, I made a new friend. Olivia may not have been as impulsive or adventurous as Suki, but she understood what it was like to have a boyfriend who felt compelled to do a dangerous job and work all hours at it. I had a feeling we'd be spending more time together in future.

Between my hangover, a cookery lesson, dinner made by Olivia, Suki's tales of what exactly Jason did to her last night in excruciating detail, and a customer who took an hour and a half to decide between two outfits, it was almost lunchtime on Monday before I got around to calling Oliver.

"I found that certificate thing."

"Excellent. Shall I send someone to collect it?"

"Or I could just post it?"

And if he'd keep talking, that would be good. I could have listened to his smooth voice all day.

"It's better I send someone from Blackwood."

"I don't want to put you to any trouble."

Although that would save me a trip to the post office.

"It's no trouble."

A man in a Blackwood uniform turned up an hour later, and I remembered to ask for ID, just as Max always drilled into me. I was getting more used to his ways with every passing day, and his overprotectiveness had grown on me. Secretly, I loved the way he glared at any man who dared to let his eyes linger in my direction.

I didn't expect to hear from Oliver for ages, but he called me back in the middle of the afternoon while I was sharing a box of cupcakes with Suki and Olivia at Black Lily. Being in the shop still made me uncomfortable, but each day got a little easier, and I was determined not to let Andrew Burns win.

That American voice made my ears tingle again. "I've contacted Mediforce's lawyers and set things in motion. The terms of the agreement ask for five thousand pounds to exercise the options."

"Do you think they're worth that?" I echoed Max's words. "It's not like one of those scams where they promise to send you a million pounds if you send them an admin fee, is it?"

"I promise it's no scam."

"Max said he'd sort out the money."

"Max Tian?"

"Yes. Are you able to speak to him about it?"

"I can do that, yes. Are you happy for me to deal with all the paperwork on your behalf?"

"Please. I'm not sure I'd understand it anyway."

His chuckle sent funny vibrations through my core, and I couldn't help wondering what Oliver looked like. Oh, what a cruel twist it would be if he was sixty-five with a pot belly and bad breath. *Stop it, Lily! You're taken.*

"In that case, I'll get all the documents filed," he said.

"Thank you."

Two weeks before Christmas, the first snowstorm of the year swept through London in the early afternoon, causing chaos all over the city. Max had taken that Thursday off, so he came on the Tube to pick me up from work rather than battling his way on the roads.

As was his custom, he greeted me with a kiss. "I've got dinner ready to go in the oven, and I've bought a replacement pan for the one you burned the cakes in last weekend."

Another oops. I'd since done a deal with Olivia— she'd make me cakes, and I'd make her sexy undies.

"My hero."

"I picked up a Christmas tree too, and all the shit you put on it."

I hadn't had a tree for years, unless you counted the mini light-up plastic one Suki got me last year to plug into my laptop's USB port, which I didn't. Max had never had one. He'd always volunteered to work at

Blackwood on Christmas Day so others could be home with their families. This year it was his turn, and we'd decided to go all out with a tree, roast turkey, and silly jumpers.

"Lovely. We can decorate it after dinner."

Or we could if we were giants. "Oh, Max. Where on earth did you get this?"

He looked ever so pleased with himself. "Bethany has a friend who's working in the Harrods Christmas shop. She sorted it out for me, and the truck to deliver it."

"You didn't think a smaller one would be enough?"

"No."

Oh well. At least we wouldn't be stuck for firewood to go in his newly renovated fireplace. For, say, a year or two. It took us hours, but we finally got the damn thing decorated. Stars, baubles, tinsel—it had the lot. I got a bit worried about shorting out the entire house when we turned the lights on, but Max assured me he'd had the whole place rewired and the electrician was top notch.

And it looked fabulous.

Max stood behind me and put his arms around my waist. "It's beautiful, just like you."

"I don't have any prickly bits."

"Apart from when it's your time of the month."

"Shut up."

He chuckled and danced out of reach. "And even then, I still love you."

"Okay, you're forgiven. Can we go to bed now?"

"I have one thing left to do." He dropped his arms and took a red-and-gold stocking out of a slim box, then hooked it over one of the branches. Green lettering spelled out a name: Fleur. "It's for my sister. I hang it up every year. Even though I don't know where she is, I never stop thinking of her."

"That's a lovely thing to do."

He swiped at his eyes, and I understood how much she meant to him. I hadn't bought his Christmas gift yet, and I knew right then what I wanted to give him. Was it even possible?

Friday morning, I was late for work and had a to-do list that spanned two pages. Second from top was call Olivia, but first I needed to pay my damn credit card bill, and my internet banking wasn't playing ball. Why did technical glitches always happen when you were in a manic hurry?

"Max! My bank account's broken."

"The internet's working fine." He should know. He had a day off and was busy watching Netflix. "What's wrong with it?"

"The numbers have gone all stupid. It thinks I've got, like, eight million pounds."

He abandoned his box set of *Orphan Black* and peered over my shoulder. "It's arrived, then."

"What's arrived? What are you talking about?"

He took the mouse from me and clicked to expand the most recent transaction. The words "CHAPS transfer from Mediforce" glared back at me, a taunting reminder of everything Andrew had taken. Dread dripped down my insides like cold porridge.

Max pointed at the screen. "The money from those share options. Oliver said it would be a nice amount."

"You mean this is *real?*" All those zeroes... My shriek probably woke the astronauts on the space station, and once the noise died away, it was replaced by the hammering of my heart as it tried to shatter my ribcage.

Max only shrugged. "Yes."

"And you knew about this?"

Another shrug. "Yes."

"Why didn't you tell me?"

"I wanted it to be a surprise. Aren't you happy?"

"I'm..."

I didn't know what I was. It wasn't every day a girl found she'd become a millionaire eight times over. But that elation was tempered because it should have been Rose shrieking with me looking over her shoulder. No amount of money could make up for the loss of the sister I still missed with every breath. She'd always be a part of me. But at the same time, I couldn't live in the past.

"I'm happy to be here with you. That's the most important thing now."

CHAPTER 31

"ARE YOU SURE you need to go to work?" Max asked.

"I have a fitting appointment at ten. Completely unavoidable. And I promised Suki she could take the afternoon off, seeing as I snuck off early yesterday."

We'd gone to visit my mum in the nursing home. Max had offered to pick her up so she could have lunch with us on Christmas Day, but I'd wriggled out of that one in case today's crazy plan came to fruition. Luckily, Mum had helped me out there when she proudly introduced her new friend Albert. According to the nurses, they'd been getting on rather well and were looking forward to sharing a turkey dinner with homemade Christmas cake. Max barely got a look-in as Mum spent most of our visit mooning over an eighty-year-old with a comb-over. Sweet.

My first instinct had been to move Mum to a private home, somewhere fancy with gardens and more activities. But then I saw her with her friends, people who understood that her mind wandered and loved her anyway, and I didn't have the heart to make her start over. Instead, Max had helped me to negotiate a bigger room for a supplement, and thanks to Rose's money, all the residents would be going on more outings in future.

And now Max leaned over to the passenger side of his car and kissed me. "I'll pick you up at half five.

Don't be late."

"I won't."

"I love you, Lily."

"Love you too, Max."

Five to nine on Christmas Eve, and the street was already crowded with last-minute shoppers. I elbowed my way through them and into the door of Black Lily.

Suki was waiting, as were Brenda and our new assistant, Rhona.

"Is it here?" I asked Suki.

"Out the back."

I dashed into the fitting room and shed my corset as fast as humanly possible, trading it in for the pair of jeans and the polo neck that Suki had laid out for me. Then I tugged on a pair of sheepskin boots and dashed out the back door, Suki hot on my heels.

Olivia was already in the Mercedes, peering out of the half-open window. "Quick, hurry up! This is so exciting."

My plans to try and bring Max the ultimate Christmas present were eased tremendously by a liberal application of my newly acquired money and two friends, one new, one old. Suki had helped with the logistics while Olivia convinced Nye to do our legwork, even if he wasn't happy about going behind his friend's back.

Another of my corsets apparently did the trick, and he spent two days tracking down Fleur Tian. Thanks to Emmy, we already knew she was in Paris, and what better way to start celebrating Christmas than with a trip to Europe's capital of culture? An associate of Nye's from Blackwood's Paris office had been keeping an eye on Fleur, and another would meet us when we arrived.

It wasn't long before our car pulled up at London City Airport, next to the private jet Suki had arranged.

"It was a bit different to hiring a cab, I'll tell you that," she'd said after a dozen phone calls. "You practically have to promise your first-born before they'll give you the time of day."

But now the sleek white plane waited on the tarmac with the steps down, inviting us in. The three of us bid goodbye to our driver and hurried on board, where someone had thoughtfully provided a bottle of champagne and some nibbles.

"Shouldn't we save it for the way back?" I asked. "If everything goes okay?"

Suki was already twisting the cork. "We can buy more for the way back. It's bloody France. They've got loads of the stuff."

"And it's Christmas," Olivia added.

"Fair enough."

I needed something to steady my nerves. Was this the smartest thing I'd ever done or the stupidest? The jury was still out.

An hour later, we descended into Charles de Gaulle Airport. According to Nye, Fleur worked as a translator and lived alone in a small apartment near the Sorbonne. We'd done the easy bit—getting to Paris. Now, I just needed to speak to a girl I'd never met before, in a country I didn't know, and convince her to make her long-lost brother's Christmas by sending him a message or a card. Something. Anything.

The car glided through the streets, taking us ever closer to our destination. My worries built with every passing block, but I had one small advantage: after everything The Florist had done, it took more to rattle me than ever before.

"Are you sure you want to go in alone?" Olivia asked.

"I think it's best. I don't want to freak her out by having a whole gang of us turn up on her doorstep."

"She's still in her apartment," our driver reported. "Pierre is watching from a café nearby."

Ten minutes later, the car drew to a halt on a quiet side street. Pierre left his newspaper and his croissant and joined us, pointing at a lit window on the first floor of the building opposite. "Fleur is in that one. *Número cinq.*"

"*Merci.*"

I drew my coat around me and crossed the street, hating the fact I had to have this conversation through a door intercom. Of all the awkward... "Hello? I mean, *bonjour?*"

Dammit, I should have paid more attention in my high school French classes.

"Hello?"

"Fleur Tian?"

"*Oui.* Who is this?"

"Uh, you don't know me, but my name's Lily. I was hoping to talk to you about your brother."

"I don't have a brother."

Okay, good start. "Do I have the right person? It's about Max."

"What kind of cruel joke is this?"

"Er, it's not a joke."

"My brother died nine years ago. Go away and leave me alone."

The intercom light died. Dammit! I buzzed through again, but this time nobody spoke. I slumped down on the step and carried on talking anyway.

"Max isn't dead. He's alive, and I live with him in London. He counts every day that passes without seeing you off in his head, and each year he hangs up a Christmas stocking with your name on it. He once told me he only has half a heart, because the other half's with you, and there's something in him I can't fix because you're still missing from his life. He doesn't talk much about you because it hurts him, but I know he thinks about you all the time, and..." Silence, nothing but silence. So much silence. Now what? I couldn't give up, not when I'd flown hundreds of miles to flipping France.

A minute passed, and I pressed the button again, just in case.

"He cares about you—" The door opened behind me and I fell inside, only to find myself looking up at someone who was unmistakably Max's sister. "My gosh, you look just like him."

"Is it true?"

"Everything I said is true."

"Max is really alive?"

"Yes."

"You'd better come in."

I scrambled to my feet and gave a thumbs up to the car as I followed Fleur inside. Part one of the operation: complete.

"I can't believe this." Fleur stood at the window, staring out as Max often did. "My parents told me he died in prison."

"He got out eight years ago. He's been living in London since then."

She clenched her fists at her sides. "Just when I think my parents couldn't do anything else to hurt me, they do."

"Maybe they thought they were helping you?"

She turned on me, eyes flashing. "Never! They only ever thought of themselves. It was always Max who looked after me. I left their home on the eve of my eighteenth birthday, and I'll never go back."

"That sounds...drastic."

"If you had my parents, you'd have run too. All I was to them was cheap labour. I spent half of my childhood ill, and they never came to visit me in hospital, that's how much they cared. Only Max did. Eventually, the nurses felt so sorry for us they clubbed together to pay his bus fares."

My heart ached for teenage Max and Fleur too. My mum might have slowly succumbed to dementia, but there had been no shortage of love in our household.

"Max is still like that. He looks out for me all the time, so much that he sometimes drives me crazy. He's saved my life twice since we met. Three times if you count the day he stopped me from burning the kitchen down."

She laughed. "I miss his cooking." Then, more quietly, "He saved my life too. With a bone-marrow transplant."

"He's a special man."

"Do you think he'll speak to me? If I call or try to visit?"

"He'd be on a plane right now if he thought you wanted to see him."

"Really?"

I nodded. "And if he couldn't get a flight, he'd swim."

She stopped her vigil and walked towards a door on the far side of the room. "I need to see him. Too many years have been lost." She disappeared for a few minutes, then came back with a bag. "Can you give me his address?"

"I can do better than that. I have a plane waiting at the airport."

Her eyes widened. "Like, a whole plane?"

"It's a long story. Do you need to get more stuff? Can I help with anything?"

She paused for a second, then walked over to the tiny Christmas tree in front of her window and picked up a gift from underneath it.

"It's for Max."

"You bought him a gift?"

"I have done every year, except after Christmas I've always donated them to charity."

"I think that's a lovely idea."

"But this year I can finally give it to him."

There was a party atmosphere on the plane as we flew back. It turned out Suki had nipped to the supermarket while I was in with Fleur and cleaned them out of Veuve Clicquot, while Olivia contributed the contents of a patisserie.

"We need a plan," Suki announced. "You can't just wander in with Lily this evening. That would be so dull."

"I want to see Max," Fleur said.

I giggled, trying not to spill my champagne. "You sound exactly like him when you say that."

Fleur may have been the physical opposite of Max—petite with a sing-song voice and expressive hands—but she shared a lot of his facial expressions, and there were definite similarities in their attitudes. Both had the same underlying determination and suffered from a lack of self-esteem. Survivors, but they'd go it alone.

I'd seen it in the way Fleur looked at her feet when Suki and Olivia introduced themselves. Granted, Suki could be a little overpowering, but it had taken three glasses of champagne to get Fleur to loosen up enough to make eye contact. We'd have to work on that.

Olivia stepped in, the voice of reason. "One more day won't make much difference. You should give Max a proper Christmas surprise."

"I'm not sure..."

"I am. We should make this special."

Between copious amounts of alcohol and chocolate eclairs, we came up with a plan. A little vague, possibly, but hey, we had bubbles.

"You really think this will work?" Fleur asked, hiccuping.

"Oh yes," Suki said, swigging straight from the bottle. "It'll definitely work."

"Are you sure you don't want to tell me what my Christmas present is?" Max asked, slipping his arms around my waist as I attempted to peel potatoes.

I glanced up at the clock. "Five minutes. That's all

you'll have to wait. And you won't tell me what mine is either."

"Afterwards. I promise."

I checked the clock again. Where were they?

Then the bell rang, right on time.

"Go on." I pointed Max towards the hallway. "Your surprise is here."

He set off, and I quickly checked the back door was unlocked before catching up to him. So far, so good.

Max opened the front door, and his jaw dropped. "What the actual fuck?"

Just as planned, Suki stood on the doorstep with the live reindeer she'd borrowed from a friend of a friend. "Surprise!" she yelled, and the reindeer jumped a foot in the air and snorted.

"It certainly is that."

She gave him a twirl in her Santa outfit. "What do you think?"

"It's like I've died and gone to hell."

She totally ignored that. "Look, I've brought your gift." The reindeer started to walk backwards as she handed over a lumpy parcel. "Oops. Got to go."

The reindeer wandered towards the front gate while Suki followed helplessly behind, and Max shut the door. "Tell me I just imagined that?"

"Wasn't it cool? A real reindeer. So cute."

He rolled his eyes. "Should I open this now?"

"Go ahead."

He peeled off the wrapping, then stared at me. "Slippers?"

"You kept saying your feet were cold."

Out of the corner of my eye, I saw Fleur peep around the door of the study. Shit! She'd ended up in the wrong place. The map I drew on the back of a pastry box yesterday may have been a little wonky.

"Slippers?" he repeated.

"They're really nice ones. Bethany recommended them." We'd only just made it back to Black Lily in time yesterday after the detour to Harvey Nichols. "So, what's my present? You promised you'd tell me now."

I needed to distract him enough for Fleur to creep past us into the lounge. Dammit, we were terrible at this espionage stuff.

He shook his head then bent a little to kiss me. "You're crazy. It's a good thing I love you so much."

"Present?"

Shitting hell, Fleur, hurry up!

Max reached a hand into his pocket then drew it out, closed. Had he got me a really tiny gift? Not slippers, then.

Fleur ran across the hallway just as Max dropped to one knee in front of me. My eyes saucered. Bloody hell, was he serious?

"Lily Matthews, will you marry me?"

Fleur leaned out the doorway and gave me a fist pump. I felt a little wobbly.

"Er, this is all a bit unexpected."

He stayed down there, looking up at me expectantly, but a modicum of doubt crept into his eyes.

"Of course I will!"

I dropped to my knees beside him, and he slid a beautiful diamond onto my finger. Goodness only knows how much he'd spent on that. Still, we could afford it, thanks to Rose. I murmured a silent thank you skywards, just in case she could hear me, then met

Max's gaze again.

"Are you ready for your real surprise now?"

"What?"

"She's waiting in the lounge."

"Huh?"

"In the lounge, Max." I pressed a soft kiss to his lips. "Happy Christmas."

Oh, I felt like dancing as Max turned towards the lounge, brow furrowed. "Who's in the lounge? She?" He suddenly smiled. "Did you get a cat?"

A cat? Max hadn't mentioned having a cat before. Not once. I'd never had a pet, but a kitten would be super cute.

"You want a cat?"

"I wanted one when I was a kid, but my parents said no. Fleur always loved horses because that's the year she was born in."

"What year were you born in?"

He grinned. "Snake."

Figured. Hang on, why were we even having this conversation? Shaking my head, I shoved him in the direction of the lounge. If Fleur really wanted a horse, we could buy her one now, although I was pretty sure it wouldn't like living in London.

Speaking of Fleur, she was standing by the sofa, and a tentative smile flickered across her lips when Max crossed the threshold. He stopped dead, and I walked into the back of him. Oops. I gave him a shove.

He half turned. "Lily?"

"Go on." I nudged him again.

"Uh, surprise?" Fleur said, then burst into tears.

But they were happy tears, and my eyes felt kind of watery too.

"Fleur?" Max asked.

He didn't wait for an answer before he closed the gap between them and swept her up in his arms. The old saying about money was true—it couldn't buy happiness—but at moments like this, it came damn close.

"Max, I can't breathe," Fleur choked out.

"Sorry," he muttered, loosening his grip enough for her to touch her tiptoes to the ground. Fleur burrowed against his chest and wrapped her arms around his waist.

"I can't believe you're alive. Mum and Dad told me you died in..." She glanced across at me. "If I'd thought for one minute..."

"Don't worry. Lily knows. And let's forget about our parents, okay? They've never caused us anything but problems. The important thing is that we've found each other again, but I still don't understand how you got here."

Fleur pointed at me. "She arrived on my doorstep yesterday."

Max's forehead crinkled, and Fleur pushed the lines away with her thumbs. It looked as if it was an unconscious gesture, something she'd done before, which didn't surprise me. Although he hid it well, Max was a worrier.

And now he turned to me. "How? How did you find Fleur?"

"Emmy gave me the first clue, then Nye helped."

"Do you live close by?" he asked Fleur.

"Paris."

"But, Lily, you were at work yesterday."

"Uh, I might have told a small fib and flown to

France with Suki and Olivia."

"Olivia? Nye said she'd gone to the spa. Am I the only person who didn't know about this?"

"I didn't want to say anything until I'd found Fleur, in case it didn't work out as well as I hoped. Plus it would have ruined the surprise."

Fleur squeezed Max again. "Good surprise, huh?"

Not once in my life had I seen him smile like that. Mind you, from what he'd told me about his upbringing, should that have surprised me?

"The best. My two favourite girls in the same room. Never thought that would happen."

Max rubbed at his eyes again, and Fleur wiped his face with a sleeve. This was too damn cute. I was definitely going to get him a cat now.

"So, are you going to show me around?" Fleur asked. "I never imagined you living in a place like this."

"Neither did I until last year," he whispered. "All the good stuff has suddenly started happening."

Fleur took one of Max's hands, and I took the other. Together, we wandered through the house as Max told Fleur the story of how we met. Just the short version, but when he'd finished, she turned and hugged me.

"I'm so sorry all that happened to you."

"I'd give anything to bring Rose back. Anything. But I can't, and I've got Max now, so life has to go on even though not a minute passes without me thinking of her." My nose began running, and I scrabbled in my pocket for a tissue. "How about you? Do you have a boyfriend?"

Fleur's hand went to her neck, brushing against a delicate gold pendant in the shape of a horseshoe, studded with... Well, they looked like diamonds.

"No, no boyfriend."

So she said, but she'd hesitated too long. Something she didn't want to tell us?

Max carried on, oblivious. "Lots of friends in Paris?"

"Just my job."

"What do you do?" Max asked. "I hate that I know nothing about your life."

"I work as a translator, which sounds far more glamorous than it is."

"How long have you been doing that?" I asked.

"Half a year. I was a student up until then." She gave another smile. "I'm Dr. Tian now."

"My little sister, a doctor. I'm so fucking proud of you." Max let go of her hand and took a step towards the kitchen. "I've got a bottle of champagne in the fridge. Seems like a good time to open it."

The perfect time. I pointed him back to the lounge. "Don't worry, I'll get it." I took half a step, then quickly turned back to kiss him, just on the cheek. "Happy Christmas, Max."

He didn't seem to care that we were in front of his sister, because he gave me a smacker on the lips. "The best Christmas I've ever had."

FLEUR

What's going on with Max's little sister? Who gave her the necklace she wears? Of course, after spending years alone in Paris, she's got her own story, and I couldn't resist telling that in a little extra book.

You can download Fleur for free via the following link:
   www.elise-noble.com/f13ur

WHAT'S NEXT?

The Blackwood UK series continues with Zander's story...

To plant a garden is to believe in the future, that's what Dove Hallam's grandmother always told her. But at twenty-two, Dove has neither. Stuck in a dead-end relationship with a job she hates, her life is going nowhere until she meets Marlene Grande.

Although Marlene is in her seventies, her appetite for hot men and spending money knows no bounds, even if her matchmaking skills leave a bit to be desired. But as Dove embraces her new life, someone isn't so keen on her having fun.

Marlene's solution? Hire a private investigator with a nice ass. Now Dove has two problems to deal with—the monster wreaking havoc on the Arndale estate and Zander Graves, a smart-mouthed womaniser she really doesn't want to like.

Will there be anything left of her heart by the time they've finished with it?

Find out more here: www.elise-noble.com/graves

If you enjoyed Roses are Dead, please consider leaving a review.

For an author, every review is incredibly important. Not only do they make us feel warm and fuzzy inside, readers consider them when making their decision whether or not to buy a book. Even a line saying you enjoyed the book or what your favourite part was helps a lot.

WANT TO STALK ME?

For updates on my new releases, giveaways, and
other random stuff, you can sign up for my newsletter
on my website:
www.elise-noble.com

Facebook:
www.facebook.com/EliseNobleAuthor

Twitter: @EliseANoble

Instagram: @elise_noble

I also have a group on Facebook for my fans to hang
out. They love the characters from my Blackwood and
Trouble books almost as much as I do, and they're the
first to find out about my new stories as well as
throwing in their own ideas that sometimes make it
into print!

And if you'd like to read my books for FREE, you
can also find details of how to join my review team.

Would you like to join Team Blackwood?

www.elise-noble.com/team-blackwood

END OF BOOK STUFF

This book covered a few firsts for me—my first go writing about a serial killer, the first story I wrote where the two main characters really didn't get on to start with (yes, Lithium got published first but I wrote Roses before it), and my first book completely set in London. UK books are always easier for me because I'm British because there's no translation into American required!

As I sit here writing this end of book stuff in not-so-sunny Egypt (it's nine o'clock in the evening, and "winter"—I use the term lightly because it's still warm enough to sit outside), I can't remember exactly how I came up with the story, other than starting with the bad guy first. The flower names and the sale of Andrew's company, as I'd just been doing some accounting work for a similar business—there's big money in medical software! Lily and Max just happened, a grumpy bodyguard and a normal girl with a big heart who occasionally makes questionable decisions.

Can you guess who's up next? Yes, it's Zander, accompanied by new girl, Dove, plus Nye's grandmother and her equally batty friend because I love ladies who grow old disgracefully. That book's in the midst of being edited, and meanwhile, I'm playing around with two new series to run alongside Blackwood. The first is an ambitious romantic suspense collection that's making my head hurt—eight standalones, each also containing clues that build up into a big mystery at the end. The other is more romantic suspense with a hint of paranormal— something a little different from me, but I'm having fun with it!

As this is (probably) going to be my last book before Christmas, I just want to take the opportunity to wish you happy holidays, and I hope you have a great 2018 :)

Elise

OTHER BOOKS BY ELISE NOBLE

The Blackwood Security Series
Pitch Black
Into the Black
Forever Black
Gold Rush
Gray is my Heart
Neon (novella)
Out of the Blue
Ultraviolet
Red Alert
White Hot (2017)
The Scarlet Affair (2018)

The Blackwood Elements Series
Oxygen
Lithium
Carbon
Rhodium (2018)

The Blackwood UK Series
Joker in the Pack
Cherry on Top (novella)
Roses are Dead
Shallow Graves

The Trouble Series
Trouble in Paradise
Nothing but Trouble
24 Hours of Trouble

Standalone
Life
A Very Happy Christmas (novella)
Twisted